The Midnight Killer

ALSO BY JEZ PINFOLD

DCI BEC POPE SERIES
Book 1: The Deptford Murder
Book 2: The Stolen Girls
Book 3: The Midnight Killer

THE
MIDNIGHT
KILLER

JEZ PINFOLD

JOFFE BOOKS

Joffe Books, London
www.joffebooks.com

First published in Great Britain in 2025

Cover art by Nebojša Zorić

ISBN: 978-1-80573-264-8

This is dedicated to the Bec Pope audience.
Thank you all for reading

CHAPTER ONE

Monday night

The cemetery really was an excellent cut-through. He estimated that it saved him around half a mile — no, more like three-quarters of a mile — when walking home from the high street.

He had started walking in the cemetery during the first pandemic lockdown. Everyone had been allowed an hour of exercise each day and someone had recommended the cemetery as a quiet, contemplative environment for the exercise. At first it had seemed strange, eerie, but after a while he had come to appreciate the solitude and the almost wild nature of the place. Now the world had returned to relative normality, it was a short cut home from the pub.

It was in total darkness now. He looked at his watch. Almost midnight. He looked around at the gravestones, barely able to see the weeds and roots dancing around them. He felt a slight unease walking through the pitch black at midnight. But the beer alleviated the feeling and he summoned up a confidence that saw off the tension.

It had been a good night. After a long day at work, he had deserved a drink. The meeting to discuss strategy had started badly, with the rest of the team and his manager unconvinced by his ideas. But he had turned it around and eventually they had seen sense and had supported him. He had felt like a Master of the Universe, and what was planned to be a quick pint had turned into an all-evening affair. First of all with several colleagues, then with other people in the pub who had drifted over and joined the revelry. The pub had finally chucked them out and now here he was, walking an erratic line home. He was happy and hoped Eric would be fine when he returned home, some six hours after finishing work. He had texted, but had received no reply. It would be fine. After today's meeting, he could talk his way out of anything.

As he walked — more briskly now, having realized how late getting home he would actually be — he heard a noise behind him. Instinctively, he turned around. But there was nothing there. The cool, dark atmosphere, the gravestones and monuments to past lives, the unkempt foliage were combining to attack his confidence. There was nothing there. He laughed at the thought of how his colleagues would react if they could see him now, jumping at any small noise. No, he was fine. All good. Power on.

He checked his watch again. Midnight. The witching hour. A suitable time for this environment. He looked up and could see the exit looming out of the darkness, gently lit by a nearby street lamp. His phone pinged. He withdrew it from his pocket. Eric. His heart sunk a little: was he in trouble? He really didn't want Eric to spoil what had been a great day.

Then there really was a noise. Footsteps? He had his phone in his hand and reacted slightly too late. As he went to turn around, there was a sharp scratch on the right side of his neck. Instinctively his hand went to the site of the pain, and he was just trying to process what might be happening to him when he felt a powerful nausea and the urge to vomit. He stared down, attempting to ground himself, utterly confused by what might be happening. Had he been stung by an insect? Was this an allergic reaction? He was suddenly aware of someone else there beside him. Or was he so disorientated that he was imagining things?

Then he felt a sharp pain to the back of his skull and everything turned black.

His phone lay face up on the ground, inches from his hand. The notification was from Eric: *Where t f are u? Call me.*

CHAPTER TWO

Tuesday morning

Bec Pope hated flying. She was firmly of the opinion that if humans were meant to zip through the air in an aluminium tube, 35,000 feet in the sky, then we would . . . well, she didn't know what we would. But she hated flying.

As she walked into the departures hall at Heathrow Airport Terminal 5, the familiar feeling in her stomach only grew worse. Her partner, Alex, walked in front and although she wasn't looking behind her, she could certainly hear Alex's daughters, Hannah and Chloe, bickering loudly. It had already been a fraught morning, with the predictable stresses of packing for a holiday causing a number of silly, pointless arguments. None of this, needless to say, was improving Pope's increasing anxiety.

'I've told you, I'm sitting by the window. I want to watch the take-off,' Hannah said, thirteen but advancing the arguments of a five-year-old.

'You can't watch the take-off from inside the plane, can you? Just the ground, so that's a stupid argument. I'm the oldest, so I should have the choice,' said Chloe. Chloe was five years older than her sister, though her behaviour suggested the opposite. Pope was attempting not to get involved.

'Dad!' called Chloe. 'Can I get the window seat?'

Alex spun around and stopped in front of his daughters. 'If you don't stop arguing then I'm having the window seat!'

Pope put her hand on his shoulder. 'Let's get in the queue for bag drop, then we can go through security and have a coffee.' She looked at him with what she hoped was a supportive smile. He nodded his agreement and turned towards one of the huge information boards, scanning for details of where they might check in. Pope had already seen it was area C, but she knew that the task of leading them through the airport would keep Alex occupied. She had to focus on her own woes, she didn't need to have to take on his too.

'Check-in area C,' said Alex, heading in that direction. Pope and the two girls followed him and he joined the back of the queue he judged was the shortest. They put their luggage on the ground and Pope took a deep breath.

Alex turned to her. 'Thanks for agreeing to come to New York,' he said. 'It's going to be amazing. Once we get rid of these bags and get through security we can start to relax a little.'

Pope returned his smile, belying how she was feeling. She nodded and Alex turned back to assessing the speed of movement of the queue.

Pope looked at the departures board again and considered the large variety of destinations displayed. She thought back to the last time she'd had a proper holiday. In fact, any type of holiday at all. She hadn't been away with Alex and the girls anywhere except to visit his parents. Twice. Neither was what she considered a holiday in the traditional sense of the word. The demands of being a DCI in the Metropolitan Police, particularly on the Homicide Squad, dictated that the job had to come before holidays, and she hadn't really challenged this view. Pope needed a holiday, as did Alex and the girls. And their relationship would certainly benefit from a change of scenery. New York. She had to agree with Alex. It would be amazing.

They shuffled forward a few feet in the queue, moving their bags with their feet, in common with the people in front of them. Pope looked at the slow-moving line. Most people looked pretty relaxed, an attitude she really couldn't relate to this morning. Maybe she was just out of practice. She hadn't flown for several years and she knew from previous flights that once she had actually survived take-off and landed safely, then the return flight wouldn't fill her with quite so much trepidation. She was rationalizing, but it wasn't really working and the familiar pre-flight anxiety returned. How was it that Bec Pope, forty-two-year-old Homicide DCI, who could deal with the toughest criminals on an almost daily basis, was reduced to a bag of nerves at the prospect of flying? Time for a distraction.

She looked at Alex. 'So, do we know how far the hotel is from JFK?'

'Well, it's downtown Manhattan, quite near Grand Central Station, I think, so shouldn't take too long. Half an hour, maybe?'

Pope knew that Alex had visited New York several times with his wife when she was alive and felt a pang of jealousy. She immediately felt bad and banished the emotion.

'What time do we land?' she asked, still attempting to distract herself.

Alex looked at the ticket on his phone and did the mental calculation. 'Around lunchtime. Just after one.'

The queue moved forward a little more and Pope dutifully edged her bag forward again. She wasn't sure she'd packed adequately. She'd been working on the final paperwork for a case yesterday and it had taken longer than she'd expected to do the handover in advance of going away. By the time she'd got home she'd had only a short period of time to get her case packed. No time for washing or ironing, so her choice had been somewhat limited. Still, she'd managed to find a pair of jeans and a couple of clean shirts. That would have to do.

Pope realized that the tension she was feeling was not simply a case of fear of flying. She'd gone through so much in the last couple of years, endured so much loss, that the cumulative stress was compounding her current nerves. She knew that the holiday was what she and Alex needed, together, but she was also aware that she needed this for herself. A complete break from work.

They had snaked round the flexible cordons and now turned into the final length of tape that would guide them to drop their bags and head to security.

'Bec?' Pope hadn't noticed that Hannah was standing by her side. Pope looked at her and nodded to signal she was listening.

'Is it true that you can't go to America if you're a communist or a terrorist?'

The question came out of the blue and Pope smiled. 'Why do you ask?'

'Because I was looking up visiting America and it said that checks were really strict there.'

Pope thought for a moment. 'Well, I think checks are really strict in lots of places these days. It's not much different if you're visiting the UK from abroad. There are lots of different criteria you have to meet to be able to get in here. But, yes, I think that is true.'

'Why do they say communists particularly? I looked it up and it said they're a political party.'

'I think you'd have to ask an American that question.'

She felt on the verge of a long discussion, but she didn't have the capacity for that at the moment. Thankfully, they inched forward again and Hannah was distracted by moving her bag.

Pope heard her phone ringing in her pocket. She felt the vibrating. Alex turned to her. Pope retrieved the phone and pressed the green answer icon, trying to ignore Alex's look.

'Pope,' she answered. Then she listened. She could feel Alex's stare. The girls were oblivious, deep in their own conversation. Pope turned and walked a couple of steps to the side, out of the queue. She tried to keep her expression as neutral as possible.

'OK. When was this?' she said quietly. She listened to the answer.

'Where was he found?' Another pause.

Pope's expression changed and as it happened she turned to Alex, who registered.

'I'm at Heathrow. In the queue for check-in. I'm on leave for the next week. Isn't there anyone else?'

After a minute or so of silence on her end, she knew Alex was getting the gist of what was about to happen.

Finally, she spoke. 'OK. I'm on my way.'

Pope ended the call and put her phone in her pocket. She looked at Alex.

'Can we have a word?' said Pope, motioning for Alex to come out of the queue and away from other people who could overhear the difficult conversation she was about to have. Alex followed her warily.

Pope looked at him and took his hand. 'I've got some bad news.' She held his gaze. He raised his eyebrows, inviting her to explain.

'That was Fletcher. There's been a murder. A young man.'

'And how does that concern you? You're on leave for a week.'

'It's pretty bad.'

'Aren't all murders "pretty bad"?'

'They are, but . . .' Pope steeled herself. Rip off the plaster. 'I've got to go in.'

Alex looked at her. His expression was neutral, but she knew this was the calm before the storm. How many times had she disappointed him before?

He held his composure. 'Tell them to get someone else.'

'There isn't anyone else.'

'Of course there is. There must be. You're not the only Homicide detective in the Metropolitan Police.'

'I know, but Fletcher says there's no one available and they need someone with experience. And it's on our patch. We have two out long-term sick and one on parental leave. The department's on its knees.'

'Why can't Brody take it?'

'Because he's a DI and Fletcher is insisting on a DCI.'

Now Alex's tone changed. 'We've booked a holiday. We're going on holiday. You can't screw this up.'

'I don't have a choice. If there was anyone else . . . But there isn't.'

'Can't you just say no?'

'Not if I want to keep my job.'

Alex's expression suggested that Pope losing her job wouldn't be such a bad thing.

'I'm so sorry, Alex.' She went to put her arms around him but he backed away. It hurt. Another Bec Pope disaster.

Alex turned and walked back to his daughters in the queue. He turned to her and his look was inviting her to explain this to Hannah and Chloe. Damn. She had hoped he might do that for her.

Pope followed Alex. She faced the girls and took a deep breath.

'Chloe, Hannah. I'm so sorry, but there's a problem at work and I'm going to have to go in.'

They both stared at her, not sure what exactly she was saying.

Hannah looked at the clock on her phone. 'Are you going to get back in time? The flight's in two hours.' She turned to her father. 'Isn't that right, Dad?'

Alex didn't say anything. He was staring just over Pope's shoulder.

'I'm afraid I'm not going to be able to make the flight. I'm not going to be able to come with you to New York. Not this time.'

'Why not?' asked Hannah.

'Something's happened and I need to go to work,' she reiterated.

Chloe glowered at Pope. Their relationship had really improved over the last few months, which was amazing given what Pope had put her through recently. She didn't want to blow it.

'I promise I'll make it up to you both.' She looked at Alex. 'To you all.'

Chloe looked away. Hannah looked like she was about to start crying. Pope swallowed hard. She put her arms around Hannah and gave her a hug. She was probably the only one of the three of them who would allow this.

'I'm so sorry. I know you guys will have a brilliant time. I can't wait to see all the pictures.' Alex's look immediately made her regret the comment.

'There must be a way you can come,' said Hannah, tearful.

'Next time,' said Pope.

'Come on girls, we've got a plane to catch,' Alex said, picking up his bag and moving it forward in the queue again.

Hannah and Chloe moved slowly in the same direction, eyes trained on Pope. Alex was looking away.

Pope didn't know what to do now. Should she go? Should she stay and watch them go through security? Should she see them off? She watched as they got closer to the check-in machines and the three of them huddled together. They were clearly having an intense conversation. Alex was shaking his head while Hannah and Chloe seemed to be arguing a case. Then Alex looked up, making a decision. He looked over to Pope. He was angry, but there was something else in his expression that she couldn't read. He looked at Hannah and Chloe and nodded. They each picked up their bags and moved out of the queue.

Pope felt a rising panic. She knew what was coming, and this was worse than having to tell them they would have to go without her.

The three of them walked over to her.

'We're not going without you,' said Chloe.

'No. You have to. You have to go.'

'We're a family,' said Alex. 'We go on holiday together.'

'But the tickets . . .'

'The four musketeers,' said Alex by way of explanation.

Pope looked at the three people standing in front of her. She felt tears in her eyes. She was half horrified that she had ruined their trip and half overwhelmed that they would decide to do this for her. To be with her.

Alex moved to Pope and put his arms around her. 'We love you. We'll book again once this case is over.'

Pope couldn't think of what to say. She nodded and gave a half smile to the girls.

Alex picked up his bag and started walking towards the exit of Heathrow Airport Terminal 5. The girls followed, with Pope bringing up the rear.

She'd screwed up. Again. But now she had to focus.

CHAPTER THREE

The drive back home from the airport was one of the longest hours Pope had ever spent. She of course felt dreadful. She had ruined the holiday. But instead of putting Alex and the girls on the plane and being left to deal with things herself, she was in a car with the people she had let down. She had thought she would have a week before she had to face the consequences.

She couldn't understand why Alex had decided not to go without her. It wouldn't have been ideal, but it was a hell of a lot better than cancelling the whole thing. Selfishly, Pope thought that it would have been much better for her if they had travelled without her. At least they would have had a good time, and maybe that would make things easier when they arrived back. She may have solved the case by then, and they could take it from there. As it was, everyone lost.

Pope had a go at some light conversation and made several poor attempts at further apologies, but most of the journey was spent in an uncomfortable silence. She was relieved when they turned into their road and she pulled the car up outside the house.

Hannah and Chloe got out without saying anything. Pope watched them walk up the path and let themselves in the house, leaving the door open for Alex.

'Looks like I'm getting the cases, then,' said Alex.

Pope could not for the life of her work out why Alex was being so damned reasonable about all this. He had every right to be furious. To be screaming and shouting about how she'd let the family down. She knew that wasn't Alex's style, but this calm was unsettling. She wondered what was going on.

She turned to him. 'I'm really sorry, Alex. It's a disaster, I know.'

He shrugged. 'Yes, it's a disaster. But we have to get to a place where we do things together. Where we can both commit. And that won't happen with you in London and us in New York.'

He made it sound as if he was moving there permanently and they were going to conduct a long-distance relationship.

'I know. I'm sorry,' she repeated.

'Look, I get that your work makes demands on you that most people don't understand. I'm trying to accept that and trying to work on dealing with the uncertainties it brings.' He looked at her and half smiled. 'You don't make it easy.'

Pope leaned over and kissed him. She didn't know what else to say. Alex had been more than generous in his acceptance of this situation. As was so often the case, she knew she would have much to do to make it up to him, and the girls.

'Let's get the bags out. Shall I go in and talk to Chloe and Hannah?'

'No, I think they'll need a bit of time. I'll talk to them. You can see them this evening.'

Pope nodded and they both got out of the car. She opened the boot and they carried the bags up to the house and put them down just inside the front door.

'I'd better go.'

'OK. Take care.'

'I will.' Pope hugged Alex and kissed him again. She looked him in the eye and tried to work him out, with no success. She ended the hug and walked back to the car. She turned to him, but Alex had gone in and closed the front door.

Pope had no idea what had just happened.

As soon as she pulled away she used the hands-free to call Fletcher.

'Pope? Where are you?'

'I'm on my way in now. I had to drop Alex and the girls off first. I'll be half an hour. Where are we?'

There was a pause on the other end of the line and Pope wasn't sure whether Fletcher was collecting his notes or gathering his thoughts. Was it that bad?

Fletcher was all business. 'Male, young, murdered near Bloomsbury. I'll text you the address. Brody is already on the way. He'll meet you there.'

'What are the circumstances?' Pope knew she'd see for herself soon enough, but she wanted the outline in advance. Her brain was still half in holiday mode.

'According to the paramedics on site . . .' Fletcher didn't seem to be able to find the words. 'They're saying there seems to be some kind of ritualistic element.'

'What do you mean "ritualistic"?' Pope had no idea what this meant.

'I think it's best if you see for yourself, DCI Pope. I'll expect to be briefed when you get there.' Fletcher ended the call.

Pope didn't really know any more than when she had spoken to him at the airport. The call ended abruptly and Fletcher's tone was as pompous as she might have expected. Her phone pinged and she saw a text arrive with the address. There was nothing else to do but head to the scene.

She followed the satnav's directions and, having had her patience tested in some thick Central London traffic, eventually pulled into a smart-looking street. It was lined with well-kept trees along the pavements on each side and small but clearly expensive houses. She thought they looked Georgian and most seemed to be converted into flats. The satnav had her pull up at the entrance to a cemetery at the end of the street.

She immediately saw the place she was aiming for. An ambulance was parked on the left-hand side of the cemetery entrance road, just inside the gate, and DI James Brody was standing by the side of it. He was dressed as smart as usual, notebook in hand. As she pulled in, Brody walked towards her. She noted his expression. Not good. She got out of the car.

'Shouldn't you be about 35,000 feet in the air?' he said by way of greeting.

Pope rolled her eyes. For a moment she'd almost forgotten. 'Did Alex and the girls get off OK?'

Pope shook her head. 'They decided not to go without me. I've just dropped them home. That's why it took me a while to get here.'

He grimaced. 'Oh, Christ. How did that go?'

'Awful. I'll fill you in later. What have we got?'

Brody looked serious. 'It's a mess. I've waited for you to do a full examination of the scene, but from what I can work out, he's been dead for a while. Maybe late twenties. Smartly dressed, suit, good shoes.'

'Cause of death?' asked Pope.

'I haven't been able to work that out yet. The paramedics wanted to wait until you'd arrived to brief us on what they found. They've been here for a while.'

'OK, better not keep them waiting too much longer.'

Brody led the way over to the two medics who were sitting in the cab of their ambulance. When they saw the two detectives approaching, they both got out. Pope was surprised by how young they looked. Maybe when you're forty-two everybody looked young. Wasn't that what they said about police officers?

Pope noticed that the man, maybe mid-twenties, walked with a slight limp. He looked tired and seemed to stoop a little as he walked. She knew what paramedics had to go through on a daily basis and wasn't surprised at his world-weary gait. His female colleague looked a couple of years younger and seemed more alert, more energetic.

Pope nodded at them both. 'DCI Pope. Thanks for waiting.'

They both nodded in return.

'Can you take us through what you found when you arrived on scene?'

The young woman spoke, and the other paramedic seemed happy to let her do the talking.

'We got the call early this morning and arrived around six thirty. A member of the public found the body on their way to work. They weren't sure if he was alive or not so they called 999 and requested an ambulance.'

'Was he not obviously dead?' asked Pope.

'I think the caller didn't want to approach the body. You see a lot of rough sleepers round here, so I don't think they were sure.'

Pope thought back to Brody's description of the victim's smart clothes and shoes and suspected that he didn't look like a rough sleeper, but she understood the reluctance to approach, especially in the dark. She nodded for the medic to continue.

'We checked him over and he's definitely dead. We noted it at 6.43 a.m.'

'OK. Anything else you can tell us at this stage?'

She looked nervous to continue. 'There are no obvious signs which point to cause of death.' She paused and looked at Pope, then at Brody.

Brody took over. 'There's a wound on the chest of the victim.'

Pope looked at the woman, confused. 'I thought you said there were no obvious signs which would point to cause of death.'

'There aren't,' she replied. 'It's . . .' She seemed unable to find the words.

'Maybe we should have a look for ourselves,' said Brody.

Pope looked at the woman impatiently, but accepted Brody's suggestion.

He led her slightly further along the path into the cemetery to where several uniforms were standing by a figure on the ground, covered in a white plastic sheet, a makeshift arrangement until the coroner arrived.

They both acknowledged the officers and walked up to the body, while Brody pulled a blue latex glove onto his right hand. Brody turned to Pope. 'Ready?'

Pope was slightly irritated by the theatrics. 'Yes.'

Brody used his gloved hand to lift the plastic sheeting. Pope saw a man who she thought looked around the age that Brody had estimated. He was dressed in business attire: a grey suit, light-blue tie and polished black brogues. Pope was surprised that he didn't look more dishevelled, given that he was lying dead in a cemetery. The tell-tale sign, however, was a large blood stain on the front of his shirt, which had pooled out over his jacket.

She walked around the body, taking in the scene.

'You're right about the suit. On his way back from work?' asked Pope.

'Could be. But it must have been late, or he would have been seen earlier by someone walking by.'

'Maybe a night out after work.' Pope looked around. 'I wonder how many people walk through here late at night. Maybe a short cut home?'

'We're not sure yet. He had a phone, but no wallet. One of the uniforms is taking it back to the station so Tech can have a look.'

'Let's have a look at where that blood's coming from.' Pope indicated with her hand for Brody to open the man's shirt.

Brody knelt down on one knee and tentatively moved the jacket to one side, then the shirt.

Then Pope saw it. 'Christ. What is that?' she asked, taking a step forward. She looked in horror at the man lying on the ground.

'Good question,' said Brody. 'I guess this is why you were called back so suddenly.'

Pope knelt down beside Brody to examine the victim's chest. She saw a great deal of blood, and the cause was clear. Someone — the killer? — had carved an emblem on the top left of his torso. She looked closely.

'Is that . . . looks like some sort of star?' she said. She was talking to Brody, but looking intently at the wound.

'It's a pentagram.'

Pope now looked at Brody. 'A pentagram?'

'Yeah. Five-pointed star.'

Pope looked again. 'There's something odd about it. Well, apart from the fact that someone has carved it onto him.'

'It's upside down,' said Brody.

Pope looked again. 'You're right. Two points at the top, they should be at the bottom.'

Pope looked confused. 'Is there a difference?'

'There is,' said Brody. 'A pentagram with a single point facing upwards is usually considered a symbol of good, of right. But an upside-down pentagram, a five-pointed star with two points facing up and one point facing down, is generally considered a symbol of evil.'

Brody always seemed to know pretty much everything and Pope needed to stop being surprised when he demonstrated this. His knowledge of obscure facts could be very useful at times in their investigations.

'Who would know about this kind of thing?' asked Pope.

'Well, you do see this sort of stuff in the movies sometimes. It's usually associated with the occult.'

'You mean witchcraft and devil worship?'

'I'm sure they wouldn't see it like that, but, yes, that's where it's often found.'

Pope looked at Brody. 'So, we've got a devil-worshipping murderer on the loose?'

Brody nodded slowly. 'Maybe. It's unusual.'

'I think that's an understatement.'

'How do you want to proceed?'

'Well, first of all we need to get a time of death, and a cause. It looks like he's been dead for a while, but we'll need something more specific so we know where to look if we're retracing his steps.' Pope looked again at the horrific wound inflicted on their victim. 'The killer must have subdued him in order to do that. It would take some time. The wound doesn't look deep enough to have been fatal. So how did he actually die? That's not clear yet.'

Brody nodded.

'And then there's the symbol itself. We'll need to talk to someone who knows more about this kind of thing than we do.'

'Where do we find an expert in the occult?' asked Brody.

'That's a very good question. Let's get back to the station and see what Tech has for us on the victim. We can't do a lot until we know the identity. Can you make sure the uniforms know what they have to do?'

Brody nodded and walked towards the two officers standing at a respectful distance. They would need to stay close to the body until the medical examiner and Scene of Crime team arrived to examine the body.

Pope looked around her. The cemetery was silent. She took in the gravestones and monuments. She had spent too long in cemeteries in the last year. She had lost people close to her, and this environment was starting to touch the parts of her she usually managed to hide away. She considered the dead body in front of them and the bloody symbol carved on him. Satanism, witchcraft, the occult. Over twenty years in the Metropolitan Police and this was another first.

Pope heard a plane flying overhead. She looked up and wondered if that was the plane she should have been in, on her way to a family holiday in New York.

* * *

The drive back to the station should only have taken ten minutes, but the traffic doubled that. Brody drove Pope's car while she checked her messages: Fletcher wanted her to call him ASAP. Nothing from Alex. Pope leaned back in her seat and closed her eyes.

'Anything interesting?' asked Brody.

Pope opened her eyes again and looked at her phone. 'Fletcher wants an update. Of course. I was hoping for a message from Alex, but no such luck.'

'So how did he take it? At the airport?'

Pope considered the question. 'He was really angry at first. I mean Alex doesn't get shout-out-loud angry, but quietly furious would describe it.'

'At first?'

'It was strange. They all had a talk and decided that they didn't want to go without me.'

'Oh no,' said Brody.

'I know. I told him to take the girls but he said we needed to start being together. Properly together. And them jetting off for a trip to New York wasn't the way to go about that.'

'And how do you feel about that?'

'Terrible. I feel bad enough about having to blow out the holiday, especially at the last minute. But then being the reason Hannah and Chloe can't go on a trip they were so looking forward to?' Pope shook her head. No further explanation was necessary.

'Do you think you'll go another time?'

'I suppose that's the plan. If Alex is even prepared to book anything again with me.'

'I'm sure he will.'

'He seemed so calm when we got back to the house. It was pretty weird.'

'How did the girls take it?'

'Neither said anything in the car. Then they walked straight into the house when we got back. Something to look forward to this evening.'

Brody steered the car onto Shaftesbury Avenue and hit another wall of traffic.

Pope changed the topic of conversation, having had enough of being reminded of her failings as a partner and stepmother.

'How's Lizzie?' Brody had been with his new partner for nearly four months now. It was the only relationship Pope had been aware of during their working partnership. She had learned the hard way that she needed to take more of an interest in the personal lives of her close colleagues.

'She's great,' replied Brody. 'Yeah. Really good.'

'Things are going well, then?'

'It's different going out with a nurse. She understands the job a bit better. And we both have antisocial shifts and random call-outs. I suppose there's less of a culture shock and it's easier to take those things in your stride.'

'That's good. I can see that would make things a bit easier.' Pope was doing her best with the small talk, but it just reminded her of the recent loss of a colleague. The realization that she didn't even know the name of his fiancée at the time had hit her hard. It was a mistake she was determined not to repeat.

Brody guided the car into the underground garage at Charing Cross Police Station and found a parking spot near the exit doors. They walked up the stairs towards the reception area.

'I'd better go and see Fletcher,' said Pope. 'He keeps texting me for updates. He's all over this already.'

'Well, he knows what's going to happen as soon as the media find out about the symbol on the body.'

Pope recalled her phone conversation with Fletcher. 'How did he know so quickly?'

'I think one of the first officers on the scene reported it in. It must have got to him early.'

Pope sighed. Superintendent Richard Fletcher didn't so much have half an eye on the media opportunities for his career as nine tenths of an eye. He was closing in on promotion and would see this as a crucial opportunity to further his ambition.

'I'll meet you in the squad room. Get the team together for a briefing.'

Brody nodded and turned right at the top of the stairs, while Pope climbed another flight and headed to her boss's office. The door was slightly ajar. She knocked. Fletcher had an annoying habit of always waiting a few seconds before inviting her in. A power game for which she had no time. Sure enough, she was left standing there a short time.

'Come in.'

Pope entered the room as Fletcher looked up from his expansive and remarkably tidy desk. He indicated for Pope to take a seat. As she sat down, she noticed that Fletcher seemed to be wearing yet another new suit, immaculately pressed, and a tie she hadn't seen before.

'Where are we?' he asked. Fletcher wasn't one for small talk, which Pope appreciated.

'I think you know the details. Young male, probably mid-to-late twenties. Found in St George's Cemetery, in Bloomsbury. Time of death to be confirmed, but probably late last night or early this morning.'

'What was he doing in a cemetery in Bloomsbury in the middle of the night?'

'We're still waiting on ID, so it's difficult to confirm until then, but we think he may have been on his way home from a late-evening engagement, either working late or some-thing social after work. He was dressed pretty smartly.'

'You saw the body?'

'Yes. It's pretty horrific. The killer has carved some sort of symbol on the body.'

'I know that. What's your take on it?' Fletcher sounded impatient. Maybe anticipating the next press conference.

'It's rudimentary. Messy. But it looks like a pentagram. An upside-down pentagram.'

'An upside-down pentagram?'

'Two points at the top and one at the bottom. It's usu-ally the other way round.'

'Any thoughts on that?'

Pope did have ideas, but she didn't want to get into a discussion of the occult connection before she knew more.

'Still working on it, sir.'

Fletcher paused. He seemed to have what he needed for the moment. He looked at his computer screen and clicked on something.

'You have a new member of the team starting this morn-ing. Zahra Khan, from Hackney station. She should be here by now.'

Pope was stunned. She had to search for the words. 'A new member of the team? Why?' was all she could manage.

Fletcher looked at Pope with something resembling compassion. A look she hadn't seen very often from her boss.

'It's been almost three months, Bec. You need a replacement. She's an excellent officer. Carefully chosen. She'll be a good addition to the team.'

'Not carefully chosen by me.'

'You've been down an officer for too long and it's putting too much strain on the team.'

'We're fine. Has there been a problem with our work?'

Fletcher ignored the question. 'Usually an extra officer is seen as a good thing. Make it work, DCI Pope. And keep me in the loop. I want to know anything you know ASAP.'

Fletcher's usual mantra signalled an end to the conversation. Pope got up and left the office without saying anything.

She walked to the end of the corridor and out into the stairwell. She stopped. Had it been almost three months since she'd lost Adam Miller? It was still so raw, so painful, that she would have guessed it was a week ago. She hadn't been able to conceive of a replacement, and this news brought the pain back. She felt her chest being crushed by an unbearable force. Pope held on to the handrail to steady herself.

'It's not a replacement for Miller,' she told herself out loud. 'Just an addition to the team.'

It didn't make things any better, and as she headed down the stairs to the squad room, she was fighting desperately to hold back the tears.

CHAPTER FOUR

Pope paused as she reached the doors to the squad room. She took a deep breath and looked at her watch. So much had already happened today and it wasn't even lunchtime. She shook her head and took another breath. Time to pull herself together. She gathered her thoughts and hoped she was ready.

When she opened the door she saw Brody talking to Sergeant Stephen Thompson, the tech wizard who had so often moved their investigations on successfully in the past. They both looked at her and nodded as she walked in. Judging by Thompson's expression, Brody had just apprised him of the scene they had found at St George's Cemetery. Pope went to her desk and sat down, switching on her computer as she sat. She'd powered everything down yesterday evening, thinking that it wouldn't be used for the next week. She didn't want to think any more about that at this point and she certainly didn't want to have to explain the situation again to Thompson.

'Give me five minutes,' she said. They both nodded and resumed their conversation. Pope waited for her computer to boot up and entered her password. As she opened her email, she had the delightful task of turning off the out-of-office message she had set the previous evening. She sighed. The

24

constant reminders seemed straight out of a comedy. A very unfunny comedy.

As she was checking the messages, the door to the office opened and Fletcher strode in, followed by a woman Pope assumed must be the new member of her team. Fletcher took to the middle of the room — marking his territory in front of the new officer, Pope thought.

'I'd like to introduce Detective Sergeant Zahra Khan.' Pope, Brody and Thompson all nodded at the woman in unison.

'DS Khan comes to us from a very successful stint in Hackney and I'm sure you'll make her welcome. This is DCI Bec Pope, DI James Brody and DS Stephen Thompson.' He indicated each of them in turn.

Khan smiled and said hello to them as they were introduced. Pope studied her. She didn't look embarrassed at Fletcher's introduction, exuding a confidence which Pope found interesting. She noticed her striking brown eyes and her neat black hijab.

Pope was conflicted. She found it almost impossible to accept that her colleague was being replaced so easily. She knew that she had not really come to terms with the loss and was not ready for this. But she also knew how difficult it was joining a new team and being expected to prove yourself from day one. No 'easing in' to a Homicide investigation. And as a minority on the force, the woman must have faced all kinds of discrimination and challenges. Pope was keen to support her, not create further obstacles as a result of her own feelings of grief. She stepped forward and held out her hand.

'Welcome to the team, DS Khan. Good to have you with us.' The woman shook her hand and smiled.

Fletcher turned to Pope. 'I'll leave DS Khan in your capable hands, DCI Pope.' Without saying anything to the new officer, Fletcher left the office, closing the door behind him.

The woman had a rucksack loosely slung over her right shoulder. Pope glanced at her colleague's old desk, which had sat empty for three months. She indicated the desk to Khan.

'You can use the free desk there,' she said, turning to her colleagues. Brody nodded slightly. Thompson, who had been closer to the desk's previous occupant than either Pope or Brody, said nothing. Pope thought that was about as good as she was going to get.

Khan walked over and put her bag down by the side of the chair.

'Right. Shall we get started?' said Pope.

The four officers each took a seat around the large conference-style table in the middle of the office space. This new dynamic felt weird to Pope, but she couldn't deny that she was pleased to have another woman on the team. Being a woman in the Met could be a lonely job at times.

'DS Khan, do you want to start by introducing yourself? Tell us a bit about your work background.'

Khan looked slightly surprised, but nodded her agreement. 'Of course. I joined the Met straight from school at eighteen. After training I spent eight years at Forest Gate, then moved to Hackney as a detective just over a year ago. Now I've moved here.'

Pope was surprised that Khan had moved up the ranks so quickly and with relatively little experience as a detective. She wondered why the officer had only spent a year in Hackney and why she had been chosen to join Pope's team, which, given that this was Homicide, was a big step up career-wise. She seemed to remember working some years ago with a detective from Hackney station, and she made a mental note to contact them to see what she could find out.

'OK, thanks. Welcome again. Let's run through what we have. DI Brody, will you start us off with the basics?' Pope used his formal job title so that their new colleague could clarify names and rank.

Brody opened his notebook and cast his eyes over the facts that he had written down so far. Zahra Khan took out her notepad and a pen and turned to a fresh page. Pope could see her writing a title at the top.

'Control received a call early this morning from a woman on the way into work. She reported an unresponsive male near the west entrance to St George's Cemetery, near Bloomsbury. Paramedics arrived at around six forty-five this morning and found the man to be deceased, with what looked like signs of foul play. They called us. When DCI Pope and I examined the scene, it was clear that the man was dead and seemed to be the victim of a homicide. Time of death is not yet certain, but the paramedics estimated that he had been dead for some hours. One possibility is that the victim had been using the cemetery for a cut-through on his way home after working late or a night out, which suggests that the murder took place late last night. The autopsy will confirm.'

Khan was making notes, while Thompson was jotting down information on his tablet.

Brody continued. 'Cause of death is at present unknown. However, of note is that someone, presumably the killer, carved what appears to be an upside-down pentagram into the flesh of the victim, on the left-hand side of his chest.'

Steven Thompson clearly already knew this, but Khan looked up in shock. Pope was watching her and Khan opened her mouth as if to say something, but clearly thought better of it. Pope wondered if she was re-evaluating her career choice.

Pope's first case in Homicide had been a child murder, so she had some sympathy with her. Police work on the streets of London could be tough and unforgiving, but it was nothing compared to the work in Homicide. Although Khan had already spent nine years in different parts of London, the nature of this crime was something different, suggesting a particularly evil murderer. It would take all the new recruit had to adjust to this case.

Brody continued. 'The wound was crudely executed and the paramedics didn't think it was the cause of death. Given how long it would take to cut that shape into a human being, we have to assume that it was carried out post-mortem, but again, the autopsy should confirm that.'

'DS Thompson, do you have any information on the victim?' Pope now took over.

Thompson nodded, his usual enthusiasm tempered by the nature of the murder.

'Yes, we have an ID,' he said, bringing up the details on his tablet. 'I'll send it to you now. I've been able to identify him as Paul Ward, aged twenty-eight. Fingerprints are in the system from a previous burglary at his workplace where employees were required to provide prints for elimination.'

'Should we have those?' asked Khan. 'I mean, still on the system?'

'Yes, it's fine.'

Pope nodded her approval to Thompson. 'Other details?'

'Yup. He works at Knight IT Solutions, based in Canary Wharf. Registered home address is 14 Milton Court, Bloomsbury.'

'That's a pretty upmarket address,' noted Brody.

'IT in Canary Wharf is a pretty upmarket business,' replied Thompson.

'Jealous?' asked Brody.

Thompson smiled. 'No. Who needs money and prestige when you can work in the public sector?'

Pope looked at each of them in turn. 'The elephant in the room. What's the carving of an upside-down pentagram telling us?'

There was silence for a moment.

'The pentagram is a very old symbol,' said Brody. 'It originally comes from religious iconography, and in general they're a symbol of good. But the inverted pentagram in the opposite. It's been associated for decades with evil, occultism and satanism. Think Aleister Crowley and those kinds of people.'

'Who is Aleister Crowley?' asked Khan.

'Crowley was a famous occultist and proponent of satanism, or a particular form of it. He died in the forties but is still popular in those circles. He's said to have had some influence on musicians like Led Zeppelin and Ozzy Osbourne back in the day, so some people know of him through music.'

Pope nodded, once again impressed with Brody's knowledge.

'So, the question is, what does the symbol mean?' asked Pope. 'Why is this killer choosing this particular symbol to leave on the body of a twenty-eight-year-old IT professional from Bloomsbury?'

There was silence for a moment. Brody broke it.

'The obvious answer is that the murderer has some form of interest in satanism or the occult. This is a very specific type of symbol with very specific connotations.'

'Would someone be likely to have a knowledge of this symbol if they didn't know something about the occult? I mean, does it have other applications, other meanings?' asked Pope.

'I don't think so, but we'll need to talk to someone who knows more about it.'

Pope nodded. 'There's clearly a psychological aspect to this murder. It doesn't seem particularly personal.'

'Why do you say that?' asked Khan.

Pope was pleased: her new colleague was asking the right questions at this stage.

'Crimes of passion or murders with a very personal motive often show signs of frenzy or overkill. This doesn't fit, and the act of carving a symbol on the body suggests that the killer is more interested in what the symbol conveys, rather than the act of the murder itself.'

Khan nodded and jotted something down in her notebook.

'Did the killer choose the cemetery in advance?' asked Pope. 'It certainly fits with the theme. If so, how did they know our victim would be there at that particular time?'

Pope could see Brody was thinking. 'Maybe the route was one that the victim often used at that time. The killer could have scoped out the location previously and seen the victim before.'

'Or they could have just waited there and it was completely random,' said Pope. 'The question then is, given the nature of the crime and the possible links with the occult, was the victim deliberately targeted or was it the location that was more important? And if so, could anyone have seen the killer previously hanging around in the cemetery?'

No one had answers to these questions at this stage, but Pope was outlining some strategies for the investigation to get started.

She looked at Steven Thompson. 'Any CCTV in that area?'

'Not around the cemetery itself. But some of the surrounding roads have coverage, so we'll scrub that to see if we can find anything.'

'OK, good. Can you get on that? Hopefully it will come up with something. Brody, Khan, let's go and see Tobias Darke at King's and see what he can tell us about this case.'

'Who's Tobias Darke?' asked Khan.

'He's a forensic psychologist we use to help profile suspects. He's often a good starting point in cases where the killer appears quite unusual.'

'Aren't all killers unusual?' asked Khan.

Brody smiled. 'Can't argue with that.'

'Shouldn't we interview the victim's friends, colleagues, partner first?'

Pope nodded. 'We will. But it's useful to have as much we can on what we're looking for before we do. It can help when interviewing if we have a sense of a possible psychological profile, particularly in a case like this.'

Pope needed to contact Darke before they left, to check he was available.

'We'll leave in ten minutes.'

Pope sat down at her computer terminal and entered her password. She watched her new colleague, who was talking to Steven Thompson about IT arrangements for her terminal. Pope was initially impressed with the woman. Young and relatively inexperienced, but doing all the right things. DS

Khan had made a positive first impression. Pope was interested to see how she would do out in the field. Then she suddenly thought again about Adam Miller and was overcome with a wave of profound sadness. She wanted him back on her team. Khan was never going to be able to fill those shoes.

CHAPTER FIVE

Tobias Darke agreed to meet with the three detectives at the King's College campus on the Strand. Pope had known him since her time at the police training college in Hendon, when she had seen him give fascinating and engaging lectures. She had been instantly impressed by his work on criminal psychology and psychiatry. She had read most of the books he had written, and he had consulted, either formally or informally, on a number of Pope's cases over the years. They had become firm friends and she knew she could trust his advice and knowledge. She regularly sought out his wisdom when cases involved an unusual aspect. This case certainly fit that criteria.

Pope collected Brody and Khan and they walked down the stairs to the underground garage. It wasn't far to King's College, but Pope decided to take the car — she wasn't sure where they'd go after meeting Darke.

'Will you drive?' she asked Brody. He nodded and fished his car keys out, pressing the automatic unlocking button on the key fob. The indicator lights on the police-issue BMW flashed and the three of them got in the car. Khan naturally went for the back door, respecting the ranks.

'Do we need to tell Superintendent Fletcher where we're going?' she asked.

'No. He'll get in touch if he needs us,' said Pope. The less contact with her boss, the better.

Brody guided the car up the steep ramp out of the garage and they drove the brief distance to King's College. Tobias Darke had an office on the second floor, confusingly numbered 307. Pope showed her badge to the security officer on duty in the reception area of the building. He called up to Darke and then pointed them in the right direction.

When they arrived at Darke's office, the door was open and he was sitting at his desk, typing an email. He beamed as soon as he saw Pope and got up immediately from his chair, bounding to the doorway.

'Bec, how delightful to see you,' he said, giving her a bear hug which lasted far more time than Pope would have wanted in front of her colleagues.

'Tobias. How are you?'

'Fighting fit, thanks for asking. Never better.'

Darke then moved to Brody and gave him an equally big hug. 'James. All well?'

'Yes. Fine. Thanks.' Brody could hardly get the words out as Darke squeezed him tight. Darke was a large man, somewhat overweight, and his affection could be mildly incapacitating. Darke released him and looked at Khan.

'And who do we have here?'

'Tobias, this is Zahra Khan. She's new on the team, just joined us from Hackney. DS Khan, meet Dr Tobias Darke,' said Pope.

Darke shot a look at Pope. He knew her well enough to understand the significance of a replacement detective on her team.

Darke shook her hand and smiled broadly. 'Very nice to meet you.'

'You too, Dr Darke.'

'Oh, Tobias please. And I'll call you Zahra if you don't object. Bec is always so professional around her colleagues but I prefer a more informal approach.'

'Yes, of course. Zahra is fine.' Darke had a knack for relaxing anyone and always welcomed any colleague of Pope's as if they were his own. His grey three-piece suit and silk tie suggested the utmost formality, but a few moments in his company demonstrated the opposite.

He indicated the two guest chairs in the corner of his office. 'Two of you can take a seat. Apologies that I don't have sufficient seating for you all.'

'I'm happy to stand,' said Brody.

Pope and Khan sat down.

'Right. What can I do for the Metropolitan Police this afternoon?'

Pope nodded to Brody, indicating for him to outline the case to Tobias Darke. Darke listened intently, jotting down a couple of notes while Brody spoke. Finally, he took out his phone and showed Darke a picture he had taken of the symbol. He took the phone from Brody and looked carefully for some time at the image.

'A pentagram,' Darke finally said.

'Yes,' said Brody.

'But notably inverted.'

'Why "notably"?' asked Pope. She needed to know if the explanation they had come up with was the only possibility.

'Well, it's a little outside my immediate area of expertise, but I do know that the pentagram is a very old symbol. As an example of the mathematical Golden Ratio, it has symbolized life, humanity and good in general. This is going back hundreds of years, of course.' Darke paused and looked at Pope. 'But you have something a little different, here.'

'In what way?'

'This pentagram is upside down, which some have conceived as the opposite. A bit like turning a lucky horseshoe upside down, it is supposed to symbolize bad luck. The inverted pentagram is widely considered to be a symbol of evil.'

Pope and Brody looked at each other. Darke was confirming their hypothesis.

'Can you tell us anything else?'

'I'm not sure I can, Bec. My understanding of this area is limited to general knowledge, I'm afraid. You need to consult an expert.'

'OK, but what could it tell us about who we're looking for? I mean, it's pretty out there.'

'Yes, it is.' Darke considered this for a minute. 'The symbol itself is clearly drawing attention to the occult, to the deification of Satan. This symbol is so closely related to this that I think there is unlikely to be any other plausible explanation.'

'Could it be an accident that it's inverted?' asked Pope.

'I think it's unlikely. The symbol has very specific connotations and it's unusual to think of a five-pointed star arranged this way. So, no, I'd say it was quite deliberate.'

'Then why carve this on a dead body?' Pope asked the direct, brutal question.

'It's drawing attention to either the killer, the victim or the cause,' said Darke.

'What do you mean?' said Pope.

'Firstly, the killer may want to be recognized. This could be a classic attention-seeking device. Do something so heinous, so out there, that everyone simply has to pay attention. It marks them out as special, even within the rarefied realms of murderers. Secondly, this symbol may be saying something about the victim. It may be a personal vendetta which, in the killer's eyes, warrants them being branded as evil in some way.'

Pope nodded. 'And the third possibility?'

'They could be drawing attention to the cause. The killer wants you to understand that this is all about satanism. They want to foreground the cause, rather than the victim. It's time, in their mind, to get people talking about the devil.'

'Which is the most likely, psychologically speaking?' she asked.

'Well, that's impossible to say at this stage. If this is a single murder, then I would think it's most likely that the killer is carrying out a vendetta against the deceased. Have there been any similar cases recently?'

'Not that we know of,' replied Pope. 'Nothing that matches this MO.'

'Then at the moment, you'll have to hope that it stays that way.'

'Yes, I think we can all agree on that. But is there a specific reason you say that?'

'Beyond the obvious, I think a single murder suggests a more traditional motive, if we can call any motive traditional. Perhaps "typical" is a better word. But if there is another similar murder then you're looking at a disturbed personality who wants to get some attention. Then you have an even greater problem.'

Pope shuddered as she remembered the recent case of the 'Cameraman' killer, as he was dubbed by the media.

'Is there anything you can tell us? Anything which might help in profiling the perpetrator?' she asked.

'It's difficult at this stage. Unfortunately, it's the case that the more murders committed, the easier it becomes to put a profile together. Similarities in cases and victims allow us to make meaningful connections, as you know.'

Pope had thought that Darke would say this.

'If we send over what we have so far, will you have a look and see what you think?'

'Have you had the autopsy report yet?'

'No. I'm hoping to get that tomorrow morning. I'll send it to you.'

'I'll have a look. But don't expect too much at this stage.'

'I won't. Thanks, Tobias. You mentioned getting an expert opinion. Do you know anybody who might be able to help?'

'I don't think I do, Bec. I do know that there is talk of the occult becoming more popular both within and outside academia. I read an article which argued that this is in response to a decline in participation in organized religion. If I recall, there is a course which has recently started at Exeter University on just this. You could try to get hold of someone there. But I don't think I know of anyone personally.'

Brody jotted down something in his notebook.

'That's a good place to start. Thanks.'

They said their goodbyes and Darke sent his regards to Alex and the girls. He made a point of saying goodbye to Khan, reminding her that they were now on first-name terms. She looked a little embarrassed, but nodded and thanked him.

As they exited the building and got back in the car, Khan spoke.

'I think I know someone who might be able to help us.'

Pope turned around to face the back seat. She waited for Khan to continue.

'A few years ago I worked a burglary of a shop in Hackney. The shop was a magic shop, you know, tricks and potions. But they were also into tarot cards and Ouija boards, that sort of thing. The guy who owns the shop knows all about the occult.'

'Do you have a relationship with him? Would he talk to us?' asked Pope.

'We solved the case and got his stuff back, so he owes me one.'

'Can you get in touch with him?'

'Now?' asked Khan.

Pope nodded. 'No time like the present.'

'OK. Hang on.' Khan searched for the name and contact details of the shop on her phone. 'Got it.' She tapped the number and put the phone on speaker. After a few rings, the call was answered.

'The Alchemist. How can I help?'

'Hi. Is that Acheron?'

Brody looked at Pope and raised his eyebrows. Pope wondered what his real name was.

'Yes. Who's this?'

'Hi, Acheron. It's DS Khan, from the police. I investigated your burglary a couple of years ago.'

'Sergeant Khan. Yes, I remember. How are you?'

'I'm well, thanks. I need to ask you a favour.'

'Go ahead. Anything for my favourite officer of the law.'

Khan rolled her eyes at Pope. 'I'm working on a case which I think you might be able to help with. Would you be happy if we visited for a quick chat?'

'Oh. That sounds exciting! Yes, of course. Do you want to come over now?'

Khan looked at Pope, who nodded.

'That would be great if you're free.'

'Yes, now's a good time.'

'Brilliant. See you in around half an hour. Thanks, Acheron.'

'No problem. See you soon.'

Khan ended the call.

'Good work,' said Pope. She looked at Brody. 'Hackney it is.'

CHAPTER SIX

Brody drove Pope's car along Fleet Street, then headed north-east towards Hackney. Khan explained that the shop they were looking for was, somewhat appropriately, located close to a graveyard next to Hackney Central station. Brody knew how to get to the station and Khan would direct them from there.

Pope, reminded of her earlier vow to get to know her officers better after recent events, decided to do just that.

'So, why the move to Charing Cross? After only a year at Hackney?' As soon as she said it, Pope realized it sounded critical. Khan answered before she was able to modify the question.

'I know. I enjoyed working at Hackney, but my Super called me in and said there was an opening here and was I interested. I'm not sure why they offered it to me. I wondered if it had come from your station.'

Perhaps Fletcher had instigated the transfer. He could move in mysterious ways at times. She knew that she should have started to do something about the gap in her team some time ago. Maybe Fletcher had avoided asking her and simply sorted it out himself.

'Not that I know of,' said Pope. 'You must have done well there to get a move so quickly.'

'I suppose so. There were other members of my team who had more experience. They weren't exactly overjoyed to find out that I'd been transferred to your team.' She paused for a moment, seemingly deciding whether to say something else. 'Charing Cross has quite a reputation in Homicide and there are a lot of officers who want to join.' Again, Khan looked a little embarrassed.

Pope knew that being new, and a woman, in Homicide was a balancing act between projecting confidence but avoiding the appearance of arrogance. Arrogance seemed to be a prized commodity in men who worked on the murder squad, but not in women. She thought Khan was doing pretty well so far on the high wire.

'Well, it's good to know our reputation is intact. It's been a difficult year.' She watched Khan for a reaction. Pope wondered how far in the Met, and beyond, the events of the recent past had reached.

Khan simply nodded. Pope saw that the new officer could be tactful when needed.

She decided to give Khan a break from the difficult questions and changed the subject.

'What is this guy's real name?'

'Acheron?'

'Yeah. Presumably no parent actually saddled their son with that as a given name?'

Khan smiled. 'No, I think he chose that all by himself. His real name is Kevin Bradley. He's clean, I think. No record. Or at least not when I worked his case.'

'Will he cooperate?'

'Yes, I think so. He was really helpful after the burglary. I know that's a different context, but he seemed pretty genuine in wanting to support the police.'

'Good to hear,' said Pope. A cooperative interviewee made life so much simpler.

'One word of warning,' said Khan.

Pope raised her eyebrows, inviting more detail.

'He's big into tarot cards. Will probably want to do your reading. He insisted on doing all the investigating officers when I was there before!'

Pope rolled her eyes. She had absolutely zero time for anything not rooted in reality.

'Great. Maybe the cards will tell us who the murderer is.'

'I hate to interrupt. DS Khan, can you direct me from here? This is about as far as I know.' Brody was pulling up at the lights on Graham Road, just next to Hackney Central station. The small, neat Victorian houses gave way to commercial and retail units as they approached.

Khan took Brody past the station and guided him to a small parade of shops a few minutes away. They passed the graveyard Khan had mentioned. Pope had seen too many cemeteries recently.

'Just there,' said Khan, indicating a small, dark-blue shop facade with The Alchemist written at the top in block gold lettering. It stood between a pizza takeaway and a betting shop and looked incongruous in these surroundings.

'Strange place for this kind of shop,' said Pope.

'Where wouldn't be a strange place for this kind of shop?' said Brody.

He pulled the car up in a space just past the premises and flicked on the hazard lights. As they got out of the car, Pope examined the outside more closely. The door was in the middle of the shop front with panelled display windows on either side. The smallish glass panels and thick surrounds gave an olde-worlde effect, which, she presumed, was deliberate. On one side was a large circle which looked like it contained the signs of the zodiac, but not exactly like any representation of this she had seen before. The other side contained various items for sale including several sets of tarot cards, a couple of board games which she didn't recognize and a display of books. She spotted *The Book of the Law* by Aleister Crowley and recalled Brody's mention of him earlier.

Pope stopped outside the doorway and turned to Khan. 'I'm going to take the lead on this, DS Khan, but I'd like you to get things started and try to put him at ease first. Use your relationship and get him in a talkative mood.'

She nodded. 'OK, will do.'

Khan went ahead and opened the door, a small bell chiming as they entered. They followed her inside and Pope immediately smelled the sweet, sickly aroma of incense. She hated incense. The interior was so dark that it took her eyes a couple of seconds to adjust to the gloom. The burgundy carpet and mahogany bookshelves that lined the left-hand side of the shop didn't help matters. The place was absolutely teeming with paraphernalia. The shelves were crammed with books, and there were display cabinets on the right-hand side filled with everything from crystals to stuffed animal heads and assorted body parts. The wall at the back was covered with medieval-looking gadgets and ominous symbols created from metal or wood. Pope instinctively scanned for an inverted pentagram but didn't see anything which resembled what they were looking for.

On the floor of the shop were a number of tables, all containing books displayed to attract the customer. Pope browsed the titles and could see that they ranged from the more lightweight titles offering an insight into popular magic tricks, to more dubious titles around witchcraft and the occult. One section was entirely devoted to books either by or about Aleister Crowley.

Pope indicated the table to Brody.

'What is it about this Crowley guy?'

'Oh, Aleister is a very important figure in the world of the occult.' The voice was deep and loud. Its owner came from a room at the back of the premises. Pope saw a tall, lean man in his mid-to-late thirties, dressed entirely in black. He wore velvet trousers and a black denim shir with a matching velvet jacket over the top. He had long blonde hair. Pope thought he looked like a wannabe 1970s rock star.

'Acheron. Nice to see you again.' Khan walked towards him and shook his hand. He smiled and seemed genuinely pleased to see the officer.

'DS Khan. How are you?'

'I'm very well, thanks. How about you?'

'Can't complain.'

'How's business?'

'Business is very good these days. The Harry Potter bounce shows no sign of slowing down, and TikTok is also helping, I'm glad to say.' He smiled and looked at Pope.

'Acheron. These are my colleagues, DCI Pope and DI Brody.'

'Pleased to meet you. Thanks for seeing us so quickly,' said Pope as she shook his hand. She noticed long, slender fingers, carefully manicured.

'What's your full name?' asked Brody, getting out his notebook.

'Just Acheron.' He didn't offer any further explanation and Pope thought they probably didn't need any. He wasn't connected to the case as far as they knew.

'Any further trouble since the burglary?' asked Khan.

Pope noticed how at ease she seemed with the man, a valuable skill these days with an ever more wary public.

'No, nothing. The new alarm system you guys recommended seems to be doing the job.' He looked around the shop. 'Although I'm not sure how many people would want to nick what I have here.'

'So, what *do* you have here?' asked Pope. 'What exactly do you sell?'

'We have two main strands to the business. The first is everyday magic equipment. Tricks, how-to manuals, outfits, that sort of stuff. The second is a bit more esoteric and specialized.'

'And what's that?' prompted Pope.

'I cater to those who are interested in the occult.'

'And what does that consist of?'

43

Acheron thought for a moment. 'The occult relates to anything mystical, supernatural, other-worldly. Anything which we can't easily explain. That which is beyond our normal range of understanding.'

'And what do you sell that fits into this category?'

'Oh, crystals—' he indicated a display case containing a number of differently coloured rocks — 'tarot decks, books and so forth.'

Pope noticed that he was looking a little less comfortable.

'Anything else? Anything a bit more interesting?'

He looked surprised at the question. 'Well, we have items that might be of interest if you are, for example, putting together some potions or elixirs. And some potent symbolic items.' He looked up at the display on the wall at the back of the shop.

'You seemed a bit reluctant to talk about those.'

Acheron looked directly at her with an intense gaze which she found rather unsettling.

'The occult is generally misunderstood by the layman. Or layperson, should I say.'

'In what way?'

'People watch movies and TV shows and get a distorted view. They think it's all witches and summoning the devil. It's much more than that and far less salacious.'

Pope decided not to get into a debate about the definition of the occult.

'Do you have anything here connected to satanism?'

'Yes, actually! It's a really fascinating branch. Again, often completely misunderstood by the layman.'

Pope wasn't sure what she was expecting. Maybe a coy acknowledgement of his interest, or outright denial. But his enthusiasm for the subject was obvious.

'Misunderstood how?'

'Very similar to what I said about the occult. Most people get their ideas about the devil from popular culture. *The Omen*, *The Exorcist*, *Rosemary's Baby* and so forth.'

Old references, thought Pope. Has he seen anything made in the last fifty years?

'And these aren't representative of what you understand by satanism?' she asked.

'No. Nothing even remotely accurate.' Acheron smiled. 'But that's Hollywood. An interest in the devil has been around for centuries. Initially conceived as a fallen angel who rebelled against God, Satan has often been used by Christians to attack anyone who differed from their beliefs. The Salem witch trials, for example.'

Brody looked up. 'Massachusetts, late seventeenth century, right?'

'Yes, exactly,' said Acheron. 'But also against Jews and Catholics and so forth. Basically a catch-all for anyone who disagreed with the dominant religious beliefs of the time.'

'How much interest is there in the practice today?' asked Pope.

'It's still very niche. There was a moral panic about it in the US in the eighties, some of it tied to music. But I must say the links with QAnon have led to more of an interest in the last couple of years. I get a fair few people through the door asking about it. Wanting to read up on the subject.'

'Here? In the UK?' Pope was surprised.

'Yeah, to an extent. I mean, not like in the States. I was at a convention last year and the Americans are all over it. Lots of interest, according to my American counterparts.'

Acheron seemed genuine to Pope. He wasn't embarrassed by his interest in what most people would call nonsense and he was only too happy to help. She walked over to the wall displaying the symbols and icons of the occult.

'We're looking for some information on a particular symbol which has come up in an investigation. Do you know much about that kind of thing?' Acheron walked over to where Pope was standing.

'Depends on the symbol,' he said, clearly intrigued.

She turned to him. 'An upside-down pentagram.' She watched his face closely for a response.

He narrowed his eyes, thinking. 'What's the context?'

'I can't really answer that. But the symbol in general. What does it represent?'

45

He walked a few steps away, then turned back. 'Is it definitely inverted? Because that's quite different to a standard pentagram.'

'Yes, two points at the top, one at the bottom.'

He fixed Pope with a stare. 'You probably already know the answer to that. Given that you're here and asking me about satanism.'

Pope couldn't read his tone. Was he scared? Hostile?

'We have an idea, yes. DS Khan thought that you might be able to give us a more educated view.'

He looked at Khan and nodded slowly.

'The traditional pentagram has one point facing upwards, which many take to represent the ascendancy of the spirit to heaven, to God. It's long been used to represent good and positivity. But the inverted pentagram, as you can probably work out, is the opposite.'

'The single point facing down being the soul's descendancy to Hell, to the devil?' suggested Brody.

'Exactly. Pretty straightforward. But also seen by some as a potent symbol of evil. It scares some people. I'm interested in why the police are asking about this.'

Pope really wanted to show him the photos of the victim and the symbol carved into his chest, but knew that she couldn't. That particular element of the crime would cause widespread panic if it became public.

'It's part of an ongoing investigation, so we can't go into detail.' Pope took a chance. 'Have you had anyone in the shop recently asking about pentagrams, or symbols in general?'

Acheron thought for a moment. 'No, I don't think so. Nothing like that.'

'Anyone buying books on the subject? Devil worship?'

'We do a steady stream of business selling books, and some of them are about the occult. Crowley is consistently popular.'

'Why him in particular?'

'He's the name everyone knows. Did you know that in a BBC poll of the greatest Britons, Crowley came seventy-third? He's still a celebrated figure.'

'Really?' Pope couldn't hide her surprise. Perhaps this branch of the occult was more popular than she thought. It certainly suggested a wider suspect pool. She looked at Brody and Khan. She wasn't sure how much new information they had learned, but she didn't have anything else to ask at this stage.

'You've been very helpful, Acheron. Do you have a card in case we need to ask you any more questions?'

He took a card from a transparent plastic holder on the counter and presented to her with a flourish.

'At your service.'

Pope looked at the card, which was a deep purple with his name in gold letters, followed by an email and mobile number.

'Talking of cards, DCI Pope, would you mind if I took a reading?' he said, producing a pack of cards from his jacket pocket.

Pope looked confused, then remembered what Khan had said.

'You have a fascinating and very powerful aura.' He walked close to her and she instinctively took a step back.

'No, thanks. I don't believe in magic. In tarot cards,' she corrected herself.

'It's not about whether you believe in the tarot, DCI Pope. They are what they are, whether you believe or not.' Acheron now had a persuasive intensity which was at odds with his earlier, more relaxed disposition. He was clearly invested in this.

'No, I . . .'

'I have been very helpful in assisting you. The least you can do is allow me to give you a reading. You never know, you might find out something interesting.'

Pope saw Brody smiling, Khan trying not to.

'Come on, DCI Pope, I'm interested in what the cards have to say,' said Brody.

Pope shot him a look to say he'd pay for this later. Again, he smiled.

She sighed inwardly. The easiest way to get out of here was to play along. 'What do I have to do?'

'Simply pick a card from the deck. Think carefully before you do it, though.' He deftly spread the cards out in his hand.

Pope hesitated, then slowly eased a card from the pack. She held it face down.

'Turn it over,' he said.

Pope did so, revealing a card with an image of a rider on a horse, holding a black flag. The word 'Death' was written in ancient-looking script at the bottom. She rolled her eyes.

'I think I saw this scene in a Bond movie years ago.'

Acheron didn't seem too perturbed.

'Don't worry too much, DCI Pope. The death card doesn't usually represent actual physical death. It's often more about change, although that change can sometimes be traumatic.'

'Good to know,' said Pope.

'But I have to say . . . you do have something of a dark aura surrounding you at the moment.'

'I'm a Homicide detective, it comes with the territory. Thanks for all your help. We'll be in touch if we need anything else.'

She turned and left the shop, followed by Brody, and after she had said her goodbyes, Khan.

When they got to the car, Brody unlocked the doors.

'Maybe you should get the bus. I'm not sure we should be riding with your dark aura in the car,' he said.

'Be careful. My dark aura will be conducting your annual review.'

Brody and Khan laughed and they all got in the car.

Brody drove them back towards the station. Pope had made light of the reading, and she genuinely didn't believe in anything like that. But she was also painfully aware that recent events in her life would have given anyone a dark aura. She just hoped that it was behind her, not still to come.

CHAPTER SEVEN

They arrived back at Charing Cross Police Station in the early evening. The journey had taken twice as long as the one there due to the rush-hour traffic in Central London. When they parked, Pope looked at her watch and turned to Brody and Khan.

'Right. We'll call it a day. Tomorrow we'll talk to the victim's partner and their work colleagues. We can follow up uniforms' interviews from earlier. And hopefully we'll have the autopsy report. We still don't know actual cause of death.'

'Do you want me to organize the interviews before I go?' asked Brody.

Pope was about to say that she'd do it herself, but she knew that if she went back inside she'd end up being there for another hour, and she really needed to get home and deal with the fallout from the holiday that she'd ruined.

'OK, that would be great. Thanks.'

'Anything you need me to do?' asked Khan.

'No, just get some good rest. We've got a busy day tomorrow.'

Khan nodded, and they all got out of the car. Brody headed towards the office, Khan walked to the pedestrian exit and Pope found her keys and unlocked her car. She felt guilty that she had sent Brody to arrange tomorrow's interviews, but he had offered. She had been up since the crack of dawn packing and getting ready for New York. Was that only this morning? It seemed like days ago. She started the engine and pulled the car out of the underground garage.

Driving home was slow. If she'd thought about it, she might have decided that spending a bit more time in the office and waiting for the traffic to subside would have made more sense. But she was so tired that she just sat, crawling over Waterloo Bridge, almost oblivious to the snail's pace.

She knew she had to steel herself for the conversation she would be having when she got home. Alex had been far less angry than she had expected, but it would come at some point, probably when she arrived home, and she had to be prepared for that. She had no comeback: it was entirely deserved. How often had Pope come to that conclusion?

In the bigger picture, there was change happening in their family dynamic. Hannah was becoming a teenager, with all that entailed. Pope had noticed that she veered between being loving, then defensive, then combative. She thought of herself at that age. A more complicated family dynamic, for sure, but the same difficulty in navigating a changing world both external and internal. She hoped that she would be able to be there for Hannah. She would never replace Hannah's mum, but she wanted to be available if and when she was needed. She knew that in the first instance that meant physically being in the house more often.

Chloe was altogether more complicated. Just about to hit eighteen and planning to go to university. Their relationship had been difficult for a while. But recently, over the past six months or so, it seemed to Pope that the two of them had grown closer. It had surprised her when Chloe had suddenly become more understanding of the commitments of Pope's work, arguably more so than Alex. She was becoming a young woman and was maturing fast. Alex perceived that Chloe was 'going off the rails', in his words. She had been staying out late, not keeping in contact, resenting questions about her life. But Pope saw it more as the difficult space between childhood and adulthood, the growing need for independence. Easy to say when it's someone else's children, Pope was aware. However, Chloe had bypassed Alex on several occasions recently and come to Pope for advice. Alex was pleased that Chloe was asking a responsible adult when she was unsure, but Pope realized that any parent would feel conflicted that their own daughter hadn't come to them first. Pope had explained to Alex that it was a female thing, that there were some topics that were easier to discuss with another woman. But there was an undeniable tension there that hadn't yet been fully resolved.

Pope's reflections on the state of her family life were interrupted by the realization that she was pulling into her street. She lived in Alex's house, just outside Greenwich, South London. She had driven home on autopilot, distracted by the catalogue of problems she had to deal with at home, the majority of which were of her own making. She pulled up outside her house and took a deep breath, preparing to face what she fully deserved.

When she went in through the front door, all seemed calm, with the faint sound of the TV coming from the living room. Pope hung up her jacket and walked in. Alex and Hannah were sitting on the large sofa, with Chloe curled up on one of the armchairs, facing the TV. Pope saw that they were watching another of the reality shows which the girls seemed to favour these days. Alex got up, seemingly pleased with the distraction. He walked over to Pope and gave her a hug, kissed her on the cheek.

'Hi, everybody,' said Pope, mustering all the positivity she could manage.

Hannah and Chloe both said 'Hi', then turned back to their programme immediately. Was she being frozen out due to her actions earlier in the day, or were the characters on screen simply more interesting? She wasn't sure which would be worse.

Pope and Alex walked to the kitchen part of the large, open-plan room to ensure they could talk without further disturbing the viewing.

She took his hands in hers. 'Alex, I'm so sorry about earlier. About New York. It's awful, I know.'

He shook his head as if to dismiss the topic. Pope knew it wasn't that an apology wasn't necessary, but Alex was unable, or unwilling, to have the conversation.

'Not now. This is a bigger conversation for another day. What's going on at work?'

Pope looked closely at Alex but decided not to force the issue. She was quite happy not to have this conversation tonight.

She lowered her voice. 'Murder. A young guy. Pretty horrific.'

'I hate to minimize it, but that doesn't sound like the kind of thing that would pull you back from leave.'

Pope paused. She didn't like to bring the grisly details of her job back to her family, but she knew Alex needed some sort of explanation.

She lowered her voice still further. 'The killer carved a symbol into the body. A religious symbol. So, pretty deranged.'

Alex looked shocked. Then he nodded slowly. Maybe Pope had done enough to explain her earlier actions for the time being.

'Have you got any leads?'

Alex would want a quick resolution, not a case that dragged on interminably, but she didn't have anything to offer him at this stage.

Pope shook her head. 'It's still early on in the investigation. We'll be interviewing family and colleagues tomorrow, so that might get us started.'

Chloe walked into the kitchen. 'You're investigating a murder?'

Pope nodded. 'Yes, I'm afraid so.'

Given what had happened to Chloe in the past, the trauma she had suffered as a result of her involvement in the

Cameraman case, she was hypersensitive about Pope's work and very wary of possible implications for her. But she had also started listening to true-crime podcasts and lately had shown genuine interest in Pope's cases.

'What was the symbol?' she asked.

Clearly she hadn't lowered her voice enough.

'I can't really discuss it, Chloe. I didn't mean for you to hear that. I'm sorry.'

She glanced over Chloe's shoulder. Thankfully, Hannah was still engrossed in the reality TV programme.

'Why not? I'm almost eighteen. I'm interested,' she persisted.

'I know. But I'm not allowed to talk to anyone outside the investigation at this stage. Your age isn't the issue.'

Pope noted that Alex was letting her deal with this without intervening. This was a fairly new dynamic. Alex was attempting to avoid conflict with his daughters where he could and giving Pope more responsibility to deal with things.

'Come on, Bec. Please.'

'OK, I'll tell you what. I can't discuss it now, but when we make an arrest, I'll tell you all about it. I'm allowed to do that. How does that sound?'

Chloe seemed to weigh up whether she should press the issue.

'Was that why you couldn't go on holiday? Because the murder was so violent?'

Pope could feel Alex looking at her with a laser focus.

'Well, it's an unusual case and they needed someone with enough experience to deal with it. There were no other DCIs available and it's on our patch. Unfortunately that's one of the downsides of my job. I have to be pretty much always available.'

Chloe seemed to understand. She was growing up.

Pope changed tack to head off any more awkward questions. 'We have a new member of the team. Started today.'

'Did you know about that?' asked Alex, surprised.

'Nope. No idea. Fletcher just brought her into the office and that was that. DS Zahra Khan.'

'That's cool,' said Chloe. 'What's she like?'

'She seems good so far. She hasn't got much experience, but she did well today. I'm hopeful that she's going to be a good fit for the team, but we'll see.'

Chloe nodded, then wandered back to her chair to catch up with the TV.

Alex waited for Chloe to settle down.

'How do you feel about the new DS?'

Pope looked up at the ceiling and let out a deep breath. 'It was hard when Fletcher told me. I felt disloyal to Miller.' She caught herself. 'To Adam. It feels too soon.'

'It's been three months, hasn't it?'

'It has, but it doesn't feel like that. I don't know . . . it just felt like I was reliving it all over again. I think that would have happened whenever someone new turned up.'

'I suppose it had to happen and maybe it's part of the healing process,' said Alex.

Pope nodded. She knew he was right, but it didn't make it any easier.

She took his hand again.

'We'll get away to New York. I promise. Soon.'

'Be careful making promises, Bec. I might hold you to them.'

She smiled. 'I'd like to be held to this one. You guys really should have gone. I feel terrible that I ruined your holiday as well as mine.'

'Look, Bec. Your job is a problem in all kinds of different ways. We both know that. There's no point in us keep having the same old conversation about priorities and how much you give to the Met. I have to accept you as you are, or we're never going to make this work. We have to do things together if we're to be a proper family.'

Pope nodded. She didn't know what to say. She squeezed his hand.

'One day, we're going to have a normal family life, whatever that is,' he said. 'Or at least as normal as we can. The girls deserve that.'

Pope smiled. 'Normal sounds good.'

'But you know what that means. What you're going to have to try to do?'

'I do. And I'm working on it. Seriously.'

They hugged.

'Let's open a bottle of wine and get some dinner cooked,' said Alex.

Pope was nonplussed. It had gone much better than she thought it would. She was really pleased, but she also felt guilty. She deserved more grief for what she had put them through. The latest in a long line.

After dinner, some wine and some inconsequential television, they went to bed. Chloe stayed up, almost certainly talking to her boyfriend on social media. It was quite early, but Pope had a busy day tomorrow and she needed the rest. Her insomnia had improved for a while last year, but had now returned with a vengeance after the death of her sergeant.

Alex said goodnight and rolled over. He had the capacity to fall asleep in a ludicrously short space of time, then sleep like a baby for eight hours. Pope wondered if she should see a doctor about getting some sleeping pills, but she had heard that they made you groggy in the morning and that was not an option for her.

As she attempted to drift off to sleep, the familiar thoughts intruded, her relationship with Alex at the forefront. She was pleased that they seemed to have reached some sort of understanding and that he had been able to articulate where they went from here. That he had accepted the holiday cancellation was great. She was really pleased about that. But she was also aware that this was a fragile situation. He said he was prepared to accept her approach to work, but often this was outside her control. Her work also had a habit of impinging on their family life in all kinds of different ways. She considered this. A work in progress was the best she could come up with.

Pope was pleased that the new recruit to the team seemed a good choice so far. Pope recognized how difficult it must be coming into her team. Khan was young, a woman and the only person of colour on the team. But that immediately sent her mind to Miller. However she thought about it — and lying in bed tonight, she thought about it in every conceivable way — it seemed like he was being replaced. Alex had pointed out the inevitability of this change, but it hurt a great deal. She wasn't going to cry herself to sleep tonight. She had done enough of that three months ago and on occasions since.

Given that Pope didn't believe in the supernatural, the occult, the devil or any associated ideas, it was ironic that as she finally managed to get to sleep in the early hours, the last thing she thought of was the tarot reading and the death card she had drawn.

CHAPTER EIGHT

After arranging the interviews of friends and work colleagues for tomorrow, Brody logged off of his computer terminal and headed home. He checked the time: not too late. Lizzie should be home by now and hopefully cooking dinner.

Brody had met Lizzie at a friend's party around four months ago. It had been an instant attraction for both of them and before long he was spending more time at her flat than at his own. Hers was much nicer, bought with a deposit loan from her parents which they had no intention of letting her pay back. She lived in a vibrant part of the city near Elephant and Castle. This was close for her job, a staff nurse at Guy's Hospital at London Bridge, and also closer to work for Brody than his own flat. The arrangement seemed to suit them both and in his estimation, things were going really well.

As he let himself in the communal door and climbed the stairs to the first floor, the smell of spaghetti bolognaise reached him. Well, her vegan version of the dish, which was absolutely excellent. Lizzie had not encouraged Brody to adopt a vegan diet at all, but by default he was eating almost exclusively vegan these days and feeling better for it. Brody realized he was starving.

He let himself in the front door. Lizzie was dressed in sweatpants and her favourite Joni Mitchell T-shirt. She turned as she heard the door open.

She gave a big smile and bounded over, putting her arms around him and delivering a slow kiss. Brody enjoyed that they were still at this stage in their relationship. He relinquished his grip and she returned to the hob, resuming stirring the bolognaise sauce.

'It's almost ready. How was your day?'

Brody took off his jacket and rolled up his shirtsleeves. He leaned against the worktop. There was only one reception space, a kitchen/diner/living room, but it was fairly big and there was plenty of space for the two of them.

'I've had better,' he replied.

Lizzie looked at him, concerned, nodding to indicate that he should go on.

'Murder in Bloomsbury. Pretty awful.'

'Oh, that's terrible. Your case?'

'Bec had to cancel her holiday.'

'No! Why? I thought they were going to New York.'

'They were. She was at the airport and got a call from Fletcher telling her she had to come back. They didn't have anyone else who could lead.'

'What about you? You could have done it.'

'Maybe. But for a case like this Fletcher wanted a DCI. Well, I think he wanted Bec.'

Lizzie knew better than to ask what 'a case like this' meant at this stage in the investigation.

'So did her family go without her?' she asked.

'Nope. They decided to cancel and do it another time.'

'Ouch. She must feel terrible.'

'She does. She was going home to face the music this evening,' said Brody.

'Poor Bec. I bet she needs a holiday.'

'Yes, I think she does. How was your day?'

'The usual. So many people in today. Some saying they can't get doctor's appointments so they come straight to A&E. Don't really need to be there at all.'

Lizzie rotated through several different departments and was currently working in emergency medicine.

'We should book a holiday. What do you think?' she said.

They hadn't been on holiday together yet and Brody hadn't even thought about it.

'That's a great idea. Where do you fancy?'

'The Maldives or the Seychelles. You're paying.' She smiled, to make sure he knew it was a joke.

'Maybe somewhere a bit less ambitious. How about New York?' he asked. He'd been jealous ever since Pope announced she was going.

She looked at him. 'Is this because you're reading that book about 9/11?' Brody's fascination with all things Twin Towers was a source of some amusement to Lizzie.

'I'd love to visit Ground Zero one day.'

'Better start saving, then. New York ain't cheap. Right, let's eat.'

She served up and put a bowl of pasta for each of them on the small dining table. She brought a bottle of white wine over and poured them both a glass.

Brody saw that Lizzie looked a little more serious.

'How do they manage a family and two jobs, when one of them is so demanding?'

'Do you mean Bec and Alex?'

She nodded, a mouth full of spaghetti.

'With difficulty, I think. Bec doesn't talk too much about it at work, but you can see the strain she's under at times. But I think what's been going on over the last couple of years with her has made it more difficult as well.'

'She's really been through it,' she said.

'I think she's OK, though. She says it's easier than it was at the start. She needed to break Alex in to the rigours of being the partner of a police officer.' He smiled.

'Is that what's happening now? You're breaking me in?' she asked, returning the smile.

'Trying to. Is it working?'

'I think it's a bit different for us, don't you?'

59

'You mean because you're a nurse?'

'Yeah. I suppose there are similarities with our jobs in terms of hours, shifts, the unpredictable work.'

'I guess so. You tell me. How do you feel about it all?'

Brody hadn't been in a relationship before where they talked so much about their feelings and about how things were going. He had learned a lot about being emotionally open with Lizzie and it seemed to be working. They were still together after four months, anyway.

'It's not a problem for me. I work more nights than you do.'

'That's true. Maybe you should be breaking me in to the rigours of being the partner of a nurse?'

They both laughed and took a sip of wine.

'Do you think it will get to us eventually? Will we find that our work gets in the way?'

Brody thought for a moment. 'I don't see why it should. I think we both knew what we were getting into.'

'Not me. Didn't give it a second thought. I just fell for your macho charms.'

'Understandable.'

They ate and drank wine in silence for a while.

'What about if we have kids?' she asked.

Brody was blindsided. They'd never even mentioned the idea of having children and he wasn't sure what to say.

Lizzie seemed to register his surprise.

'I don't mean let's get in the bedroom now and start making babies! I mean at some point in the future. If that's what we decide to do.'

She looked slightly embarrassed and was trying to make it better. Brody wanted to help.

'Well, other people cope, don't they? Plenty of working couples manage to bring up children.'

'Yes, and I suppose the shift patterns might actually help if we could work it around childcare?'

This was heading in a direction Brody had not expected. He finished his spaghetti and drained his glass of wine.

'I don't know about all this, but I seem to remember you mentioning something about heading to the bedroom.' He looked at her.

'Would those be your smouldering bedroom eyes?'

'Yes. Is it working?'

She paused. 'Yes, I think it just might be.'

CHAPTER NINE

Wednesday morning

Pope arrived at the station early, needing to catch up. She'd left home without waking Alex up like so many times before. As she was walking up the stairs to her office, she sent him a quick text to say she'd had to leave and would call him later. She'd try to remember to do that.

Sitting down at her desk, she logged on to her computer and checked her emails. There was nothing of consequence to the current case. Just as she was considering next steps, Khan came in, removing her jacket as she walked to Miller's desk. Her desk, Pope corrected herself.

'Morning,' she said to Pope. 'How was your evening?'

'Fine. I was pretty tired, so nothing exciting.'

'I know,' Khan exclaimed. 'I was absolutely shattered last night. Fell asleep really early.'

'New job. New stresses and strains, new people to meet,' said Pope.

'I suppose so. I hope it's not going to be like that every night.'

'I wouldn't count on it. Busy day today.'

Just then Brody walked briskly into the office.

'Morning all,' he said with more enthusiasm than the hour warranted.

'You're worryingly energetic this morning,' said Pope. 'Have a good evening?'

'Yes, thanks. All good.' He sat down at his desk and switched on the computer.

'Shall I make us some coffee?' asked Khan.

'Great. Milk, no sugar for me,' said Pope.

'Same for me,' said Brody.

'I'm going to call Fletcher and see if he wants to sit in on the team meeting. Can you see where Thompson is?' she asked Brody.

'Yup. I just saw him on the way in. I'll give him a buzz.'

Pope wondered what had made Brody so upbeat at this time in the morning. She assumed that his relationship must be going well if it was sending him into work with this level of enthusiasm.

Fletcher answered on the first ring. Thankfully he was available, otherwise she'd have to go through it all again. Thompson arrived within a couple of minutes of Brody calling him, closely followed by the Super, in his usual too-smart suit and highly polished shoes. Pope reflected that people who dressed like that very rarely had actual jobs. They simply kept an eye on those who did. Fletcher sat down, crossed his legs and folded his arms. He acknowledged everyone around the table with a brief nod of the head, then waited for Pope to get started.

'Right. Thanks, everyone.' She waited for Brody and Khan to join them.

'Let's go through and see what we have, how we're going to handle today. We've got a number of uniforms already on door-to-door, expanding the area after yesterday afternoon.'

'Anything so far?' asked Fletcher.

'Not yet. Time of death was sometime late at night, so there weren't many people around.'

'Do we have a more specific time of death?' asked Fletcher.

'Not as yet. We're hoping to get the autopsy report today, which might help us with a more precise time.'

Fletcher nodded thoughtfully.

'DI Brody, DS Khan and I interviewed a guy yesterday who runs a magic and occult shop in Hackney. Name of Acheron. He wasn't that helpful, but he confirmed what we thought about the symbol carved on the body. Also backed up by Tobias Darke. The inverted pentagram is a symbol often associated with evil, Satan, the descent to Hell. The other way up it has generally positive connotations, but this is the opposite.'

Pope had discussed this with Fletcher yesterday and she hoped he wouldn't ask any more questions about it until they knew more.

'The question, of course, is whether the use of this symbol was deliberate and has some specific meaning, or whether it was chosen at random. I'm not sure we're going to get an answer to that before we talk to the killer. Again, maybe the autopsy will tell us something useful about that.'

'Cause of death?' asked Fletcher.

'Not yet. Autopsy. Again,' said Pope.

Fletcher nodded, a frown on his face. 'Do we have anything more on the victim yet?'

Steven Thompson tapped the screen of his tablet to bring it to life.

'The victim's name is Paul Ward, twenty-eight, of 14 Milton Court, Bloomsbury. Lives with his partner, Eric Acevedo, thirty-one. Ward worked for Knight IT Solutions in Canary Wharf as a programmer. Acevedo is a secondary school teacher. Ward has a clean record, except for a couple of speeding offences a few years ago. Nothing relevant.'

'And Acevedo?' asked Pope.

'Clean,' said Thompson. 'He's had a preliminary interview with uniform yesterday, no red flags.'

'So, what are the next steps?' asked Fletcher.

'Uniforms are continuing their sweep of the area. That'll continue all day,' said Pope. 'Brody and I are going to interview the partner, then we'll head to Canary Wharf to talk to the victim's boss and his colleagues. Hopefully we'll also hear from Dr Okafor about the results of the autopsy. Khan and

Thompson, can you see what else you can dig up on Ward and Acevedo? Also check out Knight IT Solutions, in case there's anything we need to know. And find some CCTV from Monday night. I want to see what our victim was up to and anyone who might have been following him. Look at the last few days too, in case there's a pattern to the victim's behaviour or anyone suspicious scoping the area.'

Khan and Thompson both nodded their agreement.

Pope thought it would be useful for Khan to see how Thompson worked and get a sense of the tech in the department. She realized that she was asking Khan to slot into Miller's old role and felt an odd sensation of betrayal. She brushed it aside.

'DCI Pope, can I have a word in my office?' Fletcher strode out of the room without waiting for a reply.

Pope rolled her eyes at Brody and left to follow Fletcher.

Fletcher entered the office and sat in his large chair. Pope stood by the door, hoping to keep the meeting quick.

'Can you close the door, Bec?' He waited while she did so. 'How's DS Khan shaping up?'

'She's only been with us for a day.'

'I know. But initial impressions?'

'She seems bright, good people skills, positive attitude. So far, so good. But as I said, it's early days.'

'Make sure she gets the support she needs. I want this to work out —her being on your team, I mean.'

Pope knew what he meant. 'I'll do my best, sir.'

Fletcher paused for a moment, held her gaze. 'I need to tell you something, DCI Pope. I'm in line for a promotion to Chief Super.'

'Congratulations.' Pope knew what was coming.

'So, this is a case I don't want hanging around for long.'

She nodded. 'Understood.'

'A quick solution to this case would go a long way in helping it all along. If we can avoid any embarrassment to the Met along the way, it would be much appreciated. And not just by me.' He gave her a knowing look.

'Right, sir. As I said, understood.'

'Get this maniac, Bec. And fast.'

Pope nodded. As she left the office, closing the door behind her, she considered how Fletcher had managed to get through the conversation without using the word 'optics', one of his favourite terms.

Pope walked back to her office and sat down in her chair. Khan and Thompson had disappeared, presumably to Thompson's office. Brody walked over and sat in the empty chair opposite.

'Everything OK?'

'Yeah. He wanted to know how Khan is doing. And, of course, he was urging us to catch this guy quickly.'

'Of course,' echoed Brody.

'It's as if he thinks without telling us to solve a crime, we'll just sit around drinking coffee and doing nothing.'

'Fancy a coffee?'

Pope smiled. 'I would, actually. Thanks.'

While Brody made them a drink, Pope searched for anything connected to Paul Ward on her computer. She found several links to social media accounts. She clicked the first, but it was marked as private and she couldn't access it. She tried another. She had more luck and scrolled through the usual content. Why did every social media account look the same? Holidays, outings to bars with friends, birthdays. There were even some photos of Ward's cat, doing the same thing that everybody's cat seems to do. Nothing that could help her on initial inspection. She then returned to the list of hits for Paul Ward and found his entry on LinkedIn. He had been with Knight IT Solutions for five years and seemed to have been promoted several times within that period. Again, nothing to pique her interest.

Brody brought over the coffee and sat down again.

'I'm just looking at Paul Ward's online presence.'

'Anything interesting? I know Thompson was looking at that.'

'I just wanted to get a feeling for it myself. Nothing that's helpful. He's been in his present job for five years.

Seems to be doing well, judging by the different roles he's had.'

'Any links to the occult?'

'Nothing. One of his accounts is private so I can't see anything there, but otherwise it's just the usual stuff.'

'What about Acevedo?'

'Let's have a look.' Pope typed Eric Acevedo's name into the search engine. She clicked on a few hits and scrolled for a minute.

'Acevedo teaches maths at a secondary school in Forest Gate. I'm looking at his Facebook now.' She concentrated on the screen. 'It's locked. Profile picture has him holding a cat.'

'Black cat?'

'No. Nothing so easy, I'm afraid. Ginger. Hardly a smoking gun.'

Brody nodded. 'You see what people want you to see on social media. If they were into the occult, they might not advertise it. Especially not if he was a teacher. I don't think that would go down too well.'

'Yes, that's true. We'll see how we get on with him, but it might be worth getting uniform to go to Acevedo's school and talk to his colleagues, see what they can tell us.'

'OK.' Brody made a note to organize this.

'If Ward was in a same-sex relationship, we need to consider the possibility that this is a hate crime.'

'Yeah, although it doesn't explain the pentagram.'

'No, it doesn't. But that could be a smokescreen, to send us in the wrong direction,' said Pope.

'True. But it's so specific, and so brutal, that it doesn't seem like that. This symbolism is very important to whoever did this.'

'I think so too. It doesn't feel like something random. This was carefully planned, even if the execution wasn't quite so careful.'

They were both silent for a while.

'Have we got the interviews lined up?' asked Pope.

Brody checked his notebook.

'I've told the uniform outside Acevedo's flat that we're coming there first. He's at home and is waiting for us. Ward's boss at Knight IT Solutions is expecting us later this morning. He's apparently going to be in meetings all day but will come out to talk to us. Uniforms are on the way to interview his close colleagues. It's a big company and it'd take too long for us to get through all of them.'

'OK, great. We'll see what comes up and follow up on anyone of interest.'

Brody called up his maps app and checked the way to Paul Ward and Eric Acevedo's flat in Bloomsbury. It was very close to where they had found the body. He had only been a few minutes from safety.

'It's only a ten-minute drive to Milton Court.'

Pope drained her cup of coffee.

'OK, let's go.'

They both collected their jackets and walked out of the office, hoping to find out something more useful than Pope had discovered on social media.

CHAPTER TEN

Brody drove towards the address in Bloomsbury in light traffic.

'How was your evening? How's Lizzie?' asked Pope.

'All good. Although she did start a conversation about how we were doing with work–life balance and the difficulties of both of our jobs.'

Pope nodded but didn't say anything. This was not a subject on which she felt qualified to offer advice.

'She even mentioned the possibility of children.'

Another topic well outside Pope's wheelhouse.

'That's pretty soon. How long have you been together?'

'About four months.'

'Do you want to have kids?' she asked. They'd never discussed the topic.

'I'm not sure. I suppose so. One day. How about you?' Brody suddenly seemed unsure about the question.

Pope saw his concern. There was quite a bit to talk about here.

'It's fine.' She thought for a moment. 'I guess it's the old cliché of never enough time, never the right time, with the right person. No specific reason other than that. And our job isn't the easiest in that sense, as life with Chloe and Hannah has shown me.'

'But you get on well with them, don't you?'

'I do, yeah. But there's a big difference. Alex does all the heavy lifting.'

Brody considered that, and the conversation seemed to come to a natural end. They drove the rest of the trip in silence and it wasn't long until Brody pulled into Milton Road. He checked the satnav and they stopped outside a block of purpose-built apartments next to a sign which read *Milton Court*.

'OK, let's see what Eric Acevedo has to say for himself,' said Pope as she got out of the car and looked at the surroundings. This was an expensive part of town. Certainly not the kind of address you could afford on a schoolteacher's salary. The building was immaculate, well looked after, like all the buildings on the street. Paul Ward must have been the main breadwinner, unless the money had come from elsewhere.

Pope and Brody walked up to the communal front door and checked the list of names next to an array of buzzers. There were around twenty flats and Pope soon spotted *Ward/Acevedo*, flat number 14. She tapped the buzzer and waited.

'Hello?' The voice sounded exhausted.

'Mr Acevedo,' said Pope, 'Detectives Pope and Brody from the Metropolitan Police. I believe you're expecting us. Is it OK to come in and have a chat?'

'Get the lift to the third floor, turn left.' A practised explanation.

A further buzzer sounded and they entered the building. It was as smart inside as it was outside. Art Deco tiles on the floor and a sage-green paint on the wall gave the communal areas a calm, warm feel. The lift took quite a while to arrive. When it finally came, Pope and Brody entered an old, tiny box which had a sign on the wall proclaiming a maximum capacity of four people, although Pope doubted you could actually fit that many bodies inside. It rose slowly and noisily to the third floor.

They turned left and saw a front door with *14* in brass numbers. As they walked up, the door opened and Eric Acevedo stood in the doorway.

Pope smiled. 'Detectives Pope and Brody from the Met,' she repeated as they both showed their warrant cards. Acevedo inspected the IDs, looked back at them and nodded.

'Come in,' he said, walking back inside the flat and leaving them to close the door behind them. They followed him through a smart hallway and into an equally well-kept reception room. It was smallish but tastefully decorated with beige wallpaper and a slightly lighter but clearly co-ordinated carpet. On the wall hung several abstract paintings, originals not prints, and a large map of Manhattan and the Hudson River. There were two sofas, one grey and one lime green, and two small armchairs, both matching the grey sofa they sat opposite.

He indicated for them to sit on the chairs while he sat on one of the sofas, a phone and a box of tissues next to him.

Pope studied Acevedo. He was not a tall man, but very athletic in build. Pope speculated that he might spend quite a bit of time in the gym. He was handsome and had jet-black hair, swept back. His track pants and sports T-shirt, which read *Harvard Track and Field*, were casual but looked expensive. She started the interview.

'Mr Acevedo.'

'Eric, please.'

She smiled. 'OK, Eric. First of all, thanks for talking to us today. We're very sorry for your loss and we know what a difficult time this must be for you.'

Acevedo picked up a tissue and wiped his eyes, then blew his nose. The bin next to him was already full.

'Thank you. It's been terrible.'

'Of course,' said Pope. 'Do you need a moment?'

He shook his head wearily. 'No, I want to be of any help I can. To find who did this.'

'That's great. Really helpful. Thank you. Can I just check that we have your details right: Eric Acevedo. You work as a maths teacher at Glenwood School in Forest Gate.'

'Yes, that's right.'

'And this is your main residence? You live here full time?'

'Yes. With Paul.' He caught himself and blew his nose again.

'And how long have you lived here?'

Acevedo thought. 'Almost four years. We bought the flat together. Well, Paul mostly bought it. I put in what I could.'

Pope had the financial arrangements confirmed.

'And how long have you worked at Glenwood?'

'This is my ninth year. I'm head of maths.'

'Tough job,' said Pope.

'Takes one to know one,' he said, almost smiling.

'And how long had you and Paul been together?' She felt awful using the past tense, and from Acevedo's expression he clearly caught it.

'We were together for almost seven years. It would have been our anniversary next month. We were going to go to Barcelona for the weekend.'

'Sorry to hear that. Can you tell us a bit about Paul? What he was like, what he liked to do, hobbies?'

Brody was making notes and Pope saw that he was laser-focused on Acevedo. The partner was always a suspect.

Acevedo smiled a little. 'Paul was great. I know, I would say that. But he really was. He was intelligent, sensitive, caring. Everybody loved him. He was so full of energy, always wanting to go out and do things. He wanted to live in Central London so that we would be close to everything the city has to offer. I told him this place was too expensive, that I couldn't afford it. But he insisted on paying the lion's share. He was really generous like that.'

'Do you have a mortgage, or did you buy the flat outright?'

Acevedo looked evenly at Pope. He wasn't stupid and knew immediately what Pope was getting at. How much did he stand to gain in the event of his partner's death?

'We paid a large deposit, but we've also got a large mortgage. That I won't be able to pay. So, I'll have to sell this place and find somewhere cheaper. The life insurance covers one of us, so only half the mortgage would be paid off.'

He looked around the living room. 'We've spent the last four years making this place exactly like we wanted it. And now I'm going to have to start again somewhere else.'

Pope thought he sounded genuine, but was surprised he had picked up on her question so quickly. Grief often dulled the senses more effectively than that. She tucked the thought away to discuss with Brody after the interview.

'What did Paul like to do? When he wasn't working?'

'He liked to keep fit. He went to the gym at work most days. He loved the theatre and going to gigs. And travelling was his other passion. We had all these plans to visit . . .' His voice cracked and tears came. He took another tissue and wiped his eyes.

Pope waited until Acevedo had composed himself. He was gradually realizing that all the plans they had together were not going to materialize.

He sniffed and blew his nose again. 'I'm sorry.'

'No apology necessary. It must be incredibly difficult, but we appreciate your time. We'll try to keep it as brief as we can.'

He nodded.

'You mentioned he liked going to gigs. What type of music did he like?'

Acevedo's expression showed that he thought this was a strange question.

'He was eclectic. He liked alternative rock, pop, and was starting to get into jazz. We were supposed to be going to see Kamasi Washington this weekend.'

Pope loved Kamasi Washington, but didn't think now was the time to have that conversation. She did, however, make a mental note to check out where he was playing.

Pope now needed to ask something without explaining why she was asking. She wasn't quite sure how she would accomplish this.

'This is going to sound like a strange question.' She glanced at Brody. 'Did Paul have any interest in magic or the occult?'

Acevedo looked predictably surprised. 'Magic or . . . ? No, of course not. I mean . . . no, not that he'd ever talked about. Why do you ask?'

'I can't really go into it at this stage. We're pursuing a number of lines of investigation and this came up. I'm sure it's nothing.'

He didn't look convinced, but had the decency to respect her answer. Pope changed the subject.

'What about Paul's work life? Is it right that he worked at Knight IT Solutions in Canary Wharf?'

'Yes, that's right. He enjoyed it there. He was able to work remotely for some of the time, got to do some travelling, and got paid well. He'd been there for around five years, I think.'

'You mentioned he was popular at work. Is there anyone in particular you think we should talk to at Knight? Anyone who knew him particularly well?'

'We didn't really socialize with his colleagues. He did, but we didn't together. We kept our work lives separate. I had my work friends and he had his. Our socializing was more with communal friends. You could ask his boss, Ken Salmon. They got on pretty well. He might be able to tell you more.'

Pope thought it was unusual that they'd both been working in their current jobs for so long but hadn't formed any friendships that transcended work socializing. But then she thought of her own situation and realized that someone would say exactly the same thing about her.

'Do you know where he was the night before last? He was out late, wasn't he?'

Acevedo nodded. 'He was giving some presentation on a big project he'd been working on and I think it went well. They went out to celebrate. He said he'd be back by around ten, but stayed later. He texted me at eleven saying he'd be home soon. I wasn't happy as I had to get up early the next morning, so I didn't reply. Then after a bit I sent him a snarky message. That was the last communication I had with him. He never replied.' He dissolved in tears again.

Pope looked at Brody. She wasn't sure there was any-thing else to ask at this point. His expression suggested that he thought the same. They both got up.

'Thanks, Eric. You've been very helpful and we really appreciate you answering questions at this difficult time.' Pope took a business card from her jacket pocket. 'The fam-ily liaison officer will be in touch. If you think of anything else that might help us, call me on this number anytime. You can leave a message if you need to. And if we need to ask you anything else, is it OK if we get back in touch?'

'Yes, that's fine. I just want to know who did this.' His eyes were red and tired. Pope thought he needed to sleep.

'Will you let me know when you find this monster?'

'Yes, absolutely. Of course. We'll see ourselves out. Take care of yourself.'

They left, Pope quietly closing the door after them. They decided to take the stairs this time, rather than wait for the slowest lift Pope had ever experienced.

When they got into the car, Pope turned to Brody. 'What do you think?'

'I think he seemed pretty genuine. He's really cut up, as you'd expect. No red flags.'

'He seemed pretty on it. Very together for someone who has just lost a partner.'

'He didn't look very together to me,' said Brody.

'He knew exactly what I was getting at. That's a bit unusual, don't you think?'

'You mean with your subtle questions about his taste in music. Do you like Black Sabbath? Did he ever play his Led Zeppelin albums backwards?' Brody laughed at his own joke.

'You're showing your age.'

'Quite true.'

'But seriously, how else do we find out about any strange tendencies to do with the occult? I didn't see a Ouija board or any books in the flat, let alone any Aleister Crowley biographies.'

'I guess we might have to work on the assumption that Paul Ward was an unlucky victim, in the wrong place at the wrong time. The occult connection may just be the killer, rather than Ward.'

'Yeah, maybe. Did you get the impression that he was telling us everything? Was he holding back?' asked Pope.

'No, I didn't think so. He answered your questions and didn't seem to be playing for time or hiding anything.'

'I thought the same. He knew exactly what I was getting at when I asked him about the mortgage. But we'll need to check that he's telling us the truth about that. We also need to look into Ward's finances. See how he afforded this flat.'

'IT in Canary Wharf? Very well paid, I think. And a good bonus structure.'

'Let's check how Thompson and Khan are getting on.'

Pope called Thompson and asked if there was anything to report. So far, they hadn't found anything of great interest. Pope asked them to focus on Ward and Acevedo's finances and look into the purchase of the flat at Milton Court. She explained that they were going to Canary Wharf to talk to Ward's colleagues, then they'd be back.

Overhearing, Brody checked exactly where Knight IT Solutions was located and started the car. Just as he was pulling away and Pope was ending her call, her phone rang.

'Pope. OK, thanks, we'll be there in ten.'

'What's up?' asked Brody.

'The autopsy is done. I told Dr Okafor we're on the way.'

Brody did a U-turn and they headed for King's College Hospital at Denmark Hill.

They drove south along Kingsway towards Waterloo Bridge. The area was a mix of beautiful buildings, black taxis and a multitude of red London buses.

Brody had a thought. 'Do you think we should pick up Khan on the way? Might be good for her to hear the results first hand? To see the body?'

'We can tell her when we're back,' said Pope.

Brody hesitated. 'It might be good for her to feel part of the team. It's her first homicide with us. It's pretty much on the way.'

Pope considered his suggestion. 'OK. Good point.'

Pope called Khan and told her to be outside Charing Cross Police Station in five minutes. The delights of the autopsy report awaited.

CHAPTER ELEVEN

When Brody pulled up the car outside the main entrance to the station, Khan was standing just inside the doorway. Officers had been told not to hang around on the street outside if possible, to avoid potential surveillance by bad actors. As soon as she saw the car, she walked quickly down the stone steps and got into the back seat.

'How was Eric Acevedo?' she asked immediately.

'He was very upset, of course,' said Pope. 'He appeared genuine — nothing which rang any alarm bells. He isn't aware of anything which connects Paul Ward to the occult. They have a mortgage on the flat that he can't afford, so he'll have to move out. So, no financial motive that we can see immediately. Is Thompson looking into that?'

'He was about to. We've been looking at both of them more closely, but nothing new so far. We've got a couple of uniforms scrubbing the CCTV around the cemetery. There are plenty of cameras in the area.'

'Good. That could be key for us,' said Pope. 'How are you with autopsies?'

'OK. I haven't been to many. And then only after the fact, getting the reports and looking at the body.'

'This will be the same. Dr Okafor will take us through the report and show us the body. You don't need to be there if you don't feel comfortable.'

'No, I want to be there. I need all the experience I can get.' Khan was very enthusiastic, but Pope wondered if she'd feel the same afterwards. Still, she'd been there before, so Pope assumed the woman knew what she was letting herself in for.

Brody drove across Waterloo Bridge and onto Kennington Road, then turned right in the direction of King's College Hospital. He parked the car right in front and put a card identifying them as police officers on the dashboard. They entered through the large revolving doors and took the lift down to the basement floor, where Pathology was situated. The receptionist recognized Pope, a sign that Pope had visited this part of the hospital on too many occasions.

The receptionist checked her diary.

'DCI Pope and DI Brody. Dr Okafor just told me you were on your way.' Everything involving Dr Rachel Okafor was efficient and organized. She handed them a temporary visitor ID badge. Then she looked at DS Khan. She checked her notes for the day.

'And you are?' It sounded abrupt, but Khan took it in her stride.

'DS Khan.' She held out her warrant card. The receptionist took it and used the details to write a further visitor badge. She handed it to Khan with her own ID.

'You know the way by now,' she said, and indicated in the general direction of Dr Okafor's office.

'We do. Thanks,' said Pope.

The three officers were buzzed through a security door and followed a brightly lit corridor to the end. The last door on the left was open. Pope went in first. Rachel Okafor was standing behind her desk, ready to greet them. Pope assumed the receptionist had called ahead.

'DCI Pope, DI Brody. Nice to see you again.'

They shook hands.

'Thanks for seeing us,' said Pope.

'How are you?' asked Brody.

'Not too bad, thanks. The usual.' She looked around the office as if that explained everything. She then looked at Khan expectantly.

'Dr Rachel Okafor, this is DS Zahra Khan. She's just joined us from Hackney.'

Okafor shook hands with the new member of the team. 'So, this is your first case with DCI Pope's team?'

She nodded her head. 'Yes.'

'Baptism of fire,' said Okafor.

'Will it be possible to see the body?' asked Pope.

'Yes, I thought you might want to. Everything's ready.'

Pope always appreciated working with Rachel Okafor. In her mid-forties, a couple of years older than Pope and very experienced, she was always one step ahead. She knew what Pope would want and she was concise and specific in her reports. Pope wished everyone she had to work with was like that.

Okafor picked up an iPad and came out from behind her desk.

'Follow me.'

She led the three detectives to a heavy, imposing door, keyed in a code and took them into autopsy suite one.

'You might want these,' she said, handing each of them a disposable surgical mask from her lab coat pocket. They all put them on and Okafor walked over to a bank of small, square steel doors. She checked her iPad and found door number four. She held the lever on the left-hand side of the door and began to open it. She paused and turned to Pope.

'This is going to be brutal. Are you sure you all want to stay for this part?' Okafor was talking to Pope, but she glanced at Khan as she said it.

'I'll be fine,' said Khan. 'Don't worry about me.'

Okafor gave her a look which Pope thought was admiration, then returned to her task of pulling out the sliding tray inside the door. It held a large, white, zipped-up body bag, which contained the dead body of Paul Ward.

'OK, prepare yourself,' said Okafor. With the tray fully extended, she slowly pulled the zip down the full length of the corpse and pulled it open to reveal the contents. Pope was looking at the body, but also keeping an eye on Khan to see how she reacted. Pope had been aware of being tested on many occasions when she started in the Met. Her first boss in Homicide was eternally putting her in difficult situations in order to see if she would cope. Pope was aware that she was doing the same thing to Khan. But she also wanted to check that she was OK. She had taken an instant liking to her new colleague and she had genuine concern.

Okafor put her tablet down and got straight to business.

'I imagine you want to know four things first of all. Time of death, cause of death, what's going on with the mutilation to the torso, and whether there's any DNA evidence which will help identify the killer.'

Pope nodded. 'That'd be a good start.'

'Well, I've got good news and bad news. First the bad news. Absolutely no evidence of any foreign hairs, fibres, anything which might indicate another person. It seems your killer knew what they were doing, in this aspect at least. They probably wore gloves, maybe a hair covering so as not to leave any identifiable trace.'

Pope looked downcast. DNA evidence was often an excellent starting point in murder cases, and could often lead directly to the killer. Okafor caught the look.

'It's not all bad news. I can tell you that time of death was midnight.'

'That's very specific. What's the margin of error?'

'I don't think there's any margin of error. He wore a mechanical watch and it stopped a few seconds after twelve. The glass was smashed. Given that he was found before midday, we can assume that it suffered a severe blow at midnight and stopped working.'

'Would it definitely do that?' asked Khan.

'It would,' said Brody. He held up his wrist and showed them his own watch. An Omega Seamaster from the 1960s which he had inherited when his grandfather died.

'I wear a mechanical watch. Sometimes the slightest bump can knock the timing off. A blow such as falling on a concrete surface could easily break the mechanism so it would stop working. If the crystal was smashed, then the blow was definitely hard enough.'

'Crystal?' asked Pope.

'That's the name for the glass which covers the face.' Brody indicated his watch by way of illustration.

'Learn something new every day,' said Pope. 'What about cause of death?'

'Poison, I think. Cyanide. She took out a pen and gently eased back the material that was covering Paul Ward's neck. She used the pen to point to a spot a couple of inches below his ear. Can you see just here? The tiny puncture mark?'

The three detectives leaned in to get a look at the place Okafor was pointing. Pope had to really strain to see anything.

'Just there,' said Okafor.

'OK, I see it. It's tiny. How did you spot it?'

'Process of elimination. We checked the whole body and found no sign of any possible cause of death. There was bruising and some scrapes to the arms and legs, but they are consistent with our man falling over. The question is what caused him to fall over. So we went over the body again and found it.'

'Is that definitely it? Could it have been anything else?'

'No, I don't think so. The puncture wound looks like it has been made recently, and in the absence of any other indications, I'm fairly certain that's the injection site.'

'And how do you know it's cyanide?' asked Khan.

'Our tests confirm it, and the dose was easily large enough to kill a man Ward's size. Overkill, in fact.'

'So the killer wasn't precise. They didn't know enough to work out the exact amount to use?' said Khan.

'I wouldn't go that far,' said Okafor. 'They may have been using a belt-and-braces approach. Use much more than you need to make sure. But that is a possibility, yes.'

'Cyanide doesn't work instantly though, does it?' said Brody. 'It takes a while to act.'

'It does. I imagine it was mixed in with a fast-acting sedative, but we need more time to isolate and identify that.'

Pope thought that probably wasn't a crucial piece of information at this stage.

'So, our attacker may have incapacitated Paul Ward somehow and administered cyanide to poison him. Is it possible to tell where the attacker was standing?' asked Pope.

They leaned in close again. Brody was lifting his arm, trying to work out the angle of penetration of the needle. He nodded to himself.

'It depends on whether the attacker was right- or left-handed. As the puncture site is on the right-hand side of the neck, if the attack came from behind, the person who administered it is certainly right-handed. If they were in front of the victim, they would likely be left-handed.'

'Yes, that's the conclusion I'd come to as well, DI Brody,' said Okafor.

'Not that it's going to help us very much as we don't know where the attacker was standing, so it won't eliminate any potential suspects.'

'OK, tell me you have something for us on the wound on his chest,' said Pope.

Okafor moved the covering again to fully expose Paul Ward's chest. It was the first time Khan had seen the wound in person and she was visibly shocked. It had been cleaned up since Pope saw it, but was still utterly horrific.

'Are you OK, DS Khan?' said Pope.

She composed herself. 'Yes, I'm fine. I'm fine.'

Pope nodded for Okafor to continue.

'I'm not sure how much I can tell you here. The wound was administered post-mortem.'

'How can you tell?' asked Pope.

'Looking at the body *in situ* and examining the chest wound, it is clear that the heart had stopped beating before the wound was inflicted. There was quite a bit of blood around the body, but not enough to cause death by itself.'

'So, Paul Ward was murdered, then, when he was dead, the killer took the time to carve this into his chest?' asked Pope. She knew it was obvious, but it was still unbelievable.

'How long would it take to do this?' asked Khan.

'It's difficult to say. It's a simple design in one way, but carving it into human flesh would take some time. It's fairly deep, not a superficial wound by any means.'

'Is it difficult to do?' asked Pope.

Okafor thought about this for a moment. 'It's not that it's difficult to perform from a physical perspective. I mean, it's not easy. But it's the psychological aspect that I think would be the real challenge.'

'In what sense?' asked Pope.

'Well, the mental barrier to actually taking a knife to another human being and carving something into their body . . . that's the key issue here, I would think,' said Okafor.

'So we're looking for someone who has the stomach to do this. Who may have done something similar before?' asked Pope.

'I'm not so sure about that,' said Okafor. She used her pen again to point to the outside of the pentagram. 'If you look at the edges of this wound, you'll note that they're ragged and inconsistent. Maybe hesitant. It doesn't look like they were inflicted with confidence and expertise. If you look at cuts performed by a surgeon, they're precise, consistent, confident. This is very much not like that.'

'So potentially this is someone trying something new. A first-timer?' asked Brody.

'Difficult to say with any certainty, but if I had to bet, I'd say that was the case,' replied Okafor.

'And what type of knife was used?' asked Pope. 'Assuming it was a knife?'

'Yes, I think it was definitely a knife. Smooth-bladed, quite large. Unfortunately nothing which will narrow it down beyond the contents of your average domestic knife block.

'I think that's about everything for the moment, DCI Pope. I'll be in touch when I find out the sedative used and send the completed report over to you once it's finalized.'

'Thank you,' said Pope.

Okafor carefully zipped up the bag, gently slid the body back into the deep opening and closed the door.

She led them out of the sterile room and into the slightly more comfortable area outside her office.

'Thanks again, Dr Okafor,' said Pope.

They said their goodbyes, shook hands and turned to leave.

'No offence, DCI Pope, but hope not to see you soon,' said Okafor.

She made that comment every single time Pope came to see her. Less a joke, more a good-luck talisman. Pope hoped that one day, it might start working.

* * *

Pope, Brody and Khan made their way to the car parked in front of the hospital and got in.

'You did well in there, DS Khan,' said Pope.

'Thanks. I didn't actually mind it, to be honest. I'm not sure why, but it didn't seem to affect me as much as I thought it would.'

'That's a handy skill to have. Hold on to that.'

Brody flipped through the notes he'd made during the examination of Paul Ward's body. 'I think that was very useful. Despite the lack of DNA, Dr Okafor was able to give us some things which hopefully will help once we have a suspect.'

'Run us through them,' said Pope. This was as much for Khan as it was for her.

'Firstly, the cyanide is good. We can get Thompson on where someone can get hold of that. The time of death is also positive. Being so specific will really help when it comes to checking alibis and CCTV. And the sense that this was probably someone inexperienced and hesitant should also help to narrow things down.'

'Yes, maybe. At this stage we proceed as usual, treating this as a single murder rather than the start of something bigger. At least that's what we'll assume until we know otherwise.'

'What about the pentagram?' said Khan. 'You didn't ask Dr Okafor much about that.'

'Her job is the medical and post-mortem aspects of the case. The symbolism and importance of it is ours. That's not what she does.' Pope turned to Brody. 'Let's get over to Knight and see what Paul Ward's boss can tell us.'

Brody started the car, performed a U-turn and pulled out into the steady stream of traffic. He would head to Camberwell before turning east and crossing the Thames to Canary Wharf.

'How important do you think the satanism angle is?' asked Khan as they drove.

Pope shook her head. 'I don't think this is just a random murder. It's possible this is simply a misdirect on the part of the killer. To make us think this is key. Time will tell how important this aspect is.'

Unfortunately, Pope had a feeling in her gut that it was going to turn out to be central to this case.

CHAPTER TWELVE

The drive to Canary Wharf took just over half an hour, slowed by the amount of traffic crawling through the Rotherhithe Tunnel under the Thames. The tunnel was over a hundred years old. The small, white tiles on the walls reminded Pope of the morgue they had just left. While Brody drove, Pope updated Fletcher and Khan re-read her notes and jotted down some further thoughts.

They pulled up outside One Canada Square and got out, looking up at the imposing tower above them.

'This was the tallest building in Britain for quite some time, until the Shard was completed,' said Brody. 'For around twenty years, if I remember correctly.'

'I'm sure you do,' said Pope with a smile.

Khan looked quizzically at Brody.

'He knows more strange facts than you and I will ever forget,' said Pope. 'Come on, let's go and see what Ward's boss has to say for himself.'

They walked in through one of the entrances and showed their warrant cards to the security guards stationed there. The building allowed public access to the lower floor, but there were screens to prevent unauthorized access to the others, which all held offices. Brody called the lift and checked which floor hosted Knight IT Solutions. It arrived quickly and they started the rapid ascent to floor thirty-four.

Exiting into a large, plush concourse, Pope was struck by the fabulous views from the large windows on either side. It seemed as if all of London was on display. She thought it must be an inspiring way to start each day. Compared to the delightful vista she was greeted with most mornings, that of the ancient, tired stairs from the underground parking garage up to her office, she decided Knight won hands down.

In front of them, behind a very large desk, sat a young woman dressed in a smart, black suit. She wore a Bluetooth headset and was busy typing on her sleek desktop computer.

'How can I help you?'

Pope took out her warrant card and showed it to the receptionist.

'DCI Pope. This is DI Brody and DS Khan. We'd like to speak to Ken Salmon.'

The young woman had a look of realization. 'Is this about Paul? So terrible. Just awful.'

Pope would describe her tone as 'corporate sincerity'. She knew it was her duty to be upset, but it lacked any discernible emotion.

'Did you know Paul Ward well?' she asked.

Uniforms had already questioned all employees who knew Ward, and they were only here to follow up with his boss, but Pope thought it was worth a shot.

'Not that well. I saw him each morning he came in, but only really to say hello to. He was lovely, though. Always so polite.'

'Did you ever socialize with him?' asked Pope.

'No, not really. I mean, we went to the occasional office party, but we didn't hang out or talk much. What happened to him? We haven't heard much here.'

'I can't talk about an ongoing investigation, I'm afraid. Can you tell us where we might find Mr Salmon?'

'Yes, of course. Follow me.' She used her ID pass to open a frosted glass door with *Knight IT Solutions* printed at eye level. They seemed to occupy the entire thirty-fourth floor of the building. Inside there was a large, long corridor dotted with artfully arranged sofas. The floor was highly polished grey marble patterned with dark green diamond tiles. On each side were workspaces, some communal and open-plan, others private. She led them to an office halfway through on the left-hand side. On the door was a brass plate which read *K. Salmon, CEO*. She knocked on the door.

'Come in.'

The receptionist opened the door. 'Mr Salmon, there are some police officers here to see you.

'OK, show them in.' Ken Salmon stood up from behind his desk.

'Mr Salmon, I'm DCI Pope, this is DI Brody and DS Khan.'

He shook hands vigorously with all three of them. 'Kenny, please. Everyone calls me Kenny.'

'OK, Kenny,' said Pope.

'Please, take a seat.' He indicated four large armchairs arranged in a horseshoe facing his desk. They sat down and he walked round and sat in the fourth chair, crossing his legs and placing his hands on his knees.

Ken Salmon looked to be mid-fifties, with thick, gelled-back dark hair, greying at the temples. He was around six foot and very slim. He looked to Pope like a marathon runner. Everything about him, from his tailored, perfectly fitted suit, his leather brogues and his Rolex, told you that he was successful, at least in financial terms. If you were in a business meeting with him, you knew that his company was a success. Ken Salmon was the Richard Fletcher of the IT world.

'Can we get you a coffee, or a water?' he asked.

By 'we', Pope assumed he meant his receptionist.

'No, we're fine, thanks.'

'Thanks, Kimberley.'

The receptionist nodded and left the office, closing the door.

'Nice view,' said Pope.

The far wall consisted of floor-to-ceiling windows, show-casing much of East London, the Thames snaking its way round the Isle of Dogs. Today the sun was just at the right angle to reflect off the river, making it appear silver.

Ken Salmon looked over his shoulder. 'It is, isn't it? You just never get tired of it.'

'You're CEO here. Is that right?' asked Pope.

'Yes, for my sins,' he smiled. A bit too smug for Pope's liking, particularly given the circumstances.

'Could you tell us exactly what Paul Ward did here before he was murdered yesterday?' She wanted to jolt him out of his arrogance. It worked. He suddenly looked serious. Corporate sincerity seemed to be a thing at Knight IT Solutions.

'Yes, yes, of course. It's tragic what's happened. Just terrible.'

Salmon spoke with a slight northern lilt, possibly Leeds or Manchester originally. He'd clearly tried hard to lose it.

'Paul was a great employee. Hard-working and brilliant. He started as a programmer but moved a few years ago to project management. He was still quite hands-on, but had the vision and capability to see a project through to delivery. Clients loved him. He had a very bright future ahead of him.'

'And he'd been here for five years. Is that right?'

'Yes, I think so. There's a lot of movement in the IT world, but we know how to look after our employees.'

'And what had he been working on recently?' asked Pope.

'Paul had been developing a solution for one of our clients, Millmark Advertising in East London.'

'And what was the nature of this project?' Pope couldn't bring herself to use the word 'solution', which seemed meaningless in this context.

'It was a complete reworking of their IT infrastructure and cloud storage management. Also their customer-facing interface. He'd actually presented his ideas to me and a couple of senior execs earlier in the day. You know, the day he . . . er . . . the day he died.' Salmon clearly felt uncomfortable.

'And were there any issues with any of the employees at Millmark? Any difficulties so far?'

'Oh, no, nothing like that. Paul had had a couple of initial meetings with them, but he hadn't even presented beyond our internal board.'

'And was there anything controversial or sensitive involved?'

'No, it was a medium-sized project and nothing out of the ordinary. The kinds of issues which many companies face when they realize that they have grown out of their initial IT package. They start cheap, then when they need something serious they come to us,' said Salmon, leaning back in his chair.

'Is there anything else you can tell us that you think might be helpful?' asked Pope, keen to move Salmon away from the sales pitch.

He made a show of thinking for a moment, looking up to the right at a spot on the ceiling.

'No, I can't think of anything.'

'OK. Can you show us where Ward worked? Did he have an office?'

'Yes, he had his own office. He'd definitely earned that,' said Salmon, getting up from his chair and showing them out. He walked them down the corridor and opened a door.

'Here you go. Take all the time you need.'

Pope looked squarely at Salmon. 'We will.'

'Can I just ask, DCI Pope, will you need to share Paul's place of work? I mean, with the media, during the investigation? Erm . . . it would be really helpful if we could keep Knight away from all this. We have shareholders and, err . . . well, you know. Reputation is everything, as they say.' He smiled weakly.

'Unlikely, Mr Salmon. We'll have to share details with the public in case anyone has any useful information. And we may have to talk to some of your clients. So, I wouldn't expect that, no. You might want to do some proactive damage limitation with your shareholders. We'll let you know when we've finished in here.'

With that, Pope closed the door, leaving Salmon standing outside.

Brody smiled at Pope. 'That was a bit harsh. Proactively informing shareholders, talking to clients? Is that the plan?'

'No, I just wanted to annoy him as much as he annoyed me. I get enough Fletcher back at the office, I don't need any more.'

Pope took in the surroundings. Ward's office was not particularly large, but it was what would be called well-appointed. Everything looked smart and relatively new, but it wasn't in the same league as Salmon's larger, more luxurious office. The hierarchy was clear. A smaller desk, two chairs rather than four, although the same view. Pope thought that she definitely wouldn't mind an office with this view.

Pope sat down in Paul Ward's chair and started to go through the contents of his desk. Brody and Khan looked around the remainder of the room.

'There are no filing cabinets. No drawers full of paperwork,' said Brody. 'I guess Ward kept everything digitally.'

'But also no computer,' said Khan.

'Uniforms took that yesterday. There were two laptops, apparently. Maybe one personal and one work? They should be with Tech by now.'

Pope had found very little on the desk and in the three drawers on the right-hand side.

'It's like a new desk, or a new office,' she said. 'Unless it's been cleared of anything useful already. Ward's boss did seem very keen on keeping up appearances.'

She got out her phone and called Thompson.

'You're on speaker with Brody and Khan. Got anything?'

'Not that's going to help you too much. CCTV hasn't given us a whole lot yet. A camera on a street in Bloomsbury caught Paul Ward just before he entered the cemetery. This was at 11.58 p.m. on Monday night. He looked like he was a bit worse for wear, which fits with what we know of him spending the evening in the pub. No other captures so far and no sign of anyone following him. They may have entered from the other side of the cemetery, where there don't seem to be any cameras.'

'Did you get a chance to look into Ward and Acevedo's financials?' asked Pope.

'Yes, it all seems to accord with what Acevedo told you. He earns a reasonable schoolteacher salary, but nowhere near enough to afford the mortgage on Milton Court. No debts or issues that I could find. Clean bill of health. Ward seems to have paid a sizeable deposit for the property and he was paying the lion's share of the mortgage. His salary was much higher than Acevedo's and it looks like he got a pretty generous bonus twice each year, at Christmas and in July. But his records look clean too. Nothing that jumps out as a problem.'

'OK, thanks Steven. Have you got his laptops there?'

'Yes, got them last night. I'm going to get on to them today. I have the password for one, which the tech services at Knight gave uniform yesterday, but I don't have the password for the other machine.'

'Give Eric Acevedo a call. He might know it. We'll be on the way back soon.'

Pope ended the call.

'Another dead end,' said Brody.

'Let's get back and work out where we go from here. I want to look at the interview records from Ward's colleagues and neighbours and the people he was out with on Monday night.'

Pope stood up and Brody opened the door. Ken Salmon was waiting in the corridor, looking out of the large windows on the city below. He turned when he heard the door.

'Did you find anything interesting?' he asked.

'It all seems remarkably clean,' said Pope. 'Hardly a trace that Paul Ward was ever in there.'

'We're an IT company. We encourage our employees to work digitally, rather than cluttering the place up with paper.'

'It certainly seems to have worked.'

Pope considered if she had any more questions. She had a feeling that Salmon wouldn't give her much of any use anyway.

'OK, thanks for your time. We'll be in touch if we need anything else.'

Salmon looked like he was about to say something, but Pope shot him a look and he thought better of it. He simply nodded.

They said thank you to the receptionist as they left and took the lift to the ground floor. As they exited One Canada Square and walked towards the car, they were bathed in sunlight. Pope felt like she wanted to sit on one of the benches with a coffee and enjoy just being for an hour or so, but she knew that she wouldn't be afforded that luxury.

* * *

Back at Charing Cross Police Station, Pope divided up the witness statements collected yesterday. She gave Ward's neighbours to Khan, his work colleagues to Brody and she took the interviews with those people who had been drinking with Ward just before he was killed.

They spent the next couple of hours carefully reading through the statements. When Pope had finished hers, she called Brody, Khan and Thompson together. They sat round the communal meeting table in the middle of the open-plan office.

'Brody, do you want to start off?'

'Sure. Paul Ward seems to have been universally liked at Knight, at least according to what his colleagues told officers yesterday. Nobody had anything bad to say about him. He seems to have been very good at his job and supportive of less experienced colleagues. He'd been working on a project which had just been approved and was feeling very upbeat about it, according to two of the people he had been collaborating with. He was excited to present it to the client and hopefully get the go-ahead.'

'Any hints of discord? Anyone put out by his success, or any indication that anyone had been snubbed in the process of putting together a team?' asked Pope.

'No, nothing like that. As I said, a very popular guy at Knight.'

'And were the interviews comprehensive?'

'Yes, I think so. Apparently they spoke to all the employees who knew Ward personally. There were quite a few.'

'DS Khan, how did you get on?'

'Many of the neighbours didn't know them at all. London living, I guess. But those who did, well, similar to DI Brody, nothing bad to say about them. They always seemed keen to say 'Hi' and have a chat when they bumped into people from their block or the next-door properties. One older couple from a few doors down on their floor said that they didn't have loud parties or play loud music. Generally thought of as nice, considerate neighbours.'

'Any arguments?'

'Not according to those statements.'

Pope looked at Brody. 'You're right about the dead ends. We're not finding much to get our teeth into.'

'Did you have any luck?' asked Brody.

'Not really. Ward got to the pub around six thirty, after he left work. He travelled with a couple of colleagues who lived fairly close to him and they went to the Talbot Arms. There they got chatting to a group of other guys and Ward spent the evening drinking. He was buying a few rounds, celebrating his success that day. Everyone said he was in good spirits, nobody noticed anyone strange hanging around or following him out of the pub. Those still there said he left around half eleven, but I think it was probably a bit later, given how far the Talbot is from his flat. That's the last anyone there saw of him.'

Brody shook his head in frustration.

'Thompson, what about CCTV?' asked Pope.

Steven Thompson tapped his iPad and found the footage of Paul Ward walking towards the entrance to the cemetery. He turned it round so that the three detectives could see. It showed grainy footage of Ward walking, obviously having had a few too many drinks, but nothing, or no one, else.

'That's all we have of him so far.'

After a pause, Pope summed it up.

'So, this afternoon all we've discovered is that our victim was popular at work and didn't seem to have any enemies there. He and his partner were good, solid neighbours and Ward was also popular in the pub, although that might be because he was buying the drinks. No CCTV that helps our investigation.'

'That doesn't sound very positive.'

Pope hadn't even heard Richard Fletcher walk in the office behind her. How did he manage that? He positioned himself just behind her and to the right, so that she had to shift her position to see him properly.

'It's been a busy day, sir. Sometimes that gives us plenty of useful information and sometimes it doesn't, as you know. Today has just been one of those days.'

'That's not very helpful though, is it, DCI Pope?'

Pope was furious. She had been called away from her holiday at the last minute and now she had to listen to this. She worked very hard to hold her temper.

'If you have any good ideas, I'd love to hear them,' she said, with a clearly discernible edge.

'That's for you and your team to decide. I'd like an update first thing in the morning.'

Fletcher turned and left the office before Pope could reply.

Brody looked serious. 'You're stranded on a desert island and you can only have one companion. Fletcher or Ken Salmon?'

Khan laughed. Thompson looked confused. Pope smiled. It did the trick.

Just then Pope heard her phone ding. She checked and saw that it was a reminder she had set in her calendar. She checked the time: five thirty.

'I have an appointment. I think we need to have another talk with Tobias Darke in the morning, now we know a bit more from the autopsy. Let's have a think about where we go from here and how we get round these dead ends. 8 a.m.?'

Brody, Khan and Thompson all nodded in unison.

Pope got up, collected her jacket and walked out of the office and down the stairs. Her reminder had been for the department-mandated therapy sessions Fletcher had forced her into after the death of Adam Miller. Her least favourite part of the week. And she was going to be late.

CHAPTER THIRTEEN

Pope drove quickly onto the Strand and immediately hit traffic. She needed to cross Waterloo Bridge and head along the New Kent Road, which turned into the Old Kent Road towards Peckham where her therapy session would take place. She knew she'd be late, but that would just mean a shorter session, which was fine with her.

She'd been uncooperative when Fletcher had first brought up the idea of her attending therapy sessions, then angry when he'd insisted. He told her in no uncertain terms that her involvement in this was a prerequisite for her staying on the job. She had felt he was bluffing, but wasn't entirely sure. It was Fletcher, after all. Reluctantly, she'd agreed.

The events of the last year were the catalyst. An incredibly difficult and personally problematic case and the recent loss of her sergeant were too much for her to deal with alone, according to her boss. Pope always dealt with things alone. She didn't see the point of burdening others with her problems. They couldn't solve things for her and it only worried others. It had always been an issue with Alex. Another issue. Still, she quite liked her therapist and if that was what she needed to do to maintain her position on the Homicide Squad, so be it.

She pulled up outside the practice offices fifteen minutes late and walked quickly inside.

'Bec Pope. Here to see Dr Boyd,' she told the receptionist.

The man tapped a few keys on his screen, then a few more, then adopted a look of confusion.

'I don't have you down for an appointment with Dr Boyd this evening.'

'I have a regular six o'clock on a Wednesday.'

'Let me give Dr Boyd a call. Hang on a minute.'

A moment after the call, a consulting room door opened and Dr Boyd appeared. He had the Scandinavian look that TV therapists always seemed to have — tall, slim, blonde and with a pointed goatee. He was dressed in black jeans and a black polo-neck jumper. Pope wondered if he cultivated the look on purpose.

'Bec. Nice to see you. We don't have an appointment booked this week. I thought you were away.'

Then it hit Pope. She had cancelled the session as she should have been in New York. She had been so involved in the case that she had completely forgotten.

'Oh, God. Sorry. The trip didn't happen. I've been so busy at work, I completely forgot that we'd cancelled. OK, I'll see you next week.'

'No, don't worry. I'm free, so let's just have our session as normal.' He held open the door and indicated for Pope to go in.

'Are you sure? Don't you have other clients?'

'No, I'm free now. Come on.' Boyd smiled and Pope couldn't think of an excuse to refuse.

She entered the office and sat in her usual chair. Boyd closed the door and sat opposite her. He picked up a notepad and pen and turned to a clean page.

'So, how has your week been?' he asked. This was Boyd's standard introduction to every session.

Pope shook her head. 'I'd love to say it was good. But when I was at the airport I got a call to say there'd been a murder and I was needed on the case. I had to explain to my partner and the kids why I couldn't go to New York. They'd all been looking forward to it for weeks. Then to top it all they decided they couldn't go without me, so now I have the guilt of that to deal with.'

Pope had surprised herself with the outpouring. This was not the way she usually approached the sessions.

'And how did Alex take it?' Boyd asked. He had a gentle voice and Pope wondered if that, too, was carefully cultivated.

Brody had asked the same thing.

'Better than I thought he would.'

'And why do you think that was?'

Pope considered the question.

'He said that if we were going to work, to be a proper family, then we had to do things together, not go off in different directions.'

'And how do you feel about that?'

Pope didn't really want to have this conversation, but it was better than the other things Boyd would inevitably ask about otherwise.

'I feel guilty. They should have gone.'

'And do you agree that this is important for your relationship long-term?' he asked.

'I know what he means. But if they all rely on me being available all the time, that's going to be very difficult. I can't be all things to everyone.'

'Is that how you feel at the moment?'

'Yes, sometimes. Work pulls one way, Alex and the girls pull the other. But you know all this.'

'It's important for you to talk it through when it comes up.'

Pope raised a sceptical eyebrow.

'And how's work at the moment? You said you have a new case.'

'Yes. There wasn't anyone else available.'

'And how is the team?'

'We have a new member. She seems pretty good.' She instantly regretted the comment. She knew what was coming next.

'And how do you feel about that? It must stir some difficult emotions.'

Pope only had a certain tolerance for being asked how she was feeling and she realized she had reached it. She stood up.

'I shouldn't have come today. I've got too much on.' She turned to leave.

Boyd stayed sat down.

'Bec. Stop.'

Pope turned to face him, angry but also embarrassed at her inability to cope with the questions.

'It's exactly at these times that you need to talk about how you feel. You've got so much going on and you can't be expected to deal with it all yourself.'

'You just keep asking me how I feel. I feel shit, OK? And now worse because you keep asking the same question.'

'But this is where we start to make progress. The fact that it's difficult means we're getting to the issues which make the difference. Why don't you sit down?'

Pope didn't want to, but she was aware that if she walked out of the session, Boyd would have to include that in his report and she needed to avoid that. She reluctantly took a seat, crossed her legs and folded her arms. She looked out of the window at the tree outside Boyd's office. He waited patiently until she turned to face him.

'I know this is difficult, Bec.'

'Do you?'

'Yes, of course I do. There are generally two types of people who come to this office. Those who have accepted that they need help and are keen to be supported. The others are here against their will. They have to be here for one reason or another, but they don't think they need to be and don't think it's going to help them. Clearly you are in the latter category.' Boyd smiled at Pope. 'But that's fine. Everybody comes at this from a different perspective.'

'I suppose I just don't think you should have the final say in whether I keep working in my current job. You don't really know me, certainly not professionally. You don't know what my job entails and you don't know how I approach it. So how can you judge whether I'm OK to do it?'

Boyd nodded. 'I understand what you're saying. But that's the way it works here, and short of us refusing to see each other, we have to try to make it work.'

'That's what I'm trying to do, Dr Boyd. And I appreciate that you're working with me, even if I don't see the point. No offence.'

Boyd smiled again. 'No offence taken.'

'I don't mean you personally. Sorry if it came across like that. I mean ethically it shouldn't be you making the subjective decision. It should be me who decides if I'm fit to do my job. Or my boss.'

'Would you rather it was Superintendent Fletcher making the call?'

What a choice. She didn't reply.

'You seemed to find it problematic when I asked you about the replacement for Sergeant Miller. Has that been difficult?'

Pope took a deep breath to try to calm herself. 'Of course it has.'

'But you said the new team member seems to be good?'

'Yes, she seems good. But that doesn't help much.'

'No, of course. Why don't you tell me about her?'

'There's not much to tell. She's only been with us for two days.'

Boyd looked at Pope, waited for her to continue.

Pope sighed. 'She doesn't have experience in Homicide but she seems to have good instincts of how to work a case. So far, so good.'

'But it just reminds you of why she's here. Of your loss.'

Pope nodded. 'And don't tell me it'll help me start to process it all.'

'OK, if you say so.'

Despite her reservations, she found Boyd to be reasonably sensitive to her feelings. If she had to go through this process, she felt that he was a fairly good therapist with which to work.

'I know it's going to get easier over time. But every time we go out on a call I worry about the team.'

'Do you feel it's your responsibility to protect them?'

'It *is* my responsibility. I lead the team,' said Pope.

'But they can take care of themselves, can't they?'

'Of course. But I still have that role. I mean, after Miller died, I realized that I didn't even know the name of his fiancée. We'd worked together for ages.'

'Is that relevant?'

Pope shook her head. 'It's important. To me.'

Boyd left the exchange hanging for a moment. 'How's the sleep?'

'You told me it would be difficult to get rid of insomnia.'

'And is it proving to be the case?'

'Sometimes it's OK, but I take a long time to get to sleep and wake up a number of times every night. Sometimes for hours.'

'What do you tend to think about before you go to sleep?'

'What do you think? Some of the things we see . . . it's difficult to get that out of your head.'

Boyd had no answer for that.

They talked for a while longer, then Boyd brought the session to a close. He opened the door for Pope. 'You know that the more you engage with our sessions, the quicker you'll be done.'

'Sorry I'm such a pain in the ass.'

'You're not, Bec. Don't be so hard on yourself.'

'I'll do my best,' she said as she left the office.

* * *

As she got into the car, Pope tried not to be too angry with the whole process. Dr Boyd would tell her it was unproductive. She thought about Paul Ward and Eric Acevedo planning to see Kamasi Washington live and put on his album *The Epic*. As she pulled out of the practice car park, the euphoric intro immediately lifted her spirits. By the time the piano solo kicked in, she was well on the way to forgetting all about her therapy session.

CHAPTER FOURTEEN

The gym door slammed shut behind him. He made a mental note to get it fixed the next day. He'd forget until this time tomorrow evening, when he'd make another vow to repair it. As assistant manager, it was his job three nights per week to clear the gym, put everything back to where it should be and check all the equipment was in good order for tomorrow's early morning start. He was supposed to be on the premises until 11.30 p.m. Thankfully his manager would be here at 6 a.m. to take care of opening up.

He stood outside and ran his fingers through his hair, felt the stubble on his chin. It had been a long day. But now it was over and he just had a thirty-minute walk home. He considered getting an Uber, but thought it would be good to get a bit of extra exercise. He'd been stuck in the gym since lunchtime and as it had been so busy, he hadn't had a chance to use any of the equipment. Yes, a brisk walk would be perfect.

It was fairly busy on the streets tonight. The students were back from their holiday and out partying and drinking before heading to the local late-night bars and clubs. Locals frequented the pubs and he had to dodge a couple of drunken groups as he walked past the station and the large supermarket just beside it, long since closed for the day. There were just a couple of lone stragglers hanging around in the large car park. He wondered what they were up to.

He turned right onto a gentle hill after the dry cleaners and within a minute he was on a quiet, residential street. There were a few lights on downstairs in the small terraced houses, but most were already in darkness. These were family homes, filled with young children put to bed some hours ago by weary parents unlikely to be staying up past midnight. He looked at his phone: 11.48 p.m. He was a few minutes later than usual. It was getting colder; last week had been warm and he wasn't really dressed appropriately. He zipped his thin top right up to his chin and rolled his shoulders in. He'd step up the pace to keep himself warm.

After several more quiet, residential roads, his route took him along a wider road with no houses at all. He kept the industrial estate on the left as he walked. To the right was waste ground. He assumed nobody wanted to build houses opposite a large collection of factories and other industrial premises.

It was very dark, illuminated by only a few street lights. He had to admit — to himself, if no one else — that he always felt vulnerable walking along this stretch of road. It continued for over half a mile and he rarely encountered anyone else during the time he walked along it. He glanced at his phone again. It gave him a form of connection to the world as he walked through the desolate part of his route home. He had one message, which he'd missed earlier. It was from his dad, checking that he was still planning to go to the football with him on Saturday afternoon. He replied with a thumbs-up emoji. It was their standing joke: he'd told his dad that it was an emoji only used by old people. His dad had responded that he *was* old and had subsequently used a thumbs-up emoji at every given opportunity. Now he'd started doing the same thing.

He put the phone away and crossed over to the other side of the road. Turning left, he walked along a private road which ran along the far side of the industrial estate. He was just about to check his phone again to see if his dad had read or replied to his message when he heard a sound. He turned round but saw nothing. There was no one there. This route sometimes messed with his head and he thought he was being followed. Too many horror movies when he was a teenager.

He carried on, but quickened his pace a little. Suddenly he felt something on his neck. A sharp pain. He instinctively put his hand to the location of the pain and then was acutely aware that there was actually someone there. It was too late.

* * *

They held hands as they walked. This was the first time they had been out alone since the baby was born. Part exhilarating, part terrifying. How many times had they checked their phones during the movie? Ten? Twelve? No calls from her mum, so they knew everything was OK. But it was impossible not to worry. It would get easier.

They turned down the road which skirted the industrial estate. Normally she hated walking this way, and he knew that, but tonight they weren't thinking about the dodgy, unlit, unmade road but about the quickest way back to check on their precious daughter. They were almost home and she felt relieved.

But then she saw it. Him. Unsure at first, they both slowed, but drew closer and saw that it was indeed a body lying at the side of the road, pushed up against the wall. She screamed. He jumped back, then took out his phone and called an ambulance.

They would have to wait around for the ambulance to arrive, then for the police car. It was a terrifying sight.

The ambulance eventually pulled up and two paramedics climbed out. They introduced themselves and saw the body before they could be directed to it. They checked but saw instantly that the man was dead. The female paramedic noted that the body was still warm and commented that the man must have died very recently. She looked at her watch and saw that it was 12.55 a.m.

After a further ten minutes, one of the most agonizing waits they had ever had to endure, a marked police car arrived. Flashing lights, but no siren. Two male police officers got out. One was mid-thirties, the other seemed younger. The young one went to check on the dead body, while the older officer came over to them.

'So, you found the body?'

She was terrified. He spoke for them.

'Yes, yes, we did. Just there,' he noted unnecessarily, pointing to the location of the body. His hand was shaking.

The officer nodded while slowly writing something in his notebook. 'And what time was this?'

'Around half an hour ago.'

The officer checked his watch. 'So, about half past midnight?'

'Yes, that sounds right.'

'And where had you been this evening, sir?'

'To the cinema. The Odeon just off the high street.'

The officer looked at him. 'It's a bit late for the cinema, isn't it?'

'It was a late showing. We wanted to wait until our baby was asleep with the sitter before we went out.' Suddenly a realization dawned on him and his tone changed. 'Hey, are we suspects?'

'I just have to ask these questions, sir. We need all the information we can get in investigations.'

He nodded, partially satisfied.

Once the officer had finished, he took their details and explained that someone would probably come round in the morning to interview them properly. They walked quickly away, never so glad to be heading home.

'Sarge, come and have a look at this.' The younger officer summoned his older counterpart.

'I've never seen anything like this. Jesus!' he exclaimed, staggering backwards and leaning against the cold, brick wall.

The more experienced officer sauntered towards his colleague, expecting his experience to protect him from such a dramatic response. There wasn't much he hadn't seen. As he crouched down, he suddenly recoiled.

'Christ!' He, too, stood up and took a step backwards, keenly aware that he needed to maintain his composure in front of the junior officer. He knew that how he reacted would be spread around the station by lunchtime, good or bad. He steeled himself.

'Are you OK?' he asked.

The younger man nodded. But he certainly didn't look OK.

'I need to make a phone call.' He walked a few yards away and dialled a number. It was answered after a few rings.

'Dispatch. You need to get Homicide down here right away.'

He listened for a moment.

'Yes. It's definitely murder. I don't know exactly what's going on, but there's something . . .' He paused to consider how to explain what he had just seen. 'It looks like there's something carved on his chest . . . there's blood everywhere. Just get someone down here ASAP.'

He ended the call and replaced the phone in his jacket pocket. Now it would be their turn to wait with a dead body until Homicide decided to turn up.

CHAPTER FIFTEEN

Thursday morning

Pope's evening was going well. Kamasi Washington had soothed her on the journey home. By the time she had walked in the door and Alex had greeted her with a kiss and a glass of red wine, she had almost forgotten about her session with Dr Boyd. Chloe was out with her boyfriend and Hannah was upstairs, notionally doing her homework but in all possibility scrolling through TikTok.

Alex was cooking dinner and it smelled good. All she had to do was choose some music and sit down on the sofa and relax. She chose Coltrane's *Giant Steps*, the album that had first got her into jazz all those years ago. It would have been perfect, except for the gnawing sensation of guilt that she had a murder to solve. Red wine and John Coltrane wasn't helping with that. However, Pope remembered what Dr Boyd had said about finding time to relax, finding time to spend with family, and compartmentalizing. It was a work in progress.

After dinner they had put on a movie that Alex had wanted to watch for ages. It wasn't Pope's kind of thing. Too many guns and helicopters. She found herself tuning it out and thinking about the investigation. This, of course, happened almost every time she tried to focus on anything else during a big case. Alex was so invested in the film, he didn't seem to notice.

Afterwards they finished their wine and went upstairs to bed. Chloe wasn't back yet. Hannah's light was off and Alex called in goodnight but got no response.

He fell asleep quickly as usual, while Pope stared at the ceiling and tried to join him. It took her a while, but the relatively early return from work and the relaxed evening meant that she found sleep much more quickly than usual. She was asleep before midnight, which was a rarity.

It didn't last long.

Pope was roused by a loud, shrill sound, that she eventually realized was the persistent ringing of her phone, charging next to her side of the bed. She looked at the time on the screen: 1.05 a.m. It was a call from the station. She reluctantly answered. Then she listened.

She got up and went outside the bedroom so as not to wake Alex up. She spoke quietly. 'OK, I'll be there as soon as I can. Text me the location and also send it to DI Brody and DS Khan. Tell them to meet me there ASAP.'

Pope ended the call. She thought about what she had just heard. Well, at least she'd had an hour of sleep.

She dressed as quietly as she could, managing not to wake Alex in the process. He always slept deeply, which was a useful talent to have if living with a police officer. She crept down the stairs and let herself out of the front door.

* * *

Pope pulled up between the marked police car and the ambulance on site near Bermondsey. It was dark, secluded and inhospitable. Exactly the kind of place to commit a murder. Pope saw two police officers she didn't recognize standing some distance from the car. As she approached them, she saw that a body had been covered up nearby. They were keeping an eye on the scene, without standing too close to it.

'DCI Pope, Charing Cross Homicide. What've we got?'

The younger officer looked a bit nonplussed. The more experienced officer spoke.

'Dead body. Male, looks young, but it's difficult to tell.'

'Who found the body?'

'A couple on their way back from the cinema.'

Pope looked around. 'Where are they?'

'We took an initial statement and sent them home. Told them someone would be round in the morning to talk to them again.' He saw the look of irritation on Pope's face. 'They had to get back for their young baby. For the sitter.'

Damn. Pope wanted to talk to the couple now, but there wasn't much she could do about it.

'Is it right about what's on his chest?'

'There's definitely something there. Looks like some kind of a star. We didn't look too closely. Thought we'd leave it to you lot.' He gave a weak smile. Pope didn't find it even vaguely amusing.

She walked over to the body and realized she hadn't come prepared. She called to the paramedic standing by her ambulance.

'Do you have a pair of gloves I could borrow?'

The woman nodded, then turned and got some from the parcel shelf of the ambulance. She brought them over to Pope.

'Thanks. Have you looked at the body?' she asked.

'Yeah. We checked him. He's gone, but not long. I mean, I think he'd only been dead for a little while.'

'What time was this?'

'Just after half twelve. Judging by the body and his temperature, he can't have been dead for long.'

Pope felt her heart rate instantly quicken.

'So, time of death?'

'Maybe around midnight? Coroner will be able to confirm.'

Pope's heart rate quickened still further. She nodded slowly, then bent down and slowly peeled back the blanket covering the body.

The officer was right. The body seemed to belong to a young man and was lying on its back, with the side of the face pressed down into the dirt of the unmade road. Pope looked around and noticed the complete lack of CCTV or houses from which someone might have seen something. She wondered if this was a careful choice on the killer's part or a lucky break. She caught herself. She had to be careful not to jump to conclusions, even when they were a near certainty.

She walked around the body, watched by the two officers and the paramedic who was standing close by. The man on the ground was wearing a dark tracksuit and trainers. There didn't look to be obvious signs of a struggle, but the front of the jacket was open and the T-shirt underneath was ripped. The wound on the chest was obvious. It reminded Pope of Paul Ward. She took out her phone and took a couple of pictures of the position of the body.

Then she carefully pulled the jacket and T-shirt out of the way and inspected the victim's chest. There was a lot of blood, but it was obvious what she was looking at. An inverted pentagram.

Pope stared at the wound for a moment. So much was going through her head, but her primary thought was the realization that they were now dealing with a killer who had committed at least two murders. That they knew of.

She looked up at the paramedic. 'Can you check something for me?'

The paramedic crouched down beside her.

'Can you have a look at his neck?'

The woman looked confused. 'What am I looking for?'

'A small puncture wound. Probably the right-hand side.'

The woman took out a small torch from her pocket and bent down.

'Maybe here? Difficult to tell.' She indicated to Pope, who leaned in close.

Then she saw it. A small, neat hole in the same place as the one they had found on Paul Ward's body. A puncture wound.

Pope stood up just as she heard a car approaching. She saw that it was Brody's. He and Khan both got out of the car.

'I picked her up on the way,' Brody explained. They both looked over at the body.

Pope walked over to them. 'Bad news, I'm afraid. Pentagram carved on the chest and what looks like an injection site on the right-hand side of the neck.'

'Same guy,' said Brody.

'No doubt.'

While Brody and Khan walked over to inspect the victim, Pope called Fletcher to update him. He had an unnerving ability to sound wide awake at any time of the night. She explained that they were going to go home and regroup in the morning and ended the call.

She joined her two detectives.

'This has just escalated considerably. We now know of two murders by the same killer and that changes everything. Not least, the possibility that he will kill again. We need to find him. I want you to go home, get some rest, and we'll meet at seven at the station.'

She walked over to the two uniformed officers.

'You'll need to stay here until Forensics have finished, and make sure the body is removed before you leave.'

They didn't look too happy about the task, but neither said anything. They both simply nodded.

Pope turned, got in her car and started the engine. The journey home took twenty minutes at that time of night. She drove in silence, trying to slow the avalanche of thoughts crowding her head. Two murders, clearly one killer. A multiple murderer. She hoped that she wasn't dealing with a serial killer. But the clock was now ticking. It wasn't simply the case that they had to find the killer and have him face justice for his crime. They had to try to catch him before he killed again.

This was no misdirection. Pope was now convinced that the satanic element of this case was crucial. If that were so, it should make it easier now that there were two victims. They could join the dots and connect the victims and that would lead them to the killer. She held on to that bit of comfort. Tomorrow they would find out who the second victim was and take it from there. She hoped that the victims were connected in some way, rather than randomly chosen.

As she drew close to home, Pope recalled the tarot reading she had received. She wondered if the Death card she drew from the pack was foretelling the murder she had just discovered, or whether there was something else still to come. She shook her head, annoyed at herself for giving it any credence.

But she knew it was in her head now, and it would prevent her from getting any sleep whatsoever tonight.

CHAPTER SIXTEEN

Pope was wrong. She did manage to get a couple of hours' sleep. Not much, but enough for the moment. The adrenaline of finding a second victim powered through her. She showered, dressed and left the house by six thirty. Before she drove off, she texted Alex that she'd see him later. She didn't suggest a time.

Traffic was light this early in the morning. She made it to the station at seven and found Brody and Khan already in, making the coffee.

'Morning. Shall we meet?' Pope wanted to capitalize on her sense of momentum.

'Thompson is on his way up. He says he's got some background on our victim,' said Brody.

'Already? What time did he get in this morning?'

'Not sure. I messaged him when I got home last night. I guess he saw it and got in early.'

As they sat round the meeting table, Steven Thompson came through the door. He sat down without saying anything, absorbed in something on his tablet. He looked up and saw that the three detectives were all looking at him expectantly.

'Brody says you have some information on our victim,' said Pope.

'Yes, I do. Hold on a minute.' He finished what he had been doing and brought up another screen.

'Our victim is Tom Murray. Aged twenty-seven, lives in Bermondsey. Forensics found his gym membership card and a driving licence. He was assistant manager at Iron Core gym in New Cross, had worked there for almost three years. Not married, but judging by his social media accounts he has a girlfriend called Amy Weaver, who lives in Forest Hill. He seems clean, except for getting stopped for a red light a couple of years ago.'

'Any connections with Paul Ward?' asked Pope.

'Not that I can find so far. They lived in completely different worlds. Different areas of London, no similar interests from looking at his socials, different work spheres, opposite ends of the salary spectrum.'

Pope was frustrated. She needed connections to move the investigation along.

'I've managed to find him on CCTV, walking out of the gym and through New Cross last night.'

'What time did you start work this morning?' asked Brody. 'Did you get any sleep at all?'

Thompson looked a bit embarrassed. Clearly Pope wasn't the only one who had issues with insomnia.

He called the CCTV footage up on his tablet and turned it around. They all leaned in and peered at the screen. The first grab showed Tom Murray walking out of Iron Core gym and locking up. He turned right and went out of shot. Thompson brought up the second piece of footage, which showed him walking along a busy New Cross high street, full of young people heading for a night out. Pope noted the time. The final bit of film showed Murray turning off the high street, just after a large supermarket.

'That's the last we see of him. He must have taken a route with no CCTV after that.' Thomson put the tablet down on the table in front of him.

'So, that's just before midnight. And how far is that final piece of footage from where he was found?' asked Pope.

'Not far. About a five-minute walk.'

'OK. So, he was also killed at approximately midnight. We'll need to wait for confirmation from autopsy, but it looked like he had the same puncture wound on the right-hand side of his neck. And, of course, the inverted pentagram carved into his chest. I'd say this confirms the satanic element is crucial. No doubt we're looking for the same killer as Paul Ward. And this is not just one individual being targeted.'

They reflected on Pope's summary in silence. This was not a vendetta against an individual, or a crime of passion. This was a deranged individual who was pursuing some misguided belief in the occult. And in all likelihood, it wouldn't end here.

'I've been reading a bit about satanism and devil worship,' said Brody.

Pope narrowed her eyes. Another to add to the insomnia tally.

'For a long time, satanism was used as an accusation against anyone who religious believers felt was atheistic or had different beliefs. Think witch trials and burnings. It's only really since the sixties that people have described *themselves* as satanic and advocated devil worship. It's essentially an American import in recent years, driven by the global spread of information through the internet.'

'You mentioned music,' said Pope.

'Yeah. It was one of the moral panics which swept America and Britain in the eighties and nineties. Ozzy Osbourne, Marilyn Manson. Before that, Led Zeppelin. All of it nonsense.'

'Yeah, I remember,' said Pope. 'I had a friend who loved Marilyn Manson. Drove his parents mad.'

'I can imagine. The point is, though, it's not a widespread phenomenon by any means.' Brody checked his notes. 'There is a Church of Satan, founded in California in the sixties by Anton LaVey, and the Temple of Set, also American in origin, but they only have a few hundred members. QAnon has tried to talk up this kind of thing and capitalize on these fears, but is generally discredited now. We don't see much in the way of organized devil worship, if we can call it that, in the UK.'

'I don't recall ever encountering it. Not through work,' said Pope. 'So, where does this get us?'

'Not sure. We could talk to the academic at Exeter that Tobias Darke mentioned,' said Brody.

'We could, but I don't know how useful that's going to be. Now that you're our regular expert on all things satanic, have we got all that covered?'

Brody smiled. 'Maybe.'

'Is he branding his victims?' said Khan.

They all looked at her.

'Go on,' said Pope.

'Well, we've been thinking that the killer is trying to send a message to us through the pentagrams on the bodies. But what if it's not a message so much as a punishment? Branding the victims for something they've done.'

'But if the victims aren't connected that seems more unlikely, doesn't it?' said Brody.

'We haven't found a connection yet. But what if the connection is not between the two victims, but between each victim and the killer? Is that what we should be looking for?' said Khan.

'That makes it much more difficult,' said Brody.

'It does,' said Pope, 'but you have a good point, DS Khan. We need to look not just for connections between the two victims, but about any possible intersections where they may have separately come into contact with our killer.'

Thompson nodded. 'On it.'

Pope sat up straight in her chair. 'Right. Brody, can you make sure uniforms are talking to Tom Murray's colleagues at the gym. And any customers who were there yesterday evening. We need to know when they left and what time they got home. Also any disputes or dissatisfied customers in the past month or so. Once you've sorted that we'll go and talk to Murray's girlfriend. What was her name?'

Brody checked his notes. 'Amy Weaver.'

'Right. Let's see what she has to say.'

Just then Pope's phone rang. She leaned over to her desk and answered it.

'We'll be there in half an hour.' She ended the call. 'That was Dr Okafor. She has some initial findings from the autopsy she thinks we should know. We'll call in on the way to the girlfriend.'

Brody made a phone call to set up the uniformed officers and make sure they knew what Pope wanted them to do. Khan checked back through her notes from the previous autopsy.

'OK, let's get going,' said Pope, walking through the door without waiting for an answer.

Brody drove and at Pope's insistence put the lights and siren on to get them there quickly. They were in Okafor's office within twenty minutes of leaving the station.

'I could have told you this over the phone, DCI Pope,' said Okafor, once they were sitting down. She'd brought in an extra chair this time, so they were all able to sit.

'It's on the way, and I wanted to hear it in person. What have we got?'

Okafor opened her notes and turned to the second A4 page. 'It's still preliminary findings, but I know what I'm looking for now. Of course, the same wound inflicted on the chest, but also a similar puncture mark on the same side of the neck, the left-hand side as you're looking at the victim.'

'Were there any differences from the first victim, Paul Ward?'

'No, not really.'

'I think this is going to be an obvious question, but are we saying, then, that the victims were killed by the same killer?' asked Pope.

'I'm confident that they were, yes. The way the wound was inflicted was similar and the puncture mark on the neck looked identical.'

Pope nodded. 'Thanks, that's what we needed to know.' She got up to leave.

'I would say one thing, however, DCI Pope. From what I can see, the wound on the chest, although similar, looks like it might have been carried out with a little more confidence this time. It's almost identical, but I'd say the hand that made it was less hesitant.'

Pope turned to Brody. 'Our killer is getting more confident and refining their technique.'

'Practice makes perfect,' said Brody.

'Isn't that a common trajectory with serial killers?' asked Khan. 'As they progress they get more confident and find it more difficult to stop?'

'Which makes our job even more important,' said Pope.

CHAPTER SEVENTEEN

The journey to Forest Hill didn't take long. Brody pulled the car up outside an imposing four-storey Victorian house. He, Pope and Khan got out of the car and walked up the wide steps to the communal front door.

Pope looked up and down the street. 'This must have been quite something before they were all converted into flats. Lovely houses.'

Brody found the buzzer for Amy Weaver and gave it a short press. They waited and he was just about to try again when a voice came over the intercom.

'Hello?' The voice sounded thin and subdued.

'Ms Weaver? It's DI Brody from the Metropolitan Police. You should have been told we're coming?'

There was a pause. 'Come up to the second floor.' A different buzzer sounded. Brody pushed the door wide and they climbed the staircase in single file. There was only one flat on each floor, they found, and reaching number two, Brody knocked.

Amy Weaver opened up and stood in the doorway. She waited expectantly, so they all took out their warrant cards and she carefully inspected each one. After what had happened, Pope couldn't blame the woman.

Weaver walked back into her hallway and into the living room on the right. It was a large room, with high ceilings and expansive windows, hinting at the grandeur of its former occupants. Weaver flopped down into a large, aged armchair which had seen better days. In fact, most of the furniture was similarly shabby. Pope couldn't help but notice the difference between this room and Paul Ward's living room, which was immaculately decorated and furnished.

Weaver gestured to them to sit down. Just like Eric Acevedo, she looked as if she had been crying all night. Pope wondered at what time she had been notified of her boyfriend's death. She wore a tatty pair of jeans and a black, hooded top, zipped right up to the neck. She curled her legs up beneath her on the sofa. Weaver was doing everything she could to disappear from the nightmare in which she had found herself.

'Thanks very much for seeing us this morning,' said Pope. 'We're very sorry for your loss. I know how hard this must be and we appreciate your time.'

Weaver nodded, her expression blank.

'Is there anyone who can be with you today? A friend or family member?'

'I'm fine. Just ask me what you need to.'

She wasn't exactly hostile, but she wanted this over as quickly as possible. Pope knew she would have to tread carefully.

'Can you start by giving us a bit of background? How long had you and Tom been together?'

She looked sharply at Pope and it was clear that she had caught the use of the past tense.

'Around three years. We were due to get married next year. We'd been planning everything . . .' She tailed off as the tears came.

It was always the same when interviewing partners and family, you had to let their grief dictate the pace. Pope waited for the worst of the sobbing to subside. It took a while.

'And you lived separately, is that right?'

123

'Yes. But we were going to move in when we got married. Tom's lease was expiring soon.'

'Tom has a flat in Bermondsey?'

'Yes, that's right.'

'And were you going to move into either of your flats, or get somewhere new?'

'Tom was going to move in here with me until we'd saved up enough money to buy a bigger place together.'

'And were you planning to stay in London or move somewhere else?'

Weaver looked confused. 'I don't know why that's relevant, but we were planning to stay in London. We both have jobs here.'

She hadn't twigged that Pope was trying to find out if there were any major disagreements between her and Tom Murray.

'I'm just trying to get a full picture. Sometimes small details can be helpful,' said Pope gently. 'So, Tom worked at Iron Core gym in New Cross?'

'Yes, that's where we met. I worked out there and he was assistant manager.'

'And what do you do for work?'

'Social media and marketing.'

'And where is that?' asked Pope.

'In Greenwich. I work for an English language school, Universe Language. Mainly on recruitment abroad.'

'And do you travel abroad for your work?'

'Not often. I've been to a few recruitment fairs in Europe, but they don't result in many students.'

'And how long have you worked there?'

Weaver looked out of the window, thinking. 'Almost five years now.'

Pope paused for a moment to signal a change in the direction of the questions, but also to give Weaver a brief respite.

'I know this is difficult, but can you tell us a bit about Tom?'

She looked at Pope as if it was the hardest question she had ever had to answer.

'We just need to get a sense of who he was, what he was like, what he liked to do.'

Weaver collected her thoughts. 'Tom was the love of my life. He was quite serious. He took his health seriously. He was a vegetarian, didn't drink much, ran every other day. Don't get me wrong, he liked to go out and meet friends. But he preferred to be at home, if he wasn't out at the gym.'

'And did he work out at the gym much?'

'Yes, when he got the chance. His job kept him pretty busy, but he tried to get on the equipment when he could.'

'Were there any problems at work, as far as you know? Anybody he'd had an argument with?'

Weaver looked shocked. 'Do you think this was someone at work?'

'We need to ask these questions so we can explore every possibility.'

She lost the look of shock. 'I don't think so. Not that he'd mentioned.'

'Did Tom talk much about work to you?'

'Yes, sometimes. He enjoyed it but there were lots of late nights and weekends. He didn't like that.'

'Was he looking for another job, or would you say he was settled at Iron Core?'

'He hadn't said anything. I think he was fine there.'

'You said you were planning to get married next year. When exactly?'

'Next June. We were going to get married in church then have our reception in Greenwich. We'd visited everywhere and it was all booked.' The tears came again, but Weaver blew her nose and wiped them away.

'We're going to lose our deposits.'

'I'm sure they'll understand if you explain the situation.'

Weaver nodded, without much conviction. 'How was he killed? The police told me was attacked. But they didn't tell me how he died.'

The question wasn't unexpected. Pope considered how best to respond. There were details she didn't want to share.

'Yes, it was a homicide. But we're at the early stages so I can't tell you any more at this point.'

'You can't, or you think it's best not to tell me? Believe me, it can't be worse than I'm imagining at the moment.'

Pope doubted that.

'I can't tell you until we've had the medical report. But I promise you that as soon as I'm able to share the details, we'll be back in touch.'

Weaver looked dubious, as if she knew Pope was holding back information. 'And how long will that be?'

'I'm not sure. But as I said, as soon as I can. Would you mind if DI Brody and I had a quick look around the flat?'

Weaver again looked surprised at the question.

'We just want to get a sense of the place, as Tom obviously spent time here. See if anything jumps out to help in our investigation. While we do that, can you give DS Khan a list of Tom's friends and family, and any close colleagues that you know of?'

Weaver held her gaze then nodded and turned to Khan, who had her notebook out ready. Pope wasn't sure if the woman knew she was keeping her occupied so they could have a good look around undisturbed.

She and Brody walked through the flat. It was spacious. A corridor to the right led to a large, bright kitchen with another large sash window at the far end. Back along the corridor were two bedrooms. They looked round the first, which was clearly where the couple slept — neat and tidy, the bed made carefully despite the current situation. Pope wondered if Weaver had got to bed at all last night. Brody quietly opened a wardrobe door, which held almost exclusively woman's clothes. Only a handful of shirts and a couple of pairs of shoes looked like they had belonged to Tom Murray. Brody closed the door.

There were a couple of photos on the top of a chest of drawers. One was clearly Amy Weaver and Murray on holiday together. They looked happy and relaxed. The other seemed to be Weaver and her parents. She stood in the middle, and again they looked happy.

'So far, so normal,' said Brody.

They walked into the second bedroom, which was set up as a home office. There was a desk, office chair and Apple desktop computer. Among the other papers and documents was an A4 ring binder to the left of the computer. Pope picked it up. Printed on the front were the words 'Wedding Planner'. She opened it to see leaflets, receipts, guest lists, sketches of table layouts and myriad other plans. It seemed very personal, and not relevant to the case, so she closed it again. Pope saw a whole future just starting for this couple. The folder was the first stage in a different phase of their lives. Now it had been torn away from Amy Weaver and at some point she would have to face that. Pope felt a profound sadness for the woman next door.

'I'm not sure this is helping,' she said. 'Are we done for the moment?'

'Yeah, I think so. Let's just check the bathroom.'

They walked along to the other end of the corridor and found themselves in a small bathroom. Pope quietly opened the mirrored door of the cabinet on the wall. Inside was just a tube of toothpaste, a moisturizer Pope recognized from Chloe's bathroom, a cleansing balm, a bottle of sun cream and a spare shampoo. No pills or powders to arouse concern. Nothing unusual. Pope closed the door. 'OK, let's get going.'

They returned to the living room, where Weaver and Khan were sitting in silence. Weaver looked at Pope and Brody as they came in.

'Thanks, Ms Weaver. We have all we need for now,' said Pope. 'Someone will be back in touch if we need anything else. In the meantime, I'd really recommend you ask someone to come and be with you for a while.'

Weaver nodded, but Pope thought she had no intention of taking her advice. She placed her card on the coffee table in front of Weaver.

'All my contact details are on here. Please get in touch if you remember anything which you think might help us, or if you need to talk to me. A family liaison officer will be in touch with you. We'll let ourselves out.'

Khan stood up and they walked towards the door. Amy Weaver watched them leave, a look of palpable loss on her face.

'We were perfect together. The ideal match. Everyone thought so.'

'Again, we're very sorry for your loss.'

They went down the stairs and out of the communal front door.

'Do you think she'll be OK on her own?' asked Khan.

'There's not much else we can do but focus on finding whoever did this,' said Pope. 'If she doesn't want anybody else with her, that's her right.'

'Can we get uniform to check on her tomorrow?' asked Khan.

'OK, good idea. We'll set that up when we get back to the station.'

They got in the car.

'Have you got Tom Murray's address in Bermondsey?' asked Pope.

Khan nodded and found the details in her notebook.

'OK. Let's go and have a look round his flat, see what we can find. Forensics should have finished in there by now if we're lucky.'

Brody typed the address into the satnav and pulled the car away from the house.

'I really feel for her,' said Khan. 'She thought she had everything all mapped out, then it disappeared in an instant. It's so cruel.'

Pope couldn't help the feeling that Khan was talking from some level of experience. Either that or she was just extremely empathetic. She didn't yet know the woman well enough to decide.

Pope looked over and noticed that Brody was smiling as he drove towards Bermondsey. She considered what might be making him so happy, given the interview they had just conducted and the case they were investigating. She could only assume that the discussions about wedding planning and the sudden derailment of those plans might have got Brody thinking about his own relationship and how well it seemed to be going.

At that point, Bec Pope didn't realize what an excellent detective she was.

CHAPTER EIGHTEEN

Tom Murray's flat in Bermondsey was completely different to his fiancée's place a few miles away. It was in a purpose-built block which Pope judged to have been built in the 1980s. It had small windows and a narrow front door.

Outside the front door stood an officer Pope knew well, having worked with him on a number of cases.

'McKewan,' she said, nodding as she walked up.

'Ma'am.'

'Have Forensics finished in there?'

'Yup. About half an hour ago. Do you want to get in?'

She nodded, and he fished a set of keys out of his pocket and opened the door. He handed the keys to Pope.

'Ground floor, number two, right-hand side when you go in.'

Pope liked McKewan. No-nonsense and reliable. She was glad to see him back after his absence with an injury suffered while he was working on a case with Pope's team last year.

'Thanks very much,' she said with a smile.

The door was stiff and caught as Pope turned the key. It took a push with her shoulder to get it to open. Inside, it was immediately evident that Murray's flat was much smaller than his girlfriend's in Forest Hill. There was one bedroom, with barely enough room for a double bed and a wardrobe, a small lounge and an even smaller kitchen.

'I can see why they were planning to live in Amy Weaver's flat,' said Khan. 'This is tiny.'

Brody looked around. 'Victorians built large houses with a view to people actually living in them. Since the eighties we've built the smallest we can get away with, with a view to making as much profit as possible.'

There wasn't much natural light, despite it being fairly bright outside, so Pope turned on the light in the living room.

'I'll look here. Brody, you check the bedroom. Khan, take the kitchen and bathroom.'

They went their separate ways and Pope started to examine the main living area of the flat. It was much emptier than Weaver's apartment and she wondered how much time Tom Murray had actually spent there, or whether he spent most of his time at Weaver's. There was one sofa, but no armchairs. A large TV with a games console attached took up most of the opposite wall space. Pope had her views about grown men playing video games, but she was aware that it was a popular pastime. There was a set of dumbbells and a large medicine ball in one corner of the room, reflecting his interest in fitness. There were no photographs on display, which seemed unusual to Pope. She looked through the room with care, but found little of interest and certainly nothing which she felt helped in their investigation.

She walked over to the window. There was a small patch of grass outside, which presumably acted as a communal garden. Beyond that was a car park, currently occupied by three vehicles. Then there were several other similar blocks with car parks attached.

When Brody and Khan had returned from their tasks, Pope caught up.

'Anything?' she asked.

'Nothing useful,' said Khan. 'All the food in the kitchen is consistent with Murray being vegetarian, and otherwise the usual. Pots, pans, cooking utensils. There isn't even a medicine cabinet or any drawers in the bathroom. Shampoo and shaving gel on the edge of the bath, that sort of thing.'

Pope looked at Brody.

'Bedroom is similar. Not much space for storage. The wardrobe is full of sports gear and casual clothes. No suits, ties or anything like that. Plenty of different pairs of trainers and running shoes. Nothing interesting in the bedside drawers.'

'Were you hoping for a Ouija board and a turntable for playing Led Zeppelin albums backwards?' asked Brody.

'That would at least have been something,' said Pope. 'They all seem like such ordinary lives. There's nothing to suggest why they may have been targeted for such a violent crime. Two victims, two partners, zero clues.'

'Maybe we *are* talking random attacks,' said Khan.

'It's certainly a possibility. The more we fail to find anything, the more it looks that way.'

Pope took one last look around Tom Murray's living room, hoping for some form of inspiration. Nothing came.

'Let's get back to the station. Khan, you and Thompson can keep looking for some form of connection between the victims. I'm going to call Tobias Darke and see if he can join us. Brody, we need to update Fletcher. I have a horrible feeling that when we tell him where we are he's going to want to do a press conference. We'll see if we can dissuade him.'

* * *

When they arrived at the station, Khan headed towards the Tech office to see Thompson. Pope and Brody left their jackets in the office and went straight to see Richard Fletcher. His door was uncharacteristically open and he beckoned them in. They sat in the two chairs opposite him across his desk.

'So where are we? Any progress?' he said, leaning back into his large office chair.

'Early stages so far, but we've talked to Tom Murray's girlfriend and been to his flat,' said Pope.

'And?' Fletcher seemed even more impatient than usual.

'And not much that helps us so far.'

Fletcher frowned like a disappointed schoolteacher.

'We managed to talk to the girlfriend, Amy Weaver. She paints a picture of a very normal guy, no red flags. They were getting married next year, so were busy wedding planning. No conflicts or arguments at work that she knew of. Uniforms have been interviewing his work colleagues and friends today, so we'll get an update on that soon.'

Fletcher placed his hands on his desk and leaned forward slightly.

'Do you have *any* leads?'

'I'm not sure it's going to be a quick case, sir. We're starting to suspect that the victims might be randomly selected. Thompson and Khan are still looking for connections which might help us, but so far . . .' Pope's voice trailed off.

'We need to move this along. I've called a press conference for this afternoon and I want to be able to give them something positive.'

Fletcher chasing his promotion was a force to be reckoned with.

'Understood, sir, but I can't give you what I don't have.'

Now he looked annoyed. 'Obviously, DCI Pope, which is why you need to find something. I want you at the press conference to give an update and answer operational questions.'

Pope wasn't sure whether Fletcher was punishing her or attempting to motivate her. Probably both.

'I'm going to be busy with the case this afternoon, so it will be difficult for me to—'

'I'll need you there. Four o'clock in the briefing room. Make sure you have something useful to contribute.' Fletcher turned to his computer and started typing something in a sign that his decision was final. The meeting was over.

Now it was Pope's turn to be angry. Fletcher's attitude was nothing to do with the mechanics of the case and everything to do with trying to advance his career. He didn't understand enough about leadership to realize that setting arbitrary time limits on complex investigations was entirely unproductive. As they left his office, Pope considered the possibility of torpedoing the press conference on purpose to ruin Fletcher's promotion ambitions. Attractive though that idea was, Fletcher getting promoted meant him leaving the station, and that was something she didn't want to jeopardize.

Pope and Brody walked in silence down the flight of stairs and into their office.

'Idiot,' said Pope once the door was closed.

Brody laughed. 'Is that your minutes of the meeting?'

'I think it sums it up pretty well, don't you?'

'I couldn't possibly comment.'

'It's alright for you, you don't have to stand next to him for every local and national media outlet to photograph. Or maybe you should go in my place? Something urgent might come up.'

For a moment Brody looked like he thought she might be serious. 'That's a tempting scenario. But I think rank has its privileges and you're definitely the best person for the job.'

'Hmm. To be decided. Can you get someone from uniform to update us on progress with the interviews and door-to-doors?'

Brody made a couple of calls and then set to making coffee for everyone. 'What do you think about Khan's suggestion that the victims were unconnected? Chosen at random?'

Pope considered this. 'I think we need more time to establish a connection if there is one. It's too early to know. Fletcher wants to move things along quickly, but investigations move at their own pace and can't be forced.'

'She's asking the right questions, isn't she?'

'Khan?'

'Yeah. Seems to have good instincts.'

'Early days. But so far so good.'

'I think Miller would have liked her. He'd have approved.'

Pope avoided eye contact with Brody. Replacing Miller was the last thing she wanted to talk about at that moment.

Thankfully, the door opened and Khan walked in, followed by Thompson, and she didn't have to.

As the four of them sat down they were joined by Sergeant Mike Hawley. He was one of Pope's trusted uniformed officers. Recently promoted, he was in charge of the interviews in the case.

'Take a seat,' said Pope. 'Can you update us on how the interviews are going?'

Hawley took out his phone and checked his notes. 'We've been working through Tom Murray' colleagues at Iron Core gym. He seemed to get on with everyone. He wasn't much for socializing with others who worked there. None of them seem to have been close friends, but no one had a bad word to say about him. Professional and reliable. His boss said he was a good worker, a trustworthy assistant manager. Still some to go, but nothing flagged so far.'

'And that's ongoing?' asked Pope.

'Yes, ma'am. We have officers still on the premises. They're also talking to clients as they come in.'

'And what about the door-to-door?'

'We've finished the immediate blocks around Murray's flat. Nobody really knew him outside his own block, and even then it was just to say hello. No one we spoke to saw anything unusual that night, or in the days leading up to the attack. But quite a few of the occupants were at work by the time we got there, so we'll go back later this evening.'

'OK. Good work.'

Hawley looked pleased at the compliment, although he tried to hide it by looking down at his phone.

Pope looked at Thompson. 'Anything?'

Just then, the door opened and Tobias Darke walked into the room. Pope had called him on the way from Murray's flat. She was surprised at how quickly he had made it.

They all said their hellos, augmented by Darke's usual bear hug for Pope and Brody, and he sat down.

'Thanks for coming, Tobias. I think you know everyone by now. We're just about to get an update from Tech,' she said, indicating Steven Thompson.

Darke sat down and rifled through his briefcase for his notebook and took an ink pen from the breast pocket of his jacket.

'Financials all look fine for Murray,' said Thompson. 'He didn't earn a large salary but lived within his means. Even managed to save something most months. Maybe towards his wedding? Record is clean.'

'So, still no connections between our victims?' asked Pope.

'No, nothing so far. There seems to be absolutely nothing connecting Paul Ward and Tom Murray. They lived in different parts of London, worked in completely different fields at different locations. Ward didn't use the gym where Murray worked and they've never used the IT company where Ward worked. Ward socialized a lot but Murray didn't really. I mean, nothing.' Thompson looked like he wanted to be able to give Pope what she wanted, but it simply wasn't there.

Pope sat back and ran her hand through her hair. 'OK, what about Khan's theory that the two victims may have been unconnected to each other, but could both be connected to the killer? Any luck there?'

'I've looked at every possible area I can think of, but there would have to be at least one point of intersection for that to be the case, and I can't see it.'

Pope looked at Khan. There was a shared exasperation.

'In that case we'll need to work on the assumption that the two victims were chosen at random. And so we turn to the killer, rather than the victims,' said Pope.

Pope looked at Thompson again. 'You've searched for any similar cases in the recent past?'

'Nothing that fits this MO. As far as I can tell, these two murders are not connected to any cases we have on file.'

Pope looked at the faces around the room. She needed to inject some energy and hope into her team.

'Tobias, we need to think about our killer again. Do you have any thoughts?'

Darke turned back a couple of pages in his notebook. 'After our conversation, I connected with my colleague at Exeter University. She was most helpful in elucidating some of the characteristics inherent in devil worship. She noted that one of the typical preconditions for those who involve themselves in such things is the feeling of powerlessness. Individuals often feel alienated and anxious that the world is running away from them. They need to find a way to regain control, to exert power.'

Pope saw that Brody and Khan were taking notes, but she preferred to listen at this stage.

'Social change and instability creates a powerful, and sometimes terrifying, abyss for these people. The notion of Satan, of worshipping the devil, fills that void. The figure of Satan, however one conceives of it, starts to dominate the subject's life. They feel protected by a huge power, much greater than any other force. The consequence can be someone who feels freed of any personal responsibility for their actions and thus can act with impunity. Unfortunately this can include the taking of another life, and has done in some instances in recent and not so recent history.'

There was silence for a minute around the table as they considered Darke's assessment.

'Do these individuals tend to work alone or in groups?' asked Khan.

'I talked to my colleague about that. Both is the simple answer. Often small groups spring up, typically in the US, although nowadays these things can, of course, spread alarmingly quickly. The omnipresence of the internet and the fact that so many people obtain their news from social media rather than more conventionally trustworthy sources, means that this kind of thing can be found almost anywhere. But there have been cases where people have seemingly acted alone. Clearly the misinformation comes from somewhere, but the subject isn't involved in any groups beyond some online interaction. Sometimes not even that.'

'So how do we find this guy?' Khan asked Darke.

Darke smiled. 'Well, that's your department, DS Khan. But I'd start with looking at any online groups that deal with this kind of thing and see what you can find.'

'I'll get on to that,' said Thompson.

'So, to summarize,' said Brody, 'we have a ritualistic satanist who feels devoid of any moral responsibility, who may be acting alone or with others. And we have no further clues at present.'

Pope rolled her eyes. 'Fletcher's going to love that at the press conference.'

CHAPTER NINETEEN

Pope called into the bathroom en route to the press conference. She looked at her reflection in the mirror as she washed her hands. She felt every one of her forty-two years today. Well, most days, if she was being honest. She was pretty sure there was a new line next to her right eye. She squinted harder. Had she seen that one before? She shook her head. Not really important. Pope wasn't overly concerned about growing older. Most of the time.

She dried her hands on the cheap, scratchy paper towels the station had recently switched to and threw the balled-up paper in the bin. Press conferences were one of her least favourite parts of the job. She didn't want to be in the spotlight and have cameras trained on her. And standing next to Fletcher was perilous, given that he was always happy to throw someone else under the bus to advance his career. She understood the rationale for press conferences, but hated the execution.

It was particularly problematic this time round as they had no viable leads. Pope knew Fletcher would hand over to her once he had completed his grandstanding, and there would be nothing to say. A case like this was one of her greatest fears — an evil killer on the loose that she was unable to catch. He would simply keep killing and she would be powerless to stop it.

As she left the bathroom, Pope considered just walking out of the building, going for a coffee and returning only when it was all over. Enjoyable though that fantasy was, instead she pulled herself together and headed up the stairs to meet with Fletcher.

They had agreed to talk beforehand to clarify what they were going to say. This would be Pope's opportunity to regain some control over how the flow of information was handled.

'Bec, have a seat.'

Fletcher finished what he was doing on his phone, then turned it face down on the desk.

'How do you want to play it?' he asked.

She was fairly certain that Fletcher would have a plan already fully formed. But she played along.

'I think the key thing to emphasize is that we're making good progress in our investigation. We're following a number of leads. It's uncertain at present whether the two murders were linked and that's one key focus of our enquiries.'

Fletcher folded his arms and nodded slowly. 'How many of the details do we want the media to know?'

'Definitely not the symbol the killer carved on each body, and probably not the fact that they were both killed at midnight. I think that would cause a great deal of panic.'

'Yes, I agree with you. That's the last thing we want. What details of the investigation do we share?'

Pope noticed that Fletcher was using 'we' and wondered if he was planning on taking the limelight rather than handing over to her.

'I think it would be advisable to keep the names of the victims from the media at this stage. We don't want the families to deal with doorstepping and intrusive questions. I'd suggest keeping it brief and general — following leads, avenues of enquiry, talking to anyone who knew the victims and so on.'

Fletcher seemed amenable to her plan and so far there was an unusual consensus.

'Are you happy with that?' she asked.

'More or less, yes. I'm worried that the media will already have got hold of some of the details. The station leaks like a sieve and I don't want a repeat of the Cameraman case.'

He immediately looked like he regretted bringing it up.

'I'm sorry, Bec, I didn't mean to—'

She cut him off. 'It's fine. I know what you mean. But it happens in stations, doesn't it? We'll see what they have and take it from there. Hopefully we can control what they know as much as possible.'

Fletcher looked at his watch. 'OK, shall we get going?'

Pope followed Fletcher towards the briefing room She steeled herself. She had a horrible feeling that the media would already know a lot more than they wanted them to.

* * *

The room was already full when they arrived. As soon as Pope and Fletcher walked in, the camera flashes starting going off and the clicks of shutters went into overdrive. Pope looked ahead, but she noted Fletcher in front turning towards the cameras as they walked up onto the platform at the front of the room. There used to be a long, rectangular table behind which they could sit, offering some degree of separation from the journalists and broadcasters. But Fletcher had decided to get rid of it a few months ago so they would have to stand right in front of the crowd. Pope assumed it was so that he could be photographed and recorded more easily.

The questions started immediately. Fletcher stood silently, like a schoolteacher waiting for quiet from a rowdy class. Eventually the clamour died down. Pope was alone with Fletcher up there and she suddenly felt very isolated. She looked to her left to see an officer she vaguely recognized, who she assumed was there for crowd control.

'Ladies and gentlemen, if we're ready, shall we get started?' Fletcher's voice boomed out over the audience. A further benefit of standing rather than sitting. Fletcher was loving every minute of the limelight. 'When you're ready.'

The talking stopped.

'We're going to be giving a brief statement of the facts of the case as we know them at this stage in the investigation, then there'll be a chance for a few questions.'

'We're dealing with two attacks committed in the city in the past three days. I should emphasize that we are not sure if the attacks are linked. That is a key part of the ongoing investigation. Very sadly, two male victims have lost their lives and we of course send our sincere condolences to their families, friends and colleagues.'

'What are the names of the victims?' shouted a man towards the back of the room.

'We can't give out that information at the present time.'

'Is one victim Paul Ward?' asked a different voice, also male.

Fletcher maintained his composure, but Pope could see that he was furious. She peered into the sea of faces and outstretched phones but couldn't see who had asked the question.

'I'm afraid we can't confirm the identities of the victims at this time,' replied Fletcher.

'So it is Paul Ward?' This time Pope saw the man who was calling out. He was young and scruffily dressed, not someone who Pope recognized. A new recruit to the profession attempting to make his mark. She wondered where he had got his information.

'As I said, we can't confirm names at this stage.'

'Is it true that both victims were killed at midnight?' asked the same man.

Fletcher glanced at Pope. The conference was getting away from him and he liked to be in control. He was looking at her as if it had been her fault that the information had been leaked. But she was as angry about this as he was.

'I can tell you that we were called to a scene in Central London early on Tuesday morning where the first attack had taken place. The second attack happened the following night and we also attended that scene. Again, I would emphasize that investigations are ongoing.'

'Have you got any leads on the Midnight Killer?' asked a young woman near the front, holding her phone out towards Fletcher and Pope.

Pope had to work hard not to shake her head in resignation. Keeping information sealed in the station was like King Canute trying to stop the waves rolling in.

Fletcher ignored the question. 'I want to assure the public that we are doing everything to catch the perpetrators of these appalling crimes. There will be more officers on patrol and a visible police presence in both areas over the next few days. I know that this is a worrying time for local residents.'

Fletcher was attempting to stick to the possibility that these murders might not be linked. Pope wasn't convinced that this was the best policy, but Fletcher seemed to be holding the line.

'So both murders were carried out at midnight, but you're not sure they're linked?' asked the same young woman.

'I repeat, investigations are ongoing. When we have more information, we'll let you know.'

With that, Fletcher nodded to Pope and he walked off the small stage. Pope was stunned. It was the shortest press conference she had ever attended.

She followed him off the stage. It seemed like every person in the room was shouting at them as they walked down the side of the room and out through the door. It seemed to continue, despite there being no one in the room to answer.

Fletcher was silent as they returned to his office. Once safely inside, however, the full force of his anger surfaced.

'For fuck's sake! How the fuck did they get hold of that? The time, the names? Jesus Christ. What a shitshow!' Fletcher paced back and forth in front of his desk. He rarely swore, so it was all the more forceful when he did.

Pope was going to point out that they had only known one name, but thought better of it. Fletcher was furious that he had been made to look like a fool in front of the cameras, and she couldn't do anything about that. She also chose not to point out that she thought they should have admitted that the cases were probably linked. It risked looking like they had either lied to the press or were incompetent. Neither was ideal.

'Why don't you put out a statement which clarifies the position, stating that we think they are probably linked but don't want to give any firm answers until we can be definitive?' said Pope.

Fletcher stopped pacing and looked out of the window. He was working out the optics.

'Yes, I'll think about it. That might be a good idea.'

'I'll get back to work, then. I'll update you when we have anything.'

Fletcher nodded but said nothing as she left. Pope could tell that he was already working on the wording in his head.

As she returned to the office, Pope wondered where the information was leaking from. There were a large number of uniformed officers working on the case and it was sometimes difficult to resist a wad of cash from a reporter. Living in London on a police constable's salary was not easy.

Brody and Khan were still in the office working at their computers. Pope looked at her watch and saw it was after six. She made a decision.

'Brody, Khan, do you fancy a drink?'

They looked up, surprise on both faces.

'Are you buying?' asked Brody.

'No, you are,' she replied. 'Come on. We need it.'

144

CHAPTER TWENTY

After packing up for the day, the three detectives walked the few minutes along the Strand to the Coal Hole, an oddly named but friendly pub just near the Savoy hotel. They chose a table tucked in a quiet corner beyond the bar. Pope bought the first round while Brody and Khan sat down.

'Here we are,' said Pope as she set down the drinks. A pint for Brody, a glass of red wine for Pope and a coke for Khan.

'Don't fancy something stronger after the day we've had?' asked Brody.

'I don't drink alcohol,' said Khan.

'Oh, sorry,' said Brody, embarrassed.

'It's no problem,' she said, smiling.

They all took a drink and there was silence for a moment.

'So, how have you found your first couple of days on the squad?' asked Brody.

'Interesting. Intense. A lot has happened in a couple of days. Is it always like this?'

'Not always,' said Pope. 'Is it any different to Hackney?'

'Well, it's early days, but we never had anything like this.'

'Obviously, this is a pretty unusual case. But then we've had our fair share of unusual cases over the last few years.'

'I read about some of those,' said Khan. She didn't elaborate, and Pope wondered how much she knew about her own personal connections to one case in particular. Did she know about the Cameraman? She made the decision not to ask.

'Being based so centrally, we do spread the net wide. Some of the more challenging cases come to us.'

'That's one of the reasons why so many detectives want to come and work here,' said Khan. 'Everybody knows about your team.'

Pope hated the publicity which some of their cases attracted. She changed the subject. 'What made you want to join up, Zahra?'

She considered her answer. 'When I arrived here from Afghanistan as a kid, all I knew of authority was oppression and mistrust. This was mainly through stories my parents would tell. I don't remember much about it myself. I was only four when we left. But interactions here with the police and authorities were different. Better, mostly. Then when I got older my brother started hanging out with a bad crowd and getting in all kinds of trouble. There were big rows at home, but he wanted to go his own way. One day, when he was around fourteen, he was brought home by two police officers. One was a female officer and I remember being so impressed by her uniform and her authority. She was very kind to me and my parents, and even my brother, explaining what had happened and what would happen next. I felt I could trust her. From that day, I wanted to be like her. To be a police officer.'

'How did your parents feel about it?' asked Brody.

'They weren't exactly over the moon. Don't get me wrong, they're fairly progressive compared to some people back home. But female officers are often targeted in Afghanistan and they were worried about me. I think I've put their minds at rest a little after almost ten years. But they still worry, you know.'

'And how's your brother getting on now?' asked Pope.

Khan's look darkened. 'A work in progress. Let's just say I don't think my work with him is done yet.' She took a sip of her drink.

She clearly didn't want to elaborate.

'Do you live near your parents?' asked Pope.

'Hmm. I'm back living with them at the moment. I had to move out of my boyfriend's flat last year. Difficult break-up.'

'Oh, sorry to hear that,' said Pope.

'No, it's OK. It had run its course.'

'So, how is it living at home?' asked Pope.

'My parents are great. But it's tricky after you've had your independence for a while. Another work in progress.' Khan smiled. 'But I seem to be getting the grilling. What about you two? I guess you don't live with your parents!'

'I'll get the next round,' said Brody, standing up. 'Same again?'

They both nodded and he headed to the bar. Khan looked at Pope, encouraging her to talk.

'I live with my partner, Alex, and his two daughters.'

'How old are they?'

'Seventeen and thirteen.'

Khan smiled. 'That must present some challenges.'

'It does. But they're great and most of the time it's fine. Although neither of them are over the moon at having a homicide detective for a stepmum.'

'I can imagine. My brother and I are completely different. I think I was fine as a teenager, but him . . . not so much. He put my parents through all kinds.'

Pope nodded. She thought of Chloe's difficult moments.

'Does your brother also live at home with your parents?'

'He's in and out. To be honest, I'm not sure where he is much of the time. And he most definitely is not happy about having a police officer as a sister.'

Brody returned with the drinks.

'How are things with you, Brody? How's Lizzie?' Pope thought back to her diagnosis of his good mood earlier and wanted to check if she was right.

He turned to Khan. 'Lizzie's my girlfriend. No kids, cats or dogs.'

'Yet,' said Pope.

'What does she do?' asked Khan.

'She's a nurse at St Thomas'. Rotates around different departments, so she has an unpredictable shift pattern. I think it helps her understand some of the odd hours we have to work. At weekends when she's not on shift, she works with a food bank near where she lives which supports refugees and asylum seekers.'

'We had to use one of those when we first arrived in the UK. There's not as much support as people think,' said Khan.

'Did you say you were four?' asked Brody.

'When I arrived in the UK? Yes. My dad was a university lecturer in Kabul, but at this time they were just removing people who were critical of the regime and he had already been arrested. We had no choice but to leave.'

'How do you find it here now? Attitudes to migrants are not always friendly, are they?' said Brody.

'It's generally OK. Most people are fundamentally decent and show genuine humanity. Some of the support is amazing. It's just a shame a small minority can be very vocal and, sometimes, violent. It's another reason why I'm pleased to be in the Met. I always volunteer for overtime to work on marches and demos.'

They all took a drink and were quiet for a moment. Pope wanted to refocus on the investigation.

'So, what are we thinking for the next steps?'

'Leads seem a bit thin on the ground,' said Brody. 'Whoever's behind this is covering their tracks very well.'

'I know. I think we need to work on the occult angle tomorrow. We've hit a dead end with any connections between the victims. Nothing so far in the door-to-doors or with colleagues, friends, family. All we have is the occult angle — satanism, devil worship, whatever you want to call it. So I think that's what we look at now. That's the through line.'

Brody and Khan both nodded their agreement.

'How do we proceed?' asked Khan.

'Let's get in touch with Darke's contact at the university and see what she can tell us. I know Darke's been in contact, but I'd like it if one of us spoke to her. Just to get a different perspective. I also think we should go back to your contact at that odd shop in Hackney.'

'Acheron?'

'Yes, I want to talk to him again now we have a second victim and know a bit more. Maybe he's thought of something that could help since we spoke to him. Can you get in touch and let him know?'

'Yes, I'll do that first thing.'

'I think we also need to widen the net. If the killer is into the occult, there's a strong possibility they may have visited other, similar places.'

'Though they may equally do anything like that online,' said Brody.

'That's true. But the people who own and work in them might have contacts in online forums and that kind of thing. Something might ring a bell.'

'Are you planning to tell them about the pentagrams?' asked Khan.

'Not in relation to the murders. But maybe ask if anyone has shown any interest in the symbol. We might get lucky.'

Pope finished her drink. 'Right. I'm off. Busy day tomorrow.'

They left together and said their goodbyes outside the pub, before going their separate ways.

As Pope walked to the car park, she considered Zahra Khan. All in all, and on early impressions, she was pleased with how she seemed to be fitting in. Hard-working, proactive and keen to learn. She couldn't ask for much more at this stage. She had a team back together. It hurt every time she thought of Adam Miller, but this was some form of progress. The beginning of the healing.

Now all she had to do was make sure her team found the Midnight Killer before he struck again. The clock was ticking.

CHAPTER TWENTY-ONE

Friday morning

Pope was first in the office. When she'd arrived home last night, Chloe and Hannah had both been out and she'd spent a quiet evening with Alex. There had been no drama, no fireworks, no arguments. She almost felt like she was getting the hang of work–life balance, something she had never managed in the past.

Predictably, she'd had a terrible night's sleep, hence the early arrival at the station.

She made a coffee and sat down to check through her emails. There was nothing of any real interest: an invitation to a mandatory training course which she would do her best to avoid; a reference request for someone she had never heard of; several requests from journalists asking her for an appointment for an interview; and a strangely written appeal from someone who described themselves as a 'true-crime podcaster' insisting that they were close to breaking the Midnight Killer case and they just needed to interview Pope and get a few details to confirm their hypothesis. The email was so badly written she wondered how the sender could string two sentences together for their podcast. She deleted each one of the emails.

The only one she kept was from Fletcher. He was following up the press conference, furious about the leak and asking Pope to investigate. She didn't delete it, but she had no intention of doing anything about it.

Instead, she started an online search for any UK businesses which described themselves as 'magic' or 'occult'. She had a surprising number of hits. There were endless shops which described themselves as 'magic', but most of these seemed of the 'rabbit out of a hat' variety and seemed to cater to either professional magicians, or those aspiring to learn. Many also described themselves as bookshops. After checking a number of these, she decided to remove this from her search and try again with only 'occult' as the description. This produced a smaller number of returns and as she started looking through, Pope realized that, again, many were simply bookshops which specialized in occult material. There were only a few suppliers of products which were related to the occult and she initially concentrated on those.

She got through the list fairly quickly before they started repeating themselves on the page. This included The Alchemist, which had a fairly basic website. She started to navigate around. There was a photograph of the front of the shop on the initial page, with a menu in the top left-hand corner to allow navigation to other parts of the site. She clicked on the 'About' section and discovered an image showing the inside of the premises. Acheron, or Kevin Bradley to be accurate, was nowhere to be seen on the site. Pope browsed through the products available to order online. Books included guides to tarot reading, introductions to the occult, texts by writers such as Proudhon, who Pope had never heard of, and, of course, the ubiquitous Aleister Crowley. There were also many guides to satanism, including several of the *Beginner's Guide to Devil Worship* type.

Beyond the books you could also buy tarot cards, Ouija boards, symbols, outfits, whips, chains and all manner of merchandize which Pope considered highly dubious. She made a mental note to leave the research into online groups and chat rooms to Steven Thompson and the cyber department, if this was anything to go by.

She leaned back in her chair and checked her watch. She had been working on this for almost an hour and had found nothing to offer her anything particularly useful. Although there were not a great many physical shops in London that she could find, it was impossible to tell how popular the occult in general, and satanism in particular, actually was. The proliferation of online sales meant that without visiting each premises and asking them to check, they could only guess at numbers. That was without the number of online-only retailers she had come across in her search.

What was clear was that there was certainly an appetite out there. The question was, how could they use this to narrow the search for their killer?

By the time Brody arrived, she was getting screen fatigue.

'Morning,' he said as he walked in. 'How was your evening?'

'Fine,' said Pope distractedly. Her mind was well and truly in the case at this point.

Brody noticed. 'I thought I was early. What are you working on?' he said as he sat down and entered the password to fire up his computer.

'I've been looking at places which sell occult merchandise and books. Actual shops and online sellers. There's quite a few of the latter. Not so many shops.'

'Did you find anything useful?'

'Not so far. It's what you'd expect. Nothing that we can use yet.'

Just then Khan arrived, said her good mornings and sat down at her desk. Miller's desk.

'Shall I get in touch with Darke's contact at Exeter University?' asked Brody.

'Yes, that would be great. Khan, can I send you a list of shops which sell occult books and paraphernalia? We need to see if they have any knowledge of someone who's been interested in pentagrams, that sort of thing. It's a long shot, but it's all we have at the moment. I'm going to start checking the online retailers.'

'Yes, will do,' said Khan.

Pope made a list of the stores she had found and sent them to Khan. They then started working the phones. Pope had trouble finding an actual human being to speak to in almost all cases, so had to email and ask someone to contact her ASAP. She wondered how many she would hear back from. Khan had better luck and was taking plenty of notes as she spoke.

Brody ended his call.

'How did you get on?' asked Pope.

'I couldn't speak to the professor who runs the course. Apparently she's out of the country at some research symposium in Denmark and isn't available today. I'll try again tomorrow when she's free.'

'Khan, anything?'

'No, I've spoken to someone at most of the shops on the list. But no one seems to know anything about someone interested in that type of symbology. To be honest, if I was interested in that sort of thing, I'd probably be looking online rather than going into a shop and discussing it face to face.'

Pope was just about to complain that after several days of investigation they had nothing, when Thompson sped into the office.

'I think we might have found something interesting.'

Pope's heart rate immediately jumped. 'Go on.'

He came over and placed his tablet on her desk. Brody and Khan came over to join them.

'I was checking the social media of our victims and their partners. When I didn't find anything, I expanded it and thought I'd have a look at Kevin Bradley from The Alchemist. Partly just out of interest, but I thought we might find out a bit more about the kind of thing our killer is into. Maybe give us other avenues to explore.'

'You're looking into Acheron?' asked Khan, the surprise evident in her voice.

'I wasn't initially, just fishing around. But I found something you'll want to see.'

Khan leaned in closer.

'This is his Instagram account. Quite a few pictures of things from the shop, new books and so forth. He obviously uses his account in part to promote his business. But there's also a lot of personal stuff. He posts quite prolifically.'

Thompson was scrolling through images of Acheron at a beach bar with some friends, him in the sea, swimming in a hotel pool. The usual holiday snaps.

'I'm not sure what this is telling us,' said Pope.

Khan shook her head. 'Me either.'

'Hold on a minute.' He kept scrolling through. The next photo was of Acheron in swimming trunks, sitting on a beach. Then a few more followed that. Then Thompson stopped at one of the photos in the sequence. Acheron had bent over to get something out of a bag. It showed a different angle, where his back was visible. Pope leaned in closer. On the man's shoulder was a small tattoo. An outline, not shaded in.

Pope squinted. 'Is that . . .' She paused to take it in. 'You're kidding me!'

On Acheron's left shoulder was an inverted pentagram, inked in black.

Pope looked at Brody. 'Christ. This has to be a mistake.' She looked at the image again.

'No mistake. He has the same symbol on his shoulder that we found on our victims,' said Thompson. 'And you can see it in several of his other posts as well.'

'He said he didn't know anything about it,' said Brody. 'We specifically asked him.'

Khan was silent. She'd vouched for the man. Pope knew exactly how she'd be feeling.

'So why the hell didn't he mention it? What's he got to hide?' asked Pope, unable to keep the incredulity out of her voice.

'I mean, he did seem sort of cagey at the end of our conversation, but I didn't pick up anything too suspicious from him,' said Brody.

'Maybe the whole tarot card nonsense was to put us off track and get rid of us?' said Pope. 'It did seem to come out of nowhere. And who better to engage in an occult-themed attack than someone with an in-depth knowledge of the occult? Suddenly it makes sense.'

Khan looked uncomfortable. 'But he has no history of anything like this. He was nothing but cooperative when he worked with us a couple of years back. And his record is clean.'

'A clean record just means he's never been caught,' said Pope. 'It doesn't mean he hasn't been up to anything. Is there any connection between Acheron and either of our victims?'

Thompson shook his head. 'That's the first thing I checked out after I spotted this. I can't find anything to link him with either Paul Ward or Tom Murray. They live, work and socialize in totally different areas and groups, as far as I can tell. Can't find any friends in common. No hobbies. If there is a link, it's well hidden.'

Pope considered the situation. She was sure this had to have significance. It couldn't be a coincidence. It simply couldn't. And if it was, why didn't he mention it when they questioned him? Was she grabbing too hard at this because they didn't have anything else? No, she didn't think so.

'Shall I call him and ask him to come in?' said Khan.

Pope shook her head. 'No, let's go and see him now. I don't want him to have a chance to think up an explanation — or worse, do a runner.'

'I don't think he's the type to run,' said Khan.

Pope shot her a look. 'Did you think he was the type to have a killer's symbol tattooed on his shoulder?' Her new recruit would need to learn that you have to look at the evidence rather than let it be obscured by your feelings.

Pope grabbed her jacket and headed to the door. Then she turned to Thompson. 'Good work, Steven. Really good work.'

He nodded his appreciation at the comment.

'Come on, let's go,' said Pope. This time she didn't turn round.

* * *

Pope flew down the stairs to the underground garage and Brody and Khan had to jog to keep up with her. She got in the driver's side and immediately started the engine, while they scrambled into the car.

'Brody, sort the satnav,' Pope said as she reversed the car far too quickly out of the parking space.

Once out of the garage and onto the street, Pope gunned the engine and weaved in and out of the traffic. She didn't think the situation warranted lights and siren — Acheron had no idea they were coming for him. But she drove as quickly as the traffic allowed.

'How do you want to play it?' asked Brody.

'I think we have a conversation with him and if he can't come up with a plausible explanation for why he neglected to mention his tattoo, we'll bring him in and question him formally at the station.' Pope was weaving in and out of the traffic as she spoke.

'And if he resists?' asked Brody.

'I don't think he will,' said Khan.

'If he resists, that'll be more suspicious and we'll definitely haul him to the station.'

The three of them remained silent for the rest of the journey.

When they reached Hackney, Pope pulled up around a hundred yards before The Alchemist. She didn't want to give their suspect any advance warning of their arrival. They got out of the car and walked to the front door.

Pope saw Acheron as soon as she opened the door. He was standing facing one of the bookshelves, searching the faces of the books on display. As last time, he was dressed completely in black. He turned as they entered, and Pope noticed an uncertain expression cross his face, before he put on a welcoming smile.

'Hello again, officers. What can I do for you this time?'

Khan's face was deadly serious and Pope saw Acheron look at her, and his own expression changed.

'This all seems very serious. What's going on?' He took an instinctive step backwards towards the counter.

'We need to ask you a few questions,' said Pope, moving a step closer.

'About what?'

Pope decided to dive straight in. 'About the inverted pentagram you have tattooed on your shoulder.'

Acheron nodded slowly, maintaining eye contact with her. Suddenly, he turned and sprinted towards the back of the shop. They were all caught off guard, but moved quickly to follow.

Pope was first to the door, and as she passed through she heard a loud bang. 'I think there's another way out,' she shouted.

Sure enough, the loud noise had come from a further door leading out of the shop. Acheron had slammed it open against the wall and it was swinging back and forth.

Pope saw that there was an alley leading behind the row of shops and Acheron was sprinting away from them towards the main road, his long hair flying behind him. Pope knew that Brody was faster than her, and sure enough he overtook and gave chase. Khan, too, was quick, and Pope soon found herself in third place in the race to apprehend their suspect.

Suspect. Acheron had now jumped to the head of the list. They needed to catch him.

Pope turned onto the main road and saw that Brody was desperately trying to catch up. But Acheron was fast, and although Brody could match him, he wasn't gaining any ground. Pope knew that if they lost him on this busy street, he would go to ground and they would be back at a dead end.

Acheron turned right onto a residential side road, and she saw Brody sprint after him. But Acheron was flagging, and Brody was gaining. Suddenly, Pope saw their suspect run full speed into a waste bin, which sent him off balance and careering into a wall at the front of one of the houses. He regained his footing but it had just given Brody the extra few seconds he needed to catch up with him. Just as Acheron started to accelerate again, Brody dived and lunged at the man's torso. They both went tumbling to the ground, Brody landing hard on top of him.

Whatever else he was, Acheron didn't seem to be a fighter. He didn't struggle, kick or punch, as suspects often did in this situation. He just lay there, breathing heavily, exhausted.

Khan caught up with them and pulled out her handcuffs. Brody grabbed his wrists and bent them behind his back. Acheron grunted in pain, but didn't resist. Khan cuffed him and stood up, bent over, hands on her knees.

They all recovered their breath, steadied their nerves.

Pope walked around and knelt down by Acheron's head. He looked up at her.

'I think we need to have a chat, Kevin.'

CHAPTER TWENTY-TWO

Interview Room One had been redecorated recently. The previously white walls had been replaced with a cold, institutional grey. Fletcher had apparently chosen the colour to reflect the atmosphere in prisons, with the aim of making suspects consider their choices carefully while answering questions. It was as much a punishment for Pope and her colleagues as it was for the people they interviewed in here.

After the dramatic chase through the streets of Hackney, Acheron had come to the station quietly. He let himself be led back to Pope's car without any fuss and sat silently during the drive. Pope spent most of the journey attempting to catch her breath.

Khan had desperately wanted to be in the interview, but Pope felt that she lacked a degree of objectivity. And she wanted Acheron to feel uncomfortable. No familiar faces. Khan was not happy, but she had to settle for watching through the one-way glass in the viewing room.

Brody grabbed three cups of coffee and he and Pope made their way to the interview room. The officer standing by the door asked if Pope wanted him to remain present. Pope said yes and he retreated to the corner.

Brody handed a coffee to Pope and put the other one in front of Acheron. He looked down at the thin, steaming liquid.

'Thanks,' he said, without any enthusiasm.

Pope opened an A4 file of papers that Thompson had put together. There were copies of the photographs he had found on Acheron's Instagram account, but most of it was unrelated junk. An old, yet surprisingly effective, way to make interviewees think you had a whole file of information about them.

Sometimes she left suspects to stew for a while, building up their unease. But she wanted to interview Acheron immediately, without giving him time to think through what he might say.

Pope started the tape and carried out the required formalities. She used 'Kevin Bradley', his given name, knowing it would annoy him.

'Right, Kevin,' she said, closing the file in front of her and laying it down on the table between them.

'My name is Acheron. I'd like you to use it, please.'

'Your given name is Kevin Bradley. Is that right?'

He hesitated. 'Yes. But I go by Acheron. Everybody calls me that.'

'Even your mum?' asked Pope.

He looked evenly at her. She wondered if he knew she was baiting him.

'OK, Acheron. You've said you don't want a solicitor present, is that right?'

'Yes. I've got nothing to hide. Where is DS Khan? Is she not going to be in here too?'

'No, she won't be joining us today. DS Khan has other things to do, I'm afraid.'

Pope could almost feel Khan's irritation through the glass.

'OK. If you change your mind at any point, just let us know. You do have the right to legal representation if you choose.'

He nodded.

160

'Why did you run? You certainly gave us a good run for our money up the high street.'

Acheron looked down at his hands, absent-mindedly rubbing his wrists where the handcuffs had been. 'I wasn't sure what you would do.'

Pope raised her eyebrows. 'Most people would wait to find out, rather than racing out of the back door. You're aware that this makes you look like you have something to hide? Something serious.'

He looked like a naughty schoolboy who had been caught red-handed behind the bike sheds. He didn't have an answer. The cockiness of their previous encounter at The Alchemist was gone.

Pope tried again. 'What was it that made you run?'

He continued looking down, avoiding eye contact.

'You asked about my tattoo.' Quietly.

Pope leaned forward. 'Pardon?'

He looked at her. 'My tattoo. You asked about my tattoo.'

'Yes, why don't you tell us about that, Acheron?'

He slowly shook his head. 'It's on my shoulder.'

'We know where it is. And we know what it is. What I really want to know is, firstly, *why* you have an inverted pentagram tattooed on your shoulder. And secondly, why you neglected to mention it when we came in your shop two days ago and asked you if you knew anything about inverted pentagrams.'

He looked up. 'I just . . . when I was younger I thought it would be cool. I just . . . did it. I wasn't really thinking.'

'But not just a pentagram. An inverted pentagram. Tell us about that.'

'You already know about it.'

'I want to hear it in your words. I want to know why you chose that particular symbol.'

'I was interested in alternative belief systems. I am interested. Organized religion has been responsible for so much violence and evil in the world. I believe in something different.'

'And you think devil worship is a better option?' said Pope. She struggled to keep the sarcasm out of her voice.

'I don't expect you to understand.'

'Try me. Try to explain it, Acheron.'

'I'm interested in satanism. It's not "devil worship".'

'Is there a difference?' asked Pope.

'Most satanists don't actually worship the devil. They don't even believe in the devil as you may think of the concept. We don't believe in Satan as a being, or the embodiment of evil. It's more a reaction to religion. A revolt against traditional forms of authority.'

'So you don't worship the devil?'

'No. I don't believe there is a God, or a devil.'

'So why do people talk about satanism? That implies following the devil, doesn't it?'

'Not in the form of an actual being. For us, Satan is more like a metaphor for taking a stand against the arbitrary rules which society tries to impose upon us. It's not an evil creature with horns.'

Pope was quiet for a moment.

'You said "us". Are you part of a community?'

'Mainly online, but there are some people who come in the shop as well. In person.'

'We're going to need a list of all of those people. Online and in person.'

Acheron looked at Pope but didn't say anything.

'I'm going to ask you again. Why did you run if you haven't done anything wrong?'

'I saw your press conference yesterday. Then I read about it online. I know that's what you're investigating.'

'But if you aren't involved, what's the problem?'

He sighed deeply. It seemed to take a great deal of effort to speak.

'I've had shit about my beliefs for as long as I can remember. The other kids at school saw me as weird. When I opened the shop I got all kinds of hassle. From neighbours, other shop owners, random members of the public walking by. I've had religious groups targeting the shop, groups of teenagers throwing bricks through the windows. Local parents. They only know what they see in films and on TV. They think we're corrupting children and sacrificing virgins. It's so exhausting.'

'Surely you have to expect that. If you set yourself up as a satanist?'

'Why should I? Satanists are generally non-violent. I certainly am. We don't believe in causing anybody any harm.'

'But running from the police?'

'I knew you'd think I was involved. Whenever anything happens that's a bit out of the ordinary, people like us always get blamed.'

'People like us?'

'Nonconformists. Anyone who believes anything outside the mainstream. Maybe you hadn't noticed, but Britian is a very conservative country.'

'So you thought we'd hassle you.'

'Isn't that what you came to the shop to do? Exactly that?'

Pope had to admit, that's exactly what they had planned to do.

'Tell me about the tattoo, then. What does it symbolize?'

'In reality, it symbolizes balance and the rejection of rules, regulations, expectations. But a lot of people associate it with evil. That's not what it started out as, but it's been corrupted and used as a sign of evil. People don't understand it, like they don't understand satanism.'

Pope was beginning to wonder if Acheron was making it up as he went along in an attempt to throw them off the scent, or if he really knew his stuff and was the victim of a huge misunderstanding.

'You got the tattoo when you were younger?'

'Yes, when I was eighteen.'

'Because . . . ?'

'Because I'd read a lot about satanism and I knew what it actually represented. I thought it pretty much summed up how I felt about life and it seemed the right thing to do.'

'And do you still feel that?'

'I do. We're hemmed in by pointless rules and arbitrary moral value judgements. People don't understand. I wanted to take a stand against that.'

'And how did you get into it? When you were younger?'

'I was listening to a lot of heavy metal. There were references to the devil and to the occult, so I got interested through that.'

Pope considered how to proceed in the interview. She decided to take a chance and share the details of the deaths with Acheron. Either he already knew because he was involved, in which case it didn't matter, or he may be able to shed some light on their killer. She had nothing to lose.

'How much do you know about the murders that we're investigating?' she asked.

'Only what I've heard from your press conference and what I've read online.'

'And what have you read online?'

'That two people were killed at the same time of day. Around midnight. People are saying it has some associations with us because of the timing of the murders.'

'Anything else?'

'I don't think so. Why?'

At least the information getting out was limited. For the moment.

'What I'm going to tell you is completely confidential. I want your assurance that you don't breathe a word of this outside of this room.'

He stared at her. 'OK.'

Pope took a deep breath. She glanced at Brody, who gave a brief nod. He understood what she was going to do and approved, which made her feel better about her decision.

'The killer carved a symbol on both of the victims. An inverted pentagram. Crudely done, but obvious.'

Acheron looked shocked. Genuinely shocked, thought Pope.

'So you can see why we were asking about that when we first visited and why it looks suspicious that you professed to know nothing about it, given that you have the *exact* same symbol tattooed on your shoulder.' Pope had raised her voice in an attempt to make him feel even more uncomfortable than he already did.

'I . . . um . . . yes . . . but I had absolutely nothing to do with this. Nothing at all.'

'So you're asking us to believe that after denying you know anything about pentagrams, then running when we came to talk to you, that this is all just a complete coincidence?'

'No! I mean, yes, it's a coincidence.'

Pope was suddenly more combative. 'Oh, come on, Acheron! Tell us the truth. How are you involved in all this?'

He looked at Brody, rather than Pope, hoping for a friendlier reception.

'I swear! I don't know anything. Only what I've read.'

Brody said nothing while Pope simply stared at him. She was usually very good at working out whether a suspect was lying to her. She wasn't there yet.

'Where were you on Monday night? Between eleven and one?'

Acheron looked up, trying to remember.

Pope knew that the idea that people looked up to the left when they were lying was a myth and liars tended to maintain eye contact most of the time. She also knew liars talked too much. Acheron was doing neither of those things. But it was more than the science, the psychology. It was the gut, and only experience could teach you that.

'I was at home.'

'And what were you doing?'

'I watched TV until around midnight, then went to bed.'

'What did you watch?'

'I can't remember. I'd need to look up what was on.'

'Well, that kind of defeats the object, doesn't it? Were you alone?'

'Yes.'

'And what about on Wednesday night, same time?'

He thought back again. 'Same thing. At home. And yes, I was alone.'

Pope considered that if he had been trying to hide something, he probably would have arranged a more convincing alibi. The current one was pathetic.

'So, you have no alibi?' she said.

He looked down to the floor again and shook his head.

Pope changed tack again. 'So, what do you think about the pentagram carved on our victims? Have you ever heard of anything like that in your online groups? Anyone come into the shop and talked about anything like that?'

He shook his head again. 'No. I've never heard anything like that.'

'What's the significance? Any thoughts?'

'I don't know. It depends what type of person did it.'

'Well, obviously. That's what I'm asking you,' said Pope.

'Yes, but I mean if the person doing this is more knowledgeable about it, they will see it for what satanism really is. But if they're more into a Hollywood version, they might see it as more sensationalist. More about worshipping an actual being.'

'You mean the devil?' asked Pope.

'Yes. It's always associated with murder and satanic rituals and that kind of thing.'

'So how do we work it out?'

'You won't be able to until you talk to the killer.'

Pope shook her head. Was this another dead end in a case so full of them?

'DI Brody, can I have a word?' She walked to the door and he followed her outside. She closed the door behind her.

Pope leaned against the wall outside Interview Room One and ran her fingers through her hair.

'So, what do we think?' she asked.

Brody grimaced. 'I have to say, I'm not getting spree killer vibes from him. He's too earnest. Too . . . I don't know. What do you think?'

'I agree. He isn't doing it for me, either. Let's hold him while Thompson digs into him. We'll apply for an extension if anything crops up.'

Brody nodded. They went back inside. Acheron looked up at Pope expectantly.

'Kevin Bradley, we're going to hold you here for up to twenty-four hours while we continue our investigations. PC Rose, can you take him down to the cells, please.'

Acheron slumped in his chair. 'I haven't done anything wrong. I didn't do this.'

But his tone was resigned. She thought it sounded like the voice of someone who has been picked on for his beliefs for much of his life. She wasn't convinced he had anything to do with the murders, but due diligence won over her feelings. Bec Pope always championed the underdog and she knew that if he was proved innocent, she would feel pretty bad about putting him through this.

CHAPTER TWENTY-THREE

After watching a deflated Acheron be led down to the cells at Charing Cross Police Station, Pope returned to her office and slumped down at the meeting table. Brody joined her, shortly followed by Khan and Thompson.

'DS Khan, you know him better than us. What did you think?'

'I wouldn't say I know him, really. But I've met him a few more times, that's true. I just don't think he's got it in him.'

'OK, but ignoring what you know of him for the moment, what about the interview?'

Khan thought for a moment. 'He seemed genuine.'

'In what way?' asked Pope.

'To start with, I bought his excuse for running. He's used to being hassled, bullied for his beliefs, and this seemed like another time that was going to happen. And he had no proper alibi. I would think that if he was going to commit these murders he would at least work on some kind of plausible alibi. Given the degree of planning that must have gone into these murders, that seems like an odd thing to leave off your planning list. I mean, if he's spending time working out what tools he'd need, location, how to carve the symbol . . .'

Pope had thought exactly the same.

'Brody?'

'I agree up to a point. He did *sound* plausible in there. But he wouldn't be the first perp to put on an act and try to convince us that they're innocent. He *did* run, after failing to mention to the police something that might be material in an ongoing murder investigation. That tattoo is a hell of a coincidence.'

Pope didn't need reminding that he had run. Her legs were still doing that for her.

'OK, so we hold him for twenty-four hours. Thompson, I want you to focus on Kevin Bradley now. Dig into everything about him.'

Steven Thompson nodded.

'We can apply to keep him longer if we need to,' said Pope. 'But hopefully we can establish whether there is anything that links him to these crimes within that time frame. Beyond that stupid tattoo. What do we think about his claims that satanism is really just an alternative lifestyle? Is he telling us that as a form of smokescreen? To try to hide his involvement?'

'Maybe,' said Brody. 'But he's right — if you were to ask the average person about all this, I'm pretty sure they'd come up with the Hollywood version rather than his version. Whereas someone who was really interested in this would know the reality. There have been stories over recent years of diabolic sects engaging in sacrifices, kidnapping children and so on. But none of them have been true. All investigations have proved that. There isn't any evidence that this type of devil worship actually exists outside of books and films.'

'So are we saying that our killer is probably not a true satanist?' asked Khan. 'For whatever reason, they're copying what they've seen on the screen?'

'Possibly,' said Pope. 'It could be someone who has no interest in it at all and is just trying to put us off the scent.'

'But what's the point?' asked Brody. 'The whole carving in the chest aspect is just so much hassle if you aren't trying to say something specific. Send some kind of message.'

Pope had no answer for that.

'I think we've got someone who believes they're doing the devil's work,' said Brody. 'It's out there, but I can't see it could be anything else.'

'And Acheron's view of all this is not that,' said Khan. 'He doesn't believe in it in that way.'

'If he's telling us the truth,' replied Brody.

* * *

They spent the afternoon following up on their suspect. Khan joined Thompson in doing a deep dive on Acheron, taking apart every aspect of his digital life. Brody continued his research into every conceivable aspect of satanism, losing himself in a rabbit hole of all things occult. Pope briefed Fletcher, leaving his office predictably frustrated after his insistence that this be resolved quickly. She understood his frustration. She needed to think, so instead of returning to their shared office she continued down the stairs to the main entrance.

As she neared the bottom of the stairs she had a flashback to several months ago, when she had first encountered Alice Lowrie. Covered in blood, arms outstretched, the woman had begged for her help. She had attempted to do that and it hadn't ended well. She'd solved the case, but the collateral damage had been huge. She remembered it every time she walked down those stairs, and it weighed heavily. What would Dr Boyd think about that?

She walked out of the door onto Agar Street, turning left towards her favourite coffee place nearby. It was late afternoon and the place was fairly quiet. She ordered a coffee and found a spot facing a window out onto the busy street. She sipped the drink absent-mindedly as a range of thoughts wandered through her head. She was still feeling extremely guilty about the cancelled New York trip. She knew she had to make it up to Alex and the girls, but wasn't sure either how or when. Cases seemed to tumble in one after another, leaving her no downtime at work and no window to try to make things better at home. Not for the first time, she wondered how much longer she would be able to get away with this precarious balancing act.

As ever, her current case pushed out everything else and her focus shifted. What was the next move? If Thompson and Khan managed to find something which implicated Acheron, they were there. If they didn't, for the first time in a long time, she didn't have a way forward. The whole team needed the adrenaline rush of a significant lead, and as their leader she had nothing.

But Pope knew that feeling sorry for herself was entirely unproductive. She shook herself out of it, finished her coffee and headed back to the station. Something had to give.

As she walked to her desk she saw that the post had been delivered to her in-tray. There was an ever-smaller amount of physical mail she received these days. Although the post room tried to filter out as much as possible, there was some promotional material, some official business — legal documents and so forth.

Pope sorted through the envelopes half-heartedly, placing most in her 'open later' pile. It usually hung around for weeks until it grew so high that she felt compelled to open them. She leafed through them until one item caught her attention. An envelope with the address handwritten in neat cursive, as if with a fountain pen. Bold, thick lines in black on a very high-quality envelope. First-class stamp in the corner. She couldn't make out the postmark. She hadn't received anything like that for as long as she could remember. The only person she knew who used a fountain pen was Tobias Darke, and this wasn't his handwriting.

Pope found her keys and used her house key to slice through the top of the envelope, creating a jagged opening. She took out the contents, seeing that there were two pages.

As she started to read, her blood ran cold.

Dear DCI Pope,

I have heard you are looking for me — the one the media have called the Midnight Killer. It is nice to meet you, if a letter can be called meeting someone. I saw you on the television. You looked tired and not very pleased with the way Superintendent Fletcher handled the press conference. This must all be very difficult for you. It is odd that we still refer to them as press conferences, even though it is very little about newspapers nowadays. It is much more about the television and social media.

You will not find me. I am too good at this and you will never track me down. I wonder how long you will keep trying? What is the timescale these days for an unsolved case? At what point do you give up looking?

You will be wondering if this is a crank. I bet you get a lot of those type of letters. If I tell you that the hardest part was carving an inverted pentagram into the chest of both men that might help to clarify. The easy part was administering the cyanide injection. Most people stare at their phones while walking these days. No situational awareness whatsoever.

I am sure you know full well what an inverted pentagram represents. You will know that it represents evil, the triumph of materiality over spirituality. Also, chaos and change, the rejection of established rules and morality. But more than that, it honours the dead. It represents the great sacrifice that the victims of our rituals have made to further the cause of Satan. Rest assured, they will be rewarded in the afterlife with the eternal gratitude of our Lord.

One thing is for sure: you will know a lot more about it soon. The Antichrist is coming and this is just a foretaste. He has decreed that I should kill in advance of his arrival and has told me the manner in which I should do it. There is no choice in what or how. This is preordained. The only choice I have is who will be the victims. They were unfortunate. A case of being in the wrong place at the wrong time. But their sacrifice is nothing compared to the coming which we will soon witness. I may be the first, but you should know that I am not the only one chosen for this task. This is happening all around the world. Very soon, you will know a great deal more about us. We serve the kingdom of the devil and there is no higher power.

I thought it was important to explain why this was happening. It is vital that the world understands the imminent upheaval it faces. Only then can we begin to accept what is coming, what is inevitable. The only question was timing. Now that question has finally been answered. The time is now.

In many ways you are fortunate, DCI Pope. You are here for the start. Your name will forever be linked with these sacrifices. And you must see them as sacrifices. These are not murders. If you are able to free your mind, you will understand that.

We will never meet, but I will keep a close eye on how you are getting on. I understand that you will keep investigating, although there is no hope of resolution for you. I hope you will not think too badly of me when you finally understand.

Yours sincerely.

Pope stared at the letter. She looked up and saw that Brody was looking at her, carefully watching her expression as she read.

'Anything interesting?'

Without a word, she placed the letter on her desk. 'Don't touch it.'

He came over and silently read. 'Do you think it's genuine?' he said after reading through.

'We didn't release any information about the pentagram, or the cyanide. How else would they know that? I think we have to proceed as if it is. Can you see any other possibility?'

Brody slowly shook his head. 'No, I think you're right. What a lunatic.'

Brody reached into the pocket of his jacket, which was on the back of his chair, and pulled out a clear polythene bag. 'Here you go.'

Being careful to only touch the edges of the paper, Pope gently slid the letter into the bag, placing one sheet of the

A4 paper facing upwards and the other facing downwards, so they could be read without removing them. She took out her phone and took a photo of each sheet, then emailed them to Steven Thompson. She then texted Khan to meet her in Fletcher's office immediately.

'Come on. Let's go and see the boss.'

When they arrived at Fletcher's office and knocked, there was no answer. Pope could hear murmuring inside, suggesting he was on the phone. They waited patiently like children outside a headteacher's office. Eventually she heard the call end and after a few moments, they were summoned.

As they entered, Khan arrived, looking searchingly at Pope, then Brody.

'I've just received this,' said Pope, placing the letter on the desk in front of Fletcher. He looked at Pope for some clue as to what he was looking at, but she simply stared back at him. So he read the letter, impassively at first, but when he looked up it was clear to see his horror. For once, Superintendent Richard Fletcher was speechless. Pope picked up the letter and handed it to Khan, who read it quickly. No one spoke until she had finished. She placed it back on Fletcher's desk.

'I'm going to send it straight to Forensics, but I thought you'd want to see it as soon as possible,' said Pope.

Fletcher nodded. 'Thank you, DCI Pope. What are your initial thoughts?'

'We think it's genuine. We didn't release any details about the symbol or cyanide.'

'The writing seems quite formal. Did you notice that?' asked Fletcher.

'Yes, and it looks like it was written with a fountain pen. That's really unusual these days.'

Khan stepped forward. 'It's unusual to write at all. I wonder why it wasn't sent as an email.'

'Well, a physical letter is much more difficult to trace,' said Brody.

'Maybe,' said Khan, 'although with handwriting analysis it can be easily matched if you have a sample to compare it to.'

Brody thought about this. 'True, and it's quite straight-forward to send an email through a number of proxy servers, which make it near impossible to find the source.'

'It is, but you have to be pretty tech savvy. I wonder if this is an older person.'

'Why do you say that?' asked Fletcher.

'Writing a letter, using a fountain pen, the formal regis-ter of the language,' said Khan. 'To me it says that this isn't a young person. Middle-aged at least.'

'Or someone trying to appear that way,' said Pope. 'If you wanted to make it look like you were older, this is a good way to do it.'

'I think what is clear is that this is someone with serious mental health issues,' said Fletcher. 'All the satanist references.'

'It comes across as textbook Hollywood-style satan-ism, like you were talking about,' Pope said to Brody. 'The whole Antichrist ascending to Earth and these victims being sacrifices in deference to Satan. The author comes across as seriously disturbed, but at the same time that letter seems unnervingly calm. It could be a smokescreen to throw us off the scent, or laying the groundwork for a possible future insanity plea if they get caught.'

Fletcher looked concerned. 'So we're either dealing with a mentally disturbed serial killer who thinks they're doing the devil's bidding, or one who's extremely clever and has planned all this very carefully.'

'Both those certainly seem like possibilities,' agreed Pope.

'What's clear, in any case, is that they're planning more murders,' said Fletcher. 'And not just by this one person.'

'That's what he says.'

'What about the phrase about not thinking too badly of them?' asked Khan. 'And the fact that it isn't signed.'

'The former, I have no idea,' said Pope. 'It sounds like the killer cares about what others think of them. Murder is an odd choice if that's the case.'

'Unless you feel compelled to commit the murders but feel bad about it afterwards,' said Khan.

'The letter doesn't read as remorseful. It just lays it all out as if there's nothing they can do about it. "Preordained" was the word, if I remember rightly,' said Fletcher.

'And the fact that's it's unsigned?' repeated Khan. 'Obviously they wouldn't sign their name. But they've chosen not to adopt "the Midnight Killer".'

There was no answer to that question.

Fletcher looked at Pope, then at his watch. 'Send that to Forensics. Let's hope we can get some prints or something that might tell us something about the writer of that letter. Tell them to put a rush on it and to call me directly if they say they have other work in front of it. Then go home. All of you. There's nothing else we can do until we hear back from Forensics. Get a good night's rest and we start again in the morning.'

Pope knew this was the first solid lead they had. It had to help find this killer before there was another murder. It simply had to.

CHAPTER TWENTY-FOUR

Pope knew Fletcher was right. She was exhausted and she could see Brody and Khan were the same. Homicide investigations meant long hours. They could also take an emotional as well as physical toll on detectives. She needed her team in the best possible condition.

Pope hoped that the letter would yield some forensic detail in the morning, some clue that would set them on the path to finding this killer. Before he killed again.

The letter had unsettled Pope. It wasn't so much the fact that the author seemed unhinged. She had expected that. It was the promise that this had only just started. That it was going to happen everywhere, not just in London. And that there were going to be many more deaths which she would be powerless to prevent.

She knew she needed to try to put this aside tonight. But as she drove home through the rush-hour traffic, it was all she could think about. Occupational hazard, of course, but one she had to work on. She realized she was repeating Dr Boyd's words. Maybe he did know what he was talking about after all.

She selected a recording of John Coltrane's performance at the 1963 Newport Jazz Festival. She skipped to the second track, a long take of his version of 'My Favourite Things', one of her favourite pieces of music. If that couldn't soothe her mind, nothing could. It worked, to a point, and she could feel the tension easing out of her shoulders as she sat in thick traffic along the Old Kent Road.

When she eventually arrived home, some of the tension returned. She was still feeling bad about the aborted holiday and had again to face those she had let down. But she'd faced worse than this, she reminded herself.

Alex rose from the sofa to greet her when she arrived. They hugged and he kissed her. But something didn't feel right. He seemed tense, unsure. She was immediately on alert.

'Everything alright?' she asked.

He pulled back a little. 'Yes, fine. Why wouldn't it be?'

'No reason. Just checking. Are you sure?'

'Yes, of course. How was your day?'

Pope wanted a sounding board to help her process the letter she had received earlier, but she was aware that she needed to force a stronger separation between home and work. So she went with, 'The usual.'

Alex nodded. She knew he understood that nothing in her job was usual and that sometimes she couldn't talk about it.

'What do you fancy for dinner?' she asked, changing the subject.

'I thought we could get takeaway tonight. What do you think? Watch a movie?'

'Sounds good. What do you fancy?'

'How about Chinese? The girls would love that.'

'Yeah. Let's do that,' said Pope, relishing the normality of family life. Sometimes, after a difficult day, normal family life was all she craved.

Alex went upstairs with a copy of the menu to ascertain what Chloe and Hannah wanted to order. Pope poured herself a glass of red wine and leaned against the kitchen worktop. After almost an hour in the car, she needed to stretch her legs.

Eventually Alex returned. 'It's like UN negotiations trying to work out what to order with those two.'

Pope smiled. 'Thankfully your negotiator skills are up to the job. Did you achieve a satisfactory resolution?'

'Just about. We're ordering one of almost everything on the menu.'

While Alex put in the order, Pope laid the table between sips of wine. She actually felt herself unwinding, an unusual state of affairs.

When the food arrived half an hour later, Pope realized she hadn't eaten since breakfast and was ravenous. Alex and the girls talked about their days. Pope noticed that Hannah was quieter than usual, seemingly subdued.

'How was your day, Hannah?'

Hannah shrugged. 'OK.'

'What did you get up to?'

'I'm not hungry. I don't feel well.' She suddenly got up from the table and left, stomping heavily up the stairs.

'Hannah!' Alex called after her. 'Hannah?'

'I'd leave her,' said Chloe. 'She's had a rough day. Just needs a bit of time.'

Pope could see that Chloe had really grown up recently. In all kinds of different ways, she was impressed with Chloe's attitude and maturity.

'What happened?' asked Alex.

Chloe looked reticent. 'She just got a bit of hassle from her friends. It's fine.'

'Tell me what happened.' Alex was more insistent now.

Chloe sighed, then looked at Pope. She turned back to Alex.

'Some of her friends have been giving her a hard time. She'd been talking about going to New York for weeks to them, telling them how she was going to post content on social media. Now she isn't going, they don't believe that she ever was. They're calling her a liar.'

Pope felt the pain physically. She was instantly taken back to her own school days and how cruel teenage girls could be to each other. With age and time, you saw it for what it was. Power, control. But at the time, it really hurt.

'I'm so sorry,' said Pope. 'I'll talk to her.'

'Don't worry,' said Chloe. 'We've had that conversation. She knows the situation. I'll go up and see her after dinner. She'll be fine.'

They ate the rest of dinner in virtual silence. Pope's state of feeling unwound had abruptly come to a halt. After they had cleared up, Chloe sat down opposite Pope and Alex in the living room.

'I saw your press conference,' she said. 'The Midnight Killer. I can see why they suddenly wanted you back. It sounds terrible.'

'Yeah, it's going to be a tough one, I think.'

'In what way?'

'Chloe,' said Alex, 'Bec won't want to talk about this at home.'

Chloe seemed genuinely interested in Pope's work and she didn't want to minimize that. It was Alex who didn't want Chloe to hear all about it. And she knew only too well that her work had encroached on their family life in a real sense. Pope had to tread the line between satisfying Chloe's curiosity and placating Alex.

'We haven't got any real suspects yet and everything we chase seems to lead to a dead end. But we'll get there. These cases take time.'

'But isn't there the chance that he'll kill again? I mean, there've been two victims already, haven't there?'

'That's always a possibility. But hopefully we'll find him before that. We have a good team on it.' She chose not to mention the letter, which was the most important aspect of their investigation so far.

Pope noticed that Alex was looking a little ill at ease. She assumed that it was talk of the case. She was just about to change the subject, when Alex abruptly stood up.

'Right.' He walked somewhat stiffly to the door and called Hannah to come down.

'Is everything OK, Dad?' asked Chloe.

'Fine.'

'So why do you need Hannah?'

Alex didn't answer. Pope suddenly had a sinking feeling. With all that she'd put this family through over the past couple of years, was Alex about to deliver bad news? She felt her heart thumping. She studied his face carefully, but he avoided eye contact, instead picking up his glass of wine for what Pope could only assume was a fortifying drink. She braced herself for what was about to come.

Hannah entered the room and sulkily sat down next to her sister. 'What?'

Alex looked at Chloe and Hannah, then transferred his gaze to Pope. He walked over towards her. Pope froze. She knew exactly what was coming. Alex was going to end it with her. But then she realized that he wouldn't want an audience for that. A flood of thoughts entered her head and she couldn't untangle them in time.

And then Alex pulled a small black box out of his pocket and, as Pope looked on, stunned, bent down on one knee. He opened the box to reveal a silver ring set with a single diamond. Then she realized.

'Bec. We've had an interesting, eventful couple of years. But I love you. And I want us to be together. Will you marry me?'

He looked up at her, searching for a reaction.

Pope was genuinely flummoxed. This was completely outside her frame of reference. The adrenaline coursed through her. She looked at the girls, sitting on the sofa. Chloe was smiling. She couldn't read Hannah's expression. She looked back at Alex, realizing that she hadn't said anything and he was starting to look worried.

'OK. I mean, yes. Of course!'

He grinned, stood up and took her hand. He carefully placed the ring on her finger, then kissed her. She looked down at her finger. The ring was beautiful and fit perfectly.

'The diamond is from my grandmother's engagement ring. I had it reset in a new ring. Do you like it?'

'It's beautiful, Alex. Thank you so much. Just beautiful.'

Chloe and Hannah stood up and hugged them both in turn. Pope scanned their faces carefully. Their mother had died some years earlier and this was a big moment for them too. Their father was planning to remarry. But Hannah looked happier now and both girls seemed excited. Perhaps Hannah had realized that she had a good chance of being a bridesmaid, with all the fun that entailed.

Alex went to the fridge and picked out a bottle of champagne which he had hidden at the back of the salad drawer. He found four champagne flutes and poured them all a glass. Hannah looked shocked.

'It's a serious celebration,' said Alex. 'One glass won't hurt.'

Hannah looked really pleased. For the next hour they all talked about wedding plans, bridesmaids' outfits, Alex getting a new suit.

Pope was happy. She certainly hadn't expected this end to the day. But there was a nagging feeling in the back of her head. Why had her first thought been that Alex was going to end the relationship? Why jump to that? Was that about her personality, her experience with relationships, or something more specific about her situation with Alex?

Dr Boyd was inside her head. Enough with the cod psychoanalysis. Time to enjoy herself. She did just that and for a while forgot about the Midnight Killer.

* * *

When the girls had gone upstairs, Pope and Alex finished the bottle of champagne.

Pope looked at her glass. 'When was the last time we had this?'

'I know. But an occasion like this deserves splashing out. Are you sure you're up for this? Now?' Alex asked out of the blue.

'Yes, of course. Why do you ask?'

'Well, you seemed a bit stunned when I asked you . . .'

She put her hand on his arm. 'No. I mean, yes. I was shocked. But in a good way. It's just that you know I'm in the middle of a huge case, so I need to focus on that for the moment. But after that's finished, we can start thinking about planning. If that's OK?'

'Yes, of course. I already have some ideas!'

Pope smiled. 'I'll look forward to hearing all about them.'

Alex paused. Then, 'I wanted to do this a different way.'

'What do you mean?'

'I had planned to propose in New York. At the top of the Empire State Building.' He looked a bit embarrassed. 'Bit of a cliché.'

Suddenly it all fell into place. Pope now understood why Alex hadn't gone to New York without her.

She put her arms round him. 'Not a cliché at all. That would have been amazing. Sorry I messed it up.'

'It's OK. After a Chinese takeaway is far more memorable. One for the grandkids.'

They both laughed and, helped along by the champagne, Pope felt genuinely relaxed.

* * *

In bed, after they had made love and Alex had fallen asleep, Pope basked in a feeling she rarely, if ever, felt. Contentment. She wondered if this was the corner she had wanted to turn for a very, very long time.

CHAPTER TWENTY-FIVE

Saturday morning

Pope wanted to go into work later and have breakfast with Alex. But as soon as she woke, she thought of the letter she had received, of the two victims, and the bizarre nature of their deaths. A leisurely morning wasn't an option.

She woke Alex to say goodbye, however, and they spent a moment enjoying the aftermath of his proposal before she left.

It was early and the trip to work wasn't too slow. When she arrived, Thompson was waiting in her office.

'Morning. You're in early,' she said as she took off her jacket.

'I think we may have something.'

'From Forensics? Have they processed the letter already?'

'No, this is something else.'

Pope was immediately on alert. That moment when you knew something was coming, but not whether it was going to be significant. Thompson's serious expression hinted at the latter, but she wouldn't get her hopes up.

She nodded, indicating him to continue.

'I've been looking into our two victims, but as you know we haven't yet managed to find anything useful. So I decided to do a deep dive into their partners. Now, Eric Acevedo is completely clean. I'd looked at his financials earlier, as you wanted confirmation of how they could afford to live in a swanky flat in Bloomsbury.'

'And it was Ward's money, right? He earned a lot more than Acevedo.'

'That's right. But I hadn't been looking at Amy Weaver's financial record, because there didn't seem to be any need to. Tom Murray's were all clear and there were no obvious financial connections between them, separate flats and so on.'

'But you've looked into them now?'

'Yes. I was at a bit of a dead end, so I had a look through Amy Weaver's accounts. Most of it was as expected. But there were a number of online purchases from a store in America called Pagan Pages. Terrible name. But I looked them up online. Well, have a look for yourself.'

He handed his tablet to Pope. It was open to the front page of what looked like an occult shop. There were a number of menu headings to click through. These included 'Tarot', 'Ouija Boards', 'Witches and Wizards'. Then, a menu entitled 'Dark Magic'. She wondered if this was a euphemism. She clicked on the link and began to scroll through the sub-menus. Books about the Salem witch trials, the practice of the occult, 'real' witchcraft, and then, satanism. She looked up at Thompson.

'Satanism? What kinds of books are there here?' she asked, even as she was clicking on the link.

'Check it out.'

There were hundreds of books listed. They included historical accounts of satanism and devil worship, key figures in the history of the movement, including writings by Anton LaVey and Joseph Laycock, as well as fictional texts such as *Rosemary's Baby*. There were also a number of broader philosophical studies, as well as how-to manuals and explainers.

Pope looked up from the screen. 'Are you saying that Amy Weaver bought books from here? Online?'

'Yup. She made two online purchases. One around three months ago for forty-eight dollars, and a second three weeks later for seventy-four dollars. It seems she liked what she read in the first ones and wanted to read more.'

'Do we know what she bought?'

'No. We can try to call the bookstore a bit later on. But it's based just outside Washington, DC, so they're on Eastern Time.' He looked at his watch and did a quick mental calculation. 'It's around 3.30 a.m. there now, so we won't be able to talk to them for a few hours.'

'That's if we can actually talk to a real human and if they're prepared to tell us without a warrant.'

Pope looked back at the screen and scrolled through a few more titles while she thought.

Just then Brody arrived, looking surprised to see Pope and Thompson already deep in conversation.

'Morning,' he said. 'Everything OK?'

'Thompson's been looking into Amy Weaver,' said Pope.

'Tom Murray's fiancée?'

'It turns out she's been buying online from an occult store just outside Washington, DC. Two separate purchases, three weeks apart.' She handed Thompson's tablet to Brody. He started to scroll down.

After a moment he looked at Thompson, then at Pope. 'You're kidding me! Amy Weaver's been buying books about the occult?'

'It would seem so,' said Pope. 'Pretty big coincidence.'

He continued looking through the texts available. 'When did she make the purchases?'

'Three months ago, the first one,' said Thompson. 'Then another one soon after.'

'This is crazy.' Brody looked at Pope. 'We're not saying Amy Weaver has committed these murders?'

'We're not saying anything yet apart from it's a coincidence.'

'And you haven't found any links between Amy Weaver or Tom Murray and Paul Ward?' asked Brody.

'Nothing so far.'

'So if she's involved, where does Paul Ward fit in?'

'Good question,' said Pope. 'Maybe the first victim was random after all.'

'But if she is involved, then it doesn't make sense. Tom Murray clearly isn't a random choice, but what about Paul Ward?'

Pope sat down at her desk. She leaned back in her chair and stared up at the ceiling. 'You're right. It just doesn't make any sense.'

'What doesn't make any sense?' Zahra Khan walked in.

Steven Thompson brought her up to speed on the developments. She too scrolled through the Pagan Pages website.

'That's some pretty damning circumstantial evidence,' she said. 'Are we taking her in for questioning?'

Pope thought for a moment. 'I'm going to see Fletcher to get a warrant to search her flat. We only had a brief look last time. In the meantime we'll go and sit outside, see what she's up to. Thompson, keep digging into Amy Weaver. I don't believe she could be moved to kill two men, including her boyfriend, within three months of reading about this stuff. She must have been interested in the whole occult thing before she bought books from that site. Find some evidence.'

* * *

Brody drove the three of them to Amy Weaver's flat in Forest Hill. They parked some way down the road so that they couldn't easily be seen out of the window, but still had an unobstructed view of the front door. Pope had called Weaver's workplace en route to check if she was there. Nobody answered and she remembered that it was Saturday morning. She had already sent a squad car over to check and wait outside her work in case she showed up.

'What are you thinking?' Khan asked Pope. 'We don't even know if she's in there.'

'We don't, that's true. But she's not at work, so this is our only option. And we need to wait for the search warrant, so this is as good a place as any.'

'You don't think we should knock to see if she's in?' asked Khan.

'If we do that and she is there, we can't go into her flat for a proper search without her agreement and she may just take the time to get rid of any evidence. The warrant won't be long. Fletcher's on it.'

'We're assuming she bought the books from the States because she thought it would be more difficult to trace?' asked Brody.

Pope nodded. 'I think so. The alternative is that she couldn't get the books she wanted from the UK, but there are quite a few places here that sell that kind of thing, so I can't imagine that's the case. Unless what she was looking for was extremely niche. That's a possibility. Maybe she's been into it for a much longer time and we just haven't found any evidence of it yet.'

'Do we really think Amy Weaver is capable of committing these murders?' asked Khan. The tone of her voice suggested that maybe she didn't.

'Because she's a woman?' asked Pope.

'No, because she didn't seem like she was capable of much when we saw her. Let alone murder and disfigurement.'

Pope thought back to how frail Weaver had seemed when they interviewed her several days ago. She flashed to herself sitting in the back of an ambulance after Adam Miller had just died.

'Bear in mind she'd just found out that her fiancé had been brutally murdered. She wasn't at her best.'

'Or she was putting it all on,' said Brody.

'Either way, I'm not sure we saw the best version of Amy Weaver, so it would be rash to make any judgements based on that encounter.'

Just then Pope's phone buzzed and she saw a text from Fletcher. He'd sent the warrant. She checked her email and read through the warrant carefully. She had to make sure everything was in order so that if they found anything, it would be a legitimate discovery if and when it ended up in court.

'OK, let's see if Amy Weaver's home,' she said, getting out of the car.

As they walked the short distance to Weaver's flat, Pope's adrenaline was spiking. She looked over at Khan, who appeared remarkably calm. She suspected that wasn't the case under the surface.

They walked up the wide steps to the communal front door Pope remembered from their previous visit.

'Are we ready?'

Brody and Khan both nodded and Pope pressed the buzzer. They waited. No answer. Pope pressed again, holding it for longer this time.

'Damn. We should have brought a locksmith. I just didn't think of it.' Pope cursed herself for making such an elementary mistake. Brody leaned down and looked closely at the front door.

'I can get in. If you want me to?'

'Are you sure?' asked Pope. She looked around. No passers-by.

'Yeah, these communal front doors often just use a latch lock. Easy.'

'OK, do it.'

Brody took out a small set of tools which Pope had never seen before. He worked the lock and was in within thirty seconds.

'Impressive,' said Pope. 'From your former life as a cat burglar?'

They walked up to the second floor and Pope once again knocked. They waited, and again, nothing.

Brody inspected the lock. 'Same one here. No deadbolt, thankfully. Shall we?'

'Yes,' said Pope.

This one took a little longer, but then they were in. Brody opened the door carefully. 'Metropolitan Police,' he called out. 'Anyone home?'

Silence.

'Metropolitan Police. We have a search warrant. Make yourself known.'

The flat was silent. They checked each room in the flat. Amy Weaver wasn't home.

Pope pulled a pair of latex gloves out of her pocket and proceeded to put them on. Khan and Brody did the same.

'OK, let's split up. Take a room each. Go over everything. We need to find the books she bought online. We need something to connect her to this.'

Khan took the second bedroom, Brody the living room, Pope Weaver's bedroom.

Pope stood still and looked around, taking in the room. She hadn't paid too much attention last time she was here. Weaver wasn't a suspect then. She was a grieving partner of the victim in a violent homicide. The double bed was neatly made, two cushions placed between the two sets of pillows. The curtains were floral, a light-blue colour. They matched the bedclothes. There were bedside tables, one of which had a radio alarm, a glasses case and a drinks mat. There was also a phone charger, plugged into a socket beneath.

She opened the wardrobe. Exactly what you'd expect. Business wear and leisure wear. Five or six pairs of sneakers and four pairs of heels on a shoe rack beneath the clothes hangers.

Pope began to wonder if they'd got the wrong person. It was so normal. How could that be, given the nature of this crime? Surely there would be something obvious. Something to suggest the kind of person Amy Weaver must be to commit these crimes. She continued searching, looking through Weaver's chest of drawers.

'I've got something.' Khan's voice from the spare bedroom. Pope and Brody both joined her.

'I think I've found the books.' Khan pointed to an open wooden box sitting under the desk. Pope saw the computer and the wedding planner file she had leafed through last time she was here. The box was highly varnished, with a metal handle on each side and filled with variety of things. There were some paintbrushes and large pieces of fabric, and underneath those, Pope saw a stack of books. The top few were art books. How-to manuals and large, glossy, illustrated biographies of well-known artists such as Picasso and Van Gogh. But underneath those were the books they were looking for. Brody took some photographs on his work phone before Khan lifted them out and carefully placed them on the desk in front of the computer.

Pope looked at the first. It was a thick book on the history of satanism. The next two were more philosophical texts, one by Anton LaVey and one by Aleister Crowley. The fourth seemed to be exploring the subject from a psychological perspective, subtitled *How Good People Turn Evil*. But the final book was the one which caught Pope's eye. It was a small volume entitled *Symbology of the Occult*. She picked it up and leafed through. The book was laid out with full-page images on the right-hand side and explanatory text on the left. She stopped at one called the 'Sigil of Baphomet'. It was described as the official emblem of the Church of Satan — an inverted pentagram drawn in white on a black background. In the middle of the pentagram was a sinister-looking goat's head. Pope showed it to Brody and Khan. But the next page was the one they were looking for.

Titled simply 'Inverted Pentagram', the image was an interleaved five-pointed star, with two points facing upward. It was much plainer than the previous image. The notes explained that it was the most widespread symbol of satanism in the world.

'Got her,' said Pope. 'This is where she found it.'

They gathered round the book and studied the image. The wounds had been crudely executed, but it was clear enough where Weaver had got her inspiration.

Brody looked closely. 'If she only bought these books within the last three months or so, how does that fit with committing two murders? There must be evidence of an interest developing before this, surely?'

'Thompson's on that,' said Pope. 'There'll be some online footprint of interest before she bought those books. There has to be.'

'Unless it's a smokescreen,' said Khan.

'For what?' asked Brody.

'It doesn't make sense that she would kill Paul Ward first, then Tom Murray. I would understand her fiancé first, then a random stranger if she got the taste for it. But it makes no sense to search out a complete stranger, then come back to someone she knows. Someone she's planning to marry. So maybe the whole devil-worship angle is to hide her real motivation?'

'Motivation for what?' asked Pope. 'What's she trying to cover up? And why go to such elaborate lengths? I mean, the carving on the bodies is grotesque. There are so many easier ways to cover up a motive than that.'

'Yes, that's true,' conceded Khan.

'None of this makes much sense at the moment. We need to talk to Amy Weaver. She's the only one who'll be able to clear all this up. Brody, can you give Fletcher a call and get an APB out on her? If she's not at work and not here, there's a chance she's on the run. Include all ports, airports, stations. Can you also get SOCO out here as soon as possible?'

Brody went into the living room to make the call.

'I was sure this was a male perp,' said Pope.

'Me too,' said Khan. 'But it does explain the cyanide injection. Easier to subdue a bigger man.'

'It's all been well thought out. The planning is meticulous.' Pope glanced at the comprehensive wedding binder on the desk above the wooden box which had contained the incriminating books. 'Amy Weaver is a planner, if her upcoming wedding was anything to go by.'

'Planning to kill the groom is pretty unusual,' said Khan.

'I wonder what he did to deserve that? We need to talk to his friends and colleagues again to see if there was any disharmony between the two of them. Anything that was missed first time round.'

Brody joined them in the bedroom.

'OK?' asked Pope.

'Yeah. Fletcher pointed out that it was all circumstantial at the moment, but I explained that we really needed to sit

192

down with Amy Weaver if we were going to understand all this. He was fine with it. The APB's going out immediately.'

'Good. He's right about the evidence, but it's far too much of a coincidence. If nothing else, she needs to explain it.'

'Where's everything else?' asked Khan.

'What are you thinking?' asked Pope.

'Weaver must have used something sharp to inflict the wounds on the victims. And she would need cyanide, syringes. Where is all that?'

'Good question. Let's continue looking for that while we wait for SOCO. It has to be somewhere here.'

They continued the search of the flat. Pope started in the bathroom. If she were to find syringes, that would be the most likely place. But there was nothing. There was only a small bathroom cabinet and they weren't there.

She then moved to the kitchen, where she thought she might find a knife or sharp implement which could have caused the wounds on the victims. Brody was already searching in there. There was the typical knife block, with one empty space where the largest knife would sit. Pope withdrew each knife in turn, inspecting them carefully. But it was impossible to tell if any had been used in the crime. Maybe Forensics would be able to find something. Eventually Khan joined them.

'Anything?' asked Pope.

They both shook their heads.

'It has to be somewhere,' said Brody.

'Unless she's taken everything with her,' said Pope. 'Either because she knows we're on to her, or because she wants to use them again. Though hopefully neither of those things is true.'

'How could she know we're on to her?' asked Khan.

Pope shook her head. 'I don't know. Maybe she just assumed we'd get there eventually and she's chosen to run.'

'She might have another base,' said Brody. 'Where she keeps the paraphernalia.'

'That's possible. Hopefully Thompson will find it if so.'

There was a ring on the buzzer and Pope realized it was likely to be the forensic specialists. She found the intercom phone and buzzed them up. Once she had handed over the scene to them, they left. Pope knew that if there was something to find, it would now have to be Forensics who found it.

Pope had that familiar feeling in her gut. She knew that they had their killer. Now all she needed to do was find her before she killed again.

CHAPTER TWENTY-SIX

Fletcher was waiting for them in the office when they got back from Amy Weaver's flat. He started speaking the moment she was through the door.

'The APB is out and an all ports as well. She won't be able to leave the country and we've got every Met officer on the lookout for her. Tell me how sure you are.'

Pope hadn't had time to take off her jacket.

'We found the books Amy Weaver ordered from the online bookshop in the States. There were a number of different titles but the key one, we think, was a book about occult symbols. One of those was an inverted pentagram. Now, if you wanted a template for the kind of wound she inflicted, that picture would give you exactly what you needed. So that's pretty positive evidence, although I'm sure a brief would describe it as circumstantial.'

'Which it is,' said Fletcher, his frustration clear.

'That's why we need to talk to her. We haven't been able to find anything else yet . . .'

'Such as?' interrupted Fletcher.

'Such as the syringes she may have used, or the implement she used to inflict the wounds on the victims' bodies. But hopefully Forensics might find something. They're there now.'

'It's not much, is it?'

'I would say it's enough to warrant taking her in. I mean, as coincidences go it's pretty damning.'

'What do you think?' he asked Brody.

Fletcher had done this before. Let Pope give her opinion, then asked Brody straight afterwards as if they hadn't discussed it. Pope knew that in principle getting another opinion was a good idea, but it always made her feel as if he was second-guessing her experience and, it had to be said, asking for a male perspective. Brody glanced over at Pope.

'I agree,' said Brody. 'Too much of a coincidence. If I were to call it, I'd say it was definitely Amy Weaver. If not, she'd have to have a remarkable explanation.'

Steven Thompson walked into the office as Brody was speaking.

'Thompson's been looking into Amy Weaver,' she explained to Fletcher. 'Anything?'

He went to sit down at the meeting table and they all instinctively joined him.

'Right. Amy Weaver. Aged twenty-eight. Born here in London, always lived in the city. Currently living in Forest Hill. She's been at the same address for seven years. It seems she started renting, but now pays a mortgage, so must have made an arrangement to buy it off her landlord. No obvious issues, as we said before, except running a red light a couple of years ago. She's worked in social media and marketing for a place called Universe Language, based in Greenwich, for almost five years. Before that, after leaving school at eighteen after her A Levels, it looks like she worked mainly in hospitality, pubs and clubs, bar work, some administration.'

'And her relationship with Tom Murray?' asked Fletcher.

'They've been together for around three years,' said Pope. 'They were due to get married next year. Venues booked, flights for the honeymoon all arranged. She has a planning folder at home with lots of notes and plans for the wedding.'

'That doesn't make much sense,' said Fletcher. 'To murder your fiancé just before the wedding.'

Pope didn't have an answer for that. Something that had also been nagging at her.

'What about the cyanide?' asked Fletcher. 'Where would she get that?'

'It's straightforward to find it on the dark web, I'm afraid,' said Thompson.

'Does she travel much?' asked Fletcher. 'Is she likely to abscond abroad?'

Thompson checked his notes. 'Social media has her going on an annual holiday. She's got pictures from New York, the Canary Islands and Corfu with Murray. She also seems to have been on a couple of work trips to recruitment events for language learners. One in Basel in Switzerland and one in Turkey. She's not a big traveller, though. All fairly routine touristy stuff.'

'OK, any indications on where she might be going?' asked Fletcher.

'Not that I could find. I can't see any regular visits in the UK or abroad, nowhere she highlights as being a frequent place to visit.'

'What about family?' asked Pope.

'Her parents died some years ago and she's an only child. There's nobody else I can find. Aunts or uncles. Certainly no one she spends time with recently. According to her posts, anyway.'

'So we're going to have to hope that the APB gets us something,' said Fletcher. 'What's your next move, DCI Pope?'

Just then, Pope's phone rang on her desk.

'Excuse me a moment.' She got up and checked who was calling. Number withheld. She answered.

'DCI Pope, Charing Cross.'

'DCI Pope. Nice to talk to you again.'

Pope recognized Weaver's voice immediately. She looked over at her team and put the phone on speaker.

'Is that Amy?'

Fletcher took a moment to register, then immediately stood up and took a step towards her. The others remained seated.

'Good to see your detection skills are still working fine.'

'Amy Weaver?' Pope clarified for everyone in the room.

'Are you currently looking for any other Amys who sound like me?'

'No, Amy, we're not. I just wanted to be certain.'

'Yes, it's me.'

'Where are you?' asked Pope.

Weaver's laugh was exaggerated. 'It wouldn't be much of a cat and mouse if I told you where I was, would it? Isn't the idea that you're supposed to find me?'

'Look, Amy, we really need to talk to you. To clear up a few things. Can you come into Charing Cross Police Station?'

'Are you going to send a car for me?'

'I can do. If that's what you want.'

'Of course it's not what I fucking want! Do you think I'm an idiot?'

'No, I don't think you're an idiot. But I do want to talk to you.'

'Is that why you broke into my home this morning? To talk to me?'

Pope glanced at Brody. How did Weaver know that?

'We had a warrant to search your flat, Amy.'

'Based on what?'

'We have reason to believe that you might have been involved in the murders of Paul Ward and your fiancé, Tom Murray.'

'I know who my fiancé is. But thanks for clarifying.'

'Are you involved?'

There was a pause on the other end of the line. Weaver was trying to work out what they knew.

'You know I'm involved. That's why you broke in this morning.'

Everybody else in the room let out a breath in unison. They now knew the identity of the Midnight Killer.

'Why did you do it, Amy? Why Tom?'

'This isn't going to be some big confession, DCI Pope. You want to know, you've got to find me first.'

'We're working on it,' said Pope.

'I'm sure you are. APB, no doubt.'

Pope was silent on the line.

'A question for you, DCI Pope. Can I call you Bec, as you're calling me Amy to try to form a connection?'

Pope shook her head slowly. 'Yes, you can call me Bec if you want to.'

'OK, *Bec*.' Weaver placed a firm emphasis on Pope's name. 'My question is, how would you feel if someone broke into your home *and fucking ransacked everything in it?*'

Weaver had shouted the last part and Pope instinctively moved the phone away from her.

'Your flat wasn't ransacked—'

'Yes, it was. You trashed everything.' Weaver had stopped shouting, but her voice had changed. It had a steely edge that worried Pope.

'How do you know that?' asked Pope. Forensics were still at the property, so she clearly hadn't returned.

Weaver ignored the question.

'OK, I'll ask you something else. Why did you carve an inverted pentagram on the chests of your victims?'

Weaver paused again. 'I'm assuming you know what that symbol represents?'

'As far as we know it is a symbol of evil, of satanism, of rebellion. Depends what you read.'

'Bravo, Bec. You have been doing your homework. I'm sure Superintendent Fletcher will be very pleased with his good little DCI Pope.'

Fletcher had been pacing back and forth, but now stopped at the mention of his name and stared at Pope.

'It sounds like you've got me on speaker, so I presume you're not alone. How are DI Brody and DS Khan? All well with them?'

They all exchanged glances.

'You haven't answered my question.'

'About the pentagram? You seem to have worked that out all for yourself. I don't think you need me to tell you anything.'

Pope realized that Weaver had the upper hand. They didn't know where she was or what she was planning. Pope decided that she had to change the dynamic. She would try to catch the woman off guard and attempt to disrupt her calm.

'You got the idea from the book of satanic symbols we found in that wooden chest under your desk, right? Just under the wedding planning folder.'

'Are you fucking kidding me? You're using the fact that you rifled through all my personal possessions to try to irritate me. Well done. It worked. Now I'm angry.'

Pope instantly regretted her strategy. Why had she thought that angering Weaver was the right play? From Fletcher's expression, Pope knew that he was thinking the same.

'You know what, Bec? I know you. I know where you are. I know your team and where they are. Don't worry about finding me. You won't need to. I'll find you. And every member of your team. I want you to feel pain like I have. When you're least expecting it. You know what I'm capable of.'

Pope tried to ignore the threat. She avoided eye contact with anyone else in the room. She needed to focus on moving the conversation onto something productive.

'What pain have you felt, Amy?'

'Was the cheap police psychology course really worth the money? Am I supposed to see you as suitably empathetic and tell you all my secrets? You'll need to do better than that.'

'Amy, I'm just trying to—'

'That's enough. Just be clear, I'm coming for you. See you soon, DCI Pope.'

Weaver ended the call. Pope stood frozen to the spot, holding her phone out in front of her. They had identified their killer for certain.

CHAPTER TWENTY-SEVEN

Pope placed her phone on the desk and sat down. She looked at the shocked expressions around the room.

'Well, I think we can now confirm the identity of our killer,' she said. 'No doubt it's Amy Weaver.'

'That's good,' said Fletcher. 'We can get her identity out to the media and hopefully that will help to find her. I know what you were trying to do there, but it made her more angry.'

'It sounded like it. But we can't worry about suspects getting angry with us. It happens all the time. I was trying to ruffle her feathers.'

'I think you succeeded. What did you make of her?'

Pope thought about this for a moment. 'Either she's completely unhinged or she's playing a very clever game. I can't work out which.'

'I think anyone who commits that type of murder is most certainly unhinged,' said Fletcher.

'She's right,' said Brody. 'There's a strong possibility that she's actually not into satanism at all. She could be using it as a smokescreen for murdering her fiancé. For whatever reason.'

'And the first victim?' asked Fletcher.

'Part of the smokescreen,' said Brody. 'She' hoped to throw us off the scent, so we'd assume that the victims were random. One was, the other wasn't, but she wanted it to appear that they both were, making Weaver less of a suspect.'

'That would require an extraordinary mind,' said Fletcher. 'To be able to carry out this type of thing, killing someone at random, carving symbols on their chests, just to cover your tracks.'

Pope nodded. 'Well, you heard her. She had the bravado to call me and then threatened to come after us all. I'd say that's extraordinary.'

'Do you think she was serious about coming after us?' asked Khan.

Pope could see that the newest member of her team was rattled. 'Difficult to say. We all get this from time to time, particularly in Homicide. And it always seems worse because we know what these people are capable of. But it rarely comes to anything. Amy Weaver is just trying to scare us, to get into our heads. The important thing is to see it for what it is and try to ignore it as far as possible.'

'And we'll find her soon enough,' said Brody. 'Now we can release her identity, it'll be very difficult for her to be out in the open. She'll most likely be spotted.'

'In the meantime, we follow all the usual safety protocols when a threat is issued,' said Fletcher. 'No solo work, always travel in pairs, and if you're out and about, keep regular radio contact to inform us of your location and check in every hour. We'll alert reception to the threat and make sure they're also on the lookout.'

Khan looked dubious. 'She was pretty clear that she's coming for us.'

'But remember her MO is to creep up on her victims and catch them unaware,' said Pope. 'She won't be able to get near us if we keep our eyes open. And as Brody says, the public will be on the lookout as well, so the chances of her getting anywhere near one of us unnoticed is virtually zero.'

'We'll also update the APB to include that she's possibly armed and dangerous. I'll get the press office to issue a photo of Weaver. Sergeant Thompson, can you get me a good recent photo?'

'Yes, I'll do that now.'

'Can you also put a car on Weaver's flat?' said Pope. 'I doubt she'll go back there, but you never know.'

Fletcher nodded and left to make the calls.

'Thompson. Anything you'd suggest?'

'I'll get on the CCTV near Weaver's flat and see if there's any sign of her leaving. That way we might be able to pick up her trail and see how far we can get.'

'Are there cameras on her road?'

'I don't know. I'll have a look. I've put in a request for her phone records but I'll chase them and see if the new information we have can speed things up.'

Pope turned to Khan. 'She'll show up somewhere. She won't be able to hide. Every officer on the street will have her photo within the hour. We'll get her.'

'I know. So, what can we do?'

Pope sensed that her colleague had recovered her composure. She was about to answer when her phone rang. For a split second she thought it would be Amy Weaver again, and from her colleague's faces she could see that they thought the same. But a glance at her screen and she relaxed a little.

'Forensics.' The relief on their faces was evident. She answered.

It was a brief conversation.

'Forensics have found a pack of syringes and the remains of the cyanide.'

'How did we miss that?' asked Brody.

'It was hidden behind the wooden panel on the bath. It was removable and everything was in a metal box in there. They've also found small traces of blood on the knife block around the empty space. They'll need to get it back to the lab to check if it's human or animal.'

'That's the empty space where the largest knife should have been?' asked Brody.

'Yes. My guess is she would have disposed of it though. The syringes and cyanide would have been harder to replace, but a knife you can get easily. She's planned carefully, so disposing of the evidence could easily have been part of the play.'

'I'll get on the CCTV. I'll let you know as soon as I have anything.' Thompson gathered up his tablet and left the office.

Khan left to go to the bathroom. Pope and Brody were alone.

'She seems a bit worried,' said Brody.

'I'm not surprised. These kinds of things can be scary if you're not used to them. Even if you are. But she seemed to calm down a little. It's a lot to deal with for your first case with a new team.'

'It is. Do you think she'll be OK?'

'She'll be fine. We'll make sure she is.'

Brody looked at Pope for a few seconds. 'And how about you? How are you doing?'

Pope leaned back in her chair and rubbed the back of her neck. 'I'm fine. But I have to admit that Weaver's threats have me thinking of Miller.'

'Me too. I had a feeling you'd be thinking the same.'

'It happens from time to time. I'm used to empty threats, people just letting off steam. But what happened to Miller made me realize that it's not always the case. Sometimes the danger is real.'

'I know. But what you said to Khan is true. Everyone's on the lookout for Weaver and she won't be able to so much as show her face without someone recognizing her. These public appeals can be very effective, especially in the era of social media. And everyone has a camera now.'

'One of the unsung benefits of smartphones?'

'I guess so. From our perspective. Not so much from Amy Weaver's,' said Brody with a smile.

Pope considered that one of the great elements of their professional relationship was the ability to see a degree of humour — gallows or otherwise — in the midst of all the chaos and violence they encountered in this job.

'But she's clearly insane. And highly dangerous. We need to be very careful. And make sure that Khan's aware of it too.'

'I think she's pretty aware,' said Brody.

'Yeah, I guess so.' Pope paused and stared at Brody. 'But I'll talk to her again.' She felt her eyes welling up and wiped them with the sleeve of her shirt. She didn't want Khan to see her like this. 'I can't go through what we went through last year again, James. I just can't.'

She rarely used his first name.

'We won't have to. That was a totally different situation. We're all completely aware of the threat this time and ready for it.'

Khan walked back in the room and seemed to sense the atmosphere.

'Everything OK? What's happened?'

'Everything's fine,' said Brody. 'We were just going over the security protocols again. Are you clear on what Fletcher was saying?'

'Travel in pairs, keep on radio. And regular check-ins. Yes, got it.'

'I'm fairly certain the next time we see Amy Weaver, she'll be in handcuffs in a cell,' said Brody. 'But it pays to be careful at times like these.'

Brody went back to his desk and turned to something on his computer.

'Can I ask you something?' Khan was looking at Pope.

'Of course.'

'Why Homicide? I mean, why did you choose this over everything else in the force?'

Pope answered without missing a beat. She'd thought a lot about this in the last three months. 'Because it's the most important thing there is. There's nothing more important than getting justice for those who are unable to get it for themselves. And for the loved ones left behind.'

'And preventing people like Amy Weaver killing again,' added Khan.

'Absolutely. And we will stop her.'

'I know. Where would you go if you were her?' asked Khan.

'It depends. My first instinct would be to get out of London. Getting out of the country would be more difficult. It would involve a new passport, and you need to know what you're doing for that and have the connections. But Weaver was born in London and has lived here all her life. Much of her network will be here and it may be that she feels more secure, more confident in the places she knows.'

'If she's out for some kind of twisted revenge, she'll want to be close by, waiting for an opportunity.'

'Yeah, but as Brody said, every officer on the street has her picture and she'll be aware of that. It'll be difficult for her to move around the city. Tubes, trains, buses will all be perfect places for her to be spotted, so I imagine she'll want to avoid any form of public transport. It makes it really difficult for her.'

'She's been one step ahead of us at every turn,' said Khan.

'That's always the way. Until it isn't,' said Pope. 'If it's a known offender, we can sometimes see what they're planning and apprehend them before they commit the crime. But if it's a first-time offender, or one who hasn't been previously caught, there's no way to know and we're playing catch-up until we get a break. Sometimes we're proactive, but much of the time we're reactive. Especially in Homicide.'

'Have you let Acheron go yet?'

'Oh, I'd forgotten about him with all the excitement. No, I'll sort Acheron out in a bit.'

'He won't be very happy with us,' said Khan.

'He shouldn't have withheld potential evidence and then done a runner. Then we wouldn't have brought him here in the first place.'

Khan nodded, conceding the point.

Pope heard Brody's phone ringing and saw him pick up. Then she saw his expression and was instantly on alert.

'Thanks, Dave. Appreciate it.'

'What is it?' asked Pope.

'That was a mate of mine from uniform. They think they may have sighted Amy Weaver.'

'Jesus! Where?'

'Believe it or not, just round the corner. The Piazza.' The large central space in the middle of Covent Garden was just a few minutes' walk from the station.

'Let's go,' said Pope, probably a lot louder than she meant to.

Pope, Brody and Khan sprinted out of the office, down the stairs and out onto the street. They turned left, then right, jogging along Chandos Place and onto Henrietta Street. Then they were in the middle of the Piazza.

It was absolutely packed with early autumn tourists. There were large crowds circling one of the street performers who had their slot to entertain and hopefully make some money. It made navigation difficult and finding anybody almost impossible.

They slowed to a walk. Brody had grabbed a radio on the way out of the office and called his colleague.

'Any sign of Weaver?'

'We lost her in the north-east corner of the square. We're looking for her there now,' said the voice on the other end.

'This way.' Brody jogged as best he could through the crowds towards the location the officer had given him.

When they found the two uniforms, they were still looking.

'What happened?' asked Pope.

'We think we saw Weaver walking through this part of the Piazza. We were over there,' he said, pointing across to the middle of the space. 'But as we were coming over we lost her in the crowd.'

'How could you have lost her?' The irritation was palpable in Pope's voice.

'Look at how many people there are here, ma'am. We tried to follow her, but—'

'Are you sure it was her? Amy Weaver?'

'We think so.' He looked at his colleague, who nodded.
'You think so? Was it or wasn't it?'

'We can't be one hundred per cent, but I'm fairly certain. She was moving fast and dodging in and out of the
crowds. But I think it was her.'

'What was she wearing?' asked Pope.

'Black jeans, sneakers, I think Converse. A black hoodie.'

It certainly sounded like what Amy Weaver had been
wearing when Pope had interviewed her at her flat.

'Which direction did she go?'

The officer pointed to Russell Street, which led off the
east side of the square. 'But we have a couple of officers along
there and they say they didn't see her. So we thought she
must have doubled back into the Piazza.'

Great, thought Pope. Amy Weaver had been sighted,
then lost, in one of the busiest areas of Central London.
That's if it even was her. And she was only yards away from
the police station.

'Send that description to everyone within a couple of
miles' radius and get them on the lookout. I want you both
scouring the square. Everywhere.'

The two officers nodded, pleased to be sent away rather
than having to face more of Pope's wrath about their lack of
a definitive ID.

'Brody, Khan, head along Russell Street and work out
where she would have gone.'

Pope turned to head into the busy square.

'Ma'am, you said no solo . . .' Khan called after Pope,
but she was gone and couldn't hear. She turned to Brody.
'Should we go after her?'

'No, come on. Bec will be fine. Let's find Amy Weaver.'
Brody strode off, leaving Khan jogging to catch up.

Pope had to zig-zag through the crowds, which were
dense in most areas of the large, open space. She had a hunch
that if Amy Weaver was here, she was headed for the station.
She walked in that direction on high alert. At one point she
saw a young woman dressed in black, wearing black sneakers,

but as she approached, the woman turned and Pope realized it was an Italian tourist shouting loudly to the rest of the party from which she had become separated.

Pope spent the next hour walking around Covent Garden, walking past the police station several times, scanning every single face she could see. But it was hopeless. Amy Weaver wasn't here. Pope wondered if she had ever been here, or whether the officers had been mistaken. She might have spent the last hour on a wild goose chase.

She checked in for the third time with Brody, who had also had no luck. She told them to return to the station.

Pope desperately needed to know where to find Amy Weaver. But she had the distinct impression that, as Khan had so accurately put it, the woman was most definitely one step ahead of them. The question was, what was Weaver's next move?

CHAPTER TWENTY-EIGHT

Alex had to admit it: he was very excited. He hadn't thought that he would feel quite so nervous before proposing to Bec. Hadn't thought his heart rate would jump so immediately or to such a degree. But he had been absolutely terrified just before asking the question.

It had been a turbulent couple of years. After losing his wife, Hannah and Chloe's mother, all he had looked for was stability and calm. And although there were moments of that with Bec, her job meant that for much of the time, life was anything but stable and calm. He had found that difficult for a long time, even leaving for a period of time last year in order to work out what was best for him and the girls. But he had realized that he wanted Bec and he knew both girls had developed a strong bond with her.

Then New York had happened. Or rather, it hadn't happened. When she got the phone call and explained that she couldn't go, his immediate reaction was, that was it. The three of them should go to New York, and when they returned he would ask Bec to leave. But then it had hit him. He loved her, despite everything she had put them through. And if they could survive the last two years, they could survive anything.

Alex also realized that her job was always going to be there. A great, looming presence which she was unable to control. He knew then that he would have to change if this was going to work. He had accepted that things would not always be perfect, that stuff would get in the way. He also decided that if they were going to be a proper family, two things were going to have to happen. First, if they went on holiday, they went together. Not separately because one of them had to work. And second, they needed to get married. To formalize their relationship, their family. The New York trip was designed to achieve both of those things.

After losing his first wife, Alex didn't think he would ever get married again. But here he was. Alex had realized that he loved Bec and wanted to spend the rest of his life with her.

After the proposal, when Bec was at work, he had sat the girls down and had a long talk with them. He asked them how they felt about him getting remarried and whether they were happy. They both gave him their blessing and that meant everything. Alex didn't think he could have gone through with a wedding if his girls weren't happy.

So now he was thinking about venues, about potential honeymoon destinations and about guest lists. Bec had always seemed to like the old Routemaster buses repurposed as wedding buses, so he knew that he wanted one of them to transport guests from the wedding to the reception. His first wedding had been in a church and very traditional. He wanted this one to be different. A good opportunity to get a new suit. He was looking forward to visiting Paul Smith.

It would be a new chapter for them both. Alex was absolutely ready for it. He made a mental note to call his parents later that evening to tell them the good news. They weren't Bec's biggest fans — they had some idea what she and Alex had been through together — but they would be happy that he was happy.

Chloe walked in as Alex was contemplating these romantic developments.

'Dad, me and Hannah are going to the movies. OK?'

'Yes, of course. Sounds fun. What are you going to see?'

'Not sure. We'll see what's on when we get there.'

Alex doubted that. They almost certainly wanted to see something of which they thought he'd disapprove. But he was in such a good mood that he decided to play along.

'OK, sounds good. Do you need some cash for the tickets? Will you let me treat you?'

'That would be great. Thanks, Dad.'

Alex opened the banking app on his phone and transferred the money to Chloe's account.

'There's a bit extra for popcorn,' he said with a smile.

'Thanks, Dad.' Chloe gave him a hug, then checked the time on her phone screen. She walked to the bottom of the stairs.

'Hannah! Come on, we're going to be late.'

Alex was so tempted to point out that if they didn't know what they were going to see, how could Chloe know they were going to be late? But he resisted. He didn't want anything to spoil the current state of harmony.

Chloe came back into the living room.

'What time do you think you'll be back?' he asked.

'Not late. Are you excited? About the wedding?' she asked with a broad grin.

'I am actually.' He reciprocated the expression.

'Me too. Can me and Hannah be involved in the planning?'

'Yes, of course. I wouldn't have it any other way. I'll need someone to help me pick out a suit, shoes, a fabulous tie and all the rest of it.'

Chloe beamed. 'Do you think Bec will let us help her choose a dress?'

'I'm absolutely sure she will. You can be fashion advisers for both of us.'

'Brilliant!' said Chloe, and gave Alex another hug.

He heard Hannah racing down the stairs. She stuck her head around the door.

'Bye, Dad. See you later. Chloe, come on!'

Chloe looked at Alex and rolled her eyes. Then they were both gone and the house was quiet again.

Alex checked his watch. It was an acceptable time for a little wine. Not least as he was in celebratory mood. He opened a bottle of Merlot and poured himself a glass, then he sunk into the sofa and put his feet up. He had no idea what time Bec would be home, but he was fine with that. He knew what it was like when she was in the middle of a case. When it was over, there would likely be some downtime before the next case and they could start planning for the wedding and really enjoying the anticipation.

He picked up the remote control and started scrolling through the channels. How was it that there were so many more channels these days, but there seemed to be less and less that he actually wanted to watch? He went to Netflix, and there he found a movie that he had started some time ago but had only watched halfway through. If his daughters were watching a film, he decided he would too. He pressed play and tried to remember the first half.

After about fifteen minutes, Alex realized that he had too much adrenaline to sit through a movie. He needed to be up and about, doing something. He decided to call his parents.

They spoke for over an hour after Alex had told his mum the good news. She sounded excited, but he knew her well and he could sense that there was also an element of reservation in her voice. His parents had harboured Alex and the girls when he had walked out of the house for six months, so she knew that their relationship had not been without its difficulties. But he reassured her that all was well now and that he and Bec were stronger than they had ever been. At that point he felt that his mother had accepted that this was the right thing for Alex and from there they had started talking wedding plans. He discussed his ideas and she became animated and engaged. It became a little awkward when she asked if Bec had the same vision for the wedding as Alex. She hadn't really had the opportunity to think about any vision at all. He explained that she was in the middle of a big case and that as soon as that was over, they would have time to plan. The reservation in his mother's voice returned, so Alex promised to call again at the weekend and ended the conversation.

More or less satisfied at the outcome, he decided to call Bec and let her know about his conversation.

He dialled her number and waited, but after a lengthy wait while her phone rang, it went to answerphone. He left a message.

'Hi Bec, it's me. Just to say that I've spoken to my mum, and she's really excited at our news. She's offered to do anything she can to help, so I thought it might be an idea to delegate something to her so she can get involved. Chloe and Hannah have gone to the movies. They wouldn't tell me what they were going to see, so I'm guessing Chloe is trying to sneak Hannah into a fifteen certificate. So I'm home alone. I'll try to leave some of the wine for you. Anyway, I hope all's going well with your day and look forward to seeing you later. Let me know when you're on the way and I'll get dinner started. Love you.'

Alex had a mild feeling of anxiety in the pit of his stomach. He was well aware that Bec's job meant she was often unavailable when he called. It was totally natural. But he also understood the nature of her work and that she was regularly subjected to dangerous situations, with some of the most violent criminals, murderers, that the police ever had to deal with. When he couldn't get through to her, he couldn't help but worry.

He told himself everything was OK. Bec was at work, she would be home soon. She was brilliant at her job and she could handle anything it threw at her. He sensed a shift since they'd had to postpone their trip to New York. Bec had seemed to understand at that point that things needed to change, and over the past few days she really did seem to be making an effort.

Alex relaxed, took a sip of wine, and started to contemplate what he might cook for dinner.

There was no way that he could have known that at the same exact moment, Bec Pope was running through a packed Covent Garden Piazza, chasing a multiple murderer. A murderer who had vowed vengeance on the people closest to Pope.

CHAPTER TWENTY-NINE

Pope had been searching closer to the police station so she got back first. She made herself a coffee and sat down at her desk. Brody and Khan arrived a few minutes later.

'Busy out there today,' said Brody.

'It's always busy out there,' said Pope. 'The worst place to look for someone who doesn't want to be found.'

'You went off on your own,' said Khan suddenly, and slightly louder than she meant to.

Pope looked at her but didn't respond.

'You told me that the protocol was no one out there on their own until we catch Amy Weaver. Then you go running off on your own.'

Pope was shocked at the challenge.

'Three people walking around together is a waste of time. And I didn't want you on your own. We have a killer at large and I have to decide the best way to find her. My responsibility, my call.'

'But you put yourself in danger,' said Khan.

'You seem to have misunderstood the situation here, DS Khan. Your role in my team is not to question my decisions out in the field. Your role is to do what I ask you to do. We defer to rank and experience. If you want to question my methods, you do so later.'

'That's exactly what I'm doing,' she said coolly.

Pope had to concede that her colleague had a point. She took a decision to de-escalate.

'OK, point taken. We had agreed that, you're right. But ultimately we need to apprehend her as soon as possible, and if that means doing things in an unorthodox way, so be it. The most important thing is to catch Amy Weaver. That's what we need to focus on now. Reviews happen later.'

Khan seemed about to continue, but Brody stepped in, ever the diplomat.

'Do we think Weaver was ever actually there? The uniforms could easily have made a mistake in those crowds,' he said.

Both women looked at each other and both made the same decision to move on. For now.

Pope shook her head slowly. 'Who knows? I saw someone dressed the same, and was just about to grab her when I realized it was an Italian tourist. Black jeans and black hoodie isn't exactly a unique look. The problem is that if you're on the lookout for someone, you're more attuned to see anyone who resembles them.'

'Do you think that's what happened here?' Brody was still trying to ensure the new conversation went far enough so that the previous one would be forgotten.

'I guess we won't know until we ask Amy Weaver herself. I've already asked Thompson to check out any cameras in the vicinity, but he hasn't got back with anything yet.'

'It's so busy you could search for hours and still not be sure.'

'I know. We'll see. I've left officers out there looking for her, but if she was there, I'm guessing she's long gone by now.'

Brody had done a good job of diffusing the tension.

'So, if we accept that she might have been here, the question is why,' said Brody.

'There can only be one reason,' said Khan. 'She was heading for the police station. Or, at least, scoping it out.'

'That does seem like a possibility,' said Pope. 'But it's difficult to see what she thought she could achieve. I mean, she'll know every officer in the Met is on the lookout. You'd have to be stupid to try to get into a police station where the Homicide Squad leading the investigation is based.'

'Stupid, or reckless, or crazy,' said Brody.

'Yes, OK. But Weaver has been planning this for a while. She ordered those books months ago, so she must have hatched her plan before that. And she was careful. Locations where there was no CCTV, late at night, the whole satanism angle. She's a careful planner. This seems out of character with what she's done so far.'

'But she got angry really quickly when you spoke to her. She clearly thought that she'd get away with the murders, so the fact that we're on to her so soon might have pushed her over the edge. Maybe she's good at planning, but not so good when it comes to improvising?'

'That's a possibility. The question now is where has she gone?'

'She could be anywhere. It was over an hour ago since uniform thought they saw her. You can get a long way in an hour.' Brody thought for a moment. 'If I were Weaver, I would head along the Strand. The tourists would be unlikely to have seen the local alerts. Then out towards the city, maybe to Blackfriars or London Bridge then out of London.'

'But she has plenty of contacts here. Do we know of anyone she might go to out of town?'

'I don't think so. But she's got to show up. I've got a hunch she's not running. She was so clear about coming for us. She wants to stay and make good on that threat.'

'Or it's a ruse,' said Khan. 'She wants us to concentrate the search here while she's off far away.'

Pope looked out of the window. The sky was beginning to darken. Soon it would be evening and their job would become infinitely more difficult for the next twelve hours. That was a long time in which Weaver could disappear. Maybe Khan was right and the appearance in Covent Garden was carefully planned to give them the impression that she was staying in the area. A calculated risk to give her more chance to slip away undetected and never be found. Pope had to believe that this was not the case. They would find her. They had to.

'OK, so what's our plan?' she asked.

Brody spoke first. 'If she's left town, or is in the process of leaving, there's nothing we can do from here. We'll have to rely on uniforms and the stations, ports, airports keeping vigilant and catching her. If she's still close by, then I guess she'll come to us. Then she'll be intercepted.'

'Then what can we do in the meantime?' asked Khan.

'See how Thompson and Tech are getting on. Help with the CCTV search. Brody and I will try to dig into Weaver's background and see if anything pops up.'

Khan headed out of the office.

'She's got a point, Bec. That wasn't the most sensible thing you've ever done,' said Brody.

'I know. But if she was there, we had to give ourselves the best chance of catching her. I thought splitting up gave us the best chance.'

'True. But remember she's pretty inexperienced in Homicide. We all have to set an example. Make sure she has the basics to grow into the team. Part of that is actually working as a team.'

'OK, but you know what it's like in the heat of the moment. You have to make quick decisions, and sometimes that's going to involve a dangerous situation. Anyway, there are so many people around — nothing's going to happen in the middle of Covent Garden.'

Brody looked at her and grinned. 'You know your problem? You're a maverick detective who doesn't play by the rules. You get the job done at any cost.'

'Piss off,' said Pope. But it did make her smile.

'Seriously, though. Don't give her too much of a hard time. She's just worried about you. About all of us.'

'I know. Come on. Let's see if we can find anything that Thompson missed.'

Brody raised his eyebrows. 'You mean see if we can out-tech the tech genius?'

'Something like that. Let's have a look at her social media.'

Surprisingly, Weaver's Instagram account was public. Brody pulled up a chair and sat down next to Pope as she started scrolling through the posts. It was fairly standard stuff. No cats, but a fair number of food pictures.

'What is it with people taking pictures of what they're eating?' asked Pope. 'Do they really think that everyone is interested in what they had for dinner?'

'You're out of touch,' said Brody. 'Important stuff on social media. Lizzie always posts her food if it looks good. People do seem to be interested in that type of thing.'

Pope shook her head and continued scrolling. 'What's interesting is that she hasn't posted that much over the past six months. Just a handful of photos, a sunset, a couple from a country park she visited, a video from a concert. But go back six months and she's a much more regular poster. I mean, look at this stuff. It's virtually every day.'

She moved through the posts. There were holidays, more food, more concerts, a couple of festivals, Weaver with friends. And lots of pictures of her and Tom.

'The pictures of her and Murray become much less frequent too. Go back a year or more, and every other photo has Murray in it, or Weaver and Murray in a selfie. But then he more or less disappears. What's that about?'

'Maybe something happened between them around that time,' said Brody. 'Maybe they fell out, which would explain the lack of photos and Weaver planning to murder him. The timing fits. Six months ago there was a problem, maybe an argument, or maybe they split up? Then Weaver stews on it for a while, then has an idea and orders the books. We know the rest.'

'I don't get the impression they split up. Weaver said they were full-steam ahead planning the wedding. And none of his friends or colleagues mentioned that. And it's something I'm sure they'd tell us.'

'If they knew,' said Brody. 'Maybe they kept it quiet?'

'We need to talk to her colleagues,' said Pope. 'We didn't do that because there seemed no need to. It was a random attack, so why talk to her circle? But we'll do that on Monday morning. We'll get uniforms to her place of work. Someone must know what happened to cause her to commit this brutal crime.'

* * *

Pope checked her watch. It was getting late and was dark outside. She knew she should head home but she also felt that she needed to be here in case there were any sightings of Amy Weaver. Or, even better, if she was apprehended. Weaver had threatened her colleagues. She had threatened Pope herself. She was dangerous, clever and possibly close by.

In the morning she would first call Tobias Darke and update him on the case. She would ask his opinion on Weaver, given all the new information they now had. Maybe he would be able to tell them something which might help to understand her better and help them catch her.

She looked over at what used to be Adam Miller's chair. She had to find Weaver before . . . she couldn't finish the thought. It was still too painful.

Pope decided she could do no more tonight. She had a few loose ends to tie up, then she would go home to spend an evening with Alex. She checked her phone and saw that she had a voicemail from him some time ago. She listened and it made her smile. Hannah and Chloe were out at the cinema and he was home alone. She would go back and spend some much-needed quality time with her fiancé. That felt very strange. Pope hadn't got her head around it yet by any means. But it felt good. It felt very good indeed.

CHAPTER THIRTY

Alex looked out of the window to the back garden. Should they have the wedding reception here? At the house? A few years ago he had attended a friend's wedding and they'd had their reception in their garden. It had been really nice. Personal. And cheap, of course. Alex's initial research into possible venues had demonstrated just how expensive venue hire could be. He surveyed the space. Yes, it might just work. Maybe fifty to sixty people. A small marquee. A caterer. He would talk to Bec about it when she got back this evening. She had texted to say she was just finishing up at work, so he gave up on watching the movie and decided to get started on dinner. He perused his phone to decide which music to listen to while he cooked. Bec liked vinyl, or at a pinch, CDs. But he preferred the ease of streaming. He decided on Primal Scream's *Screamadelica* album to fire him up for his cooking.

As the first song started playing, Alex considered the contents of the fridge. Not a great selection of ingredients. But on closer inspection he decided there was enough for a stir fry. He retrieved some brown rice from the back of one cupboard and put it on to get started. Then he set about chopping the vegetables. He chopped in time to the music, which made him smile, feeling good about, well, pretty much everything.

As he was slicing a large head of broccoli, there was a knock at the door. He looked at his watch. Too early for Bec to be home, judging by the timing of her text. He put down the knife and wiped his hands on a tea towel. As he walked towards the front door, Alex looked through the front window and saw a black VW parked outside on the road. Did he know anyone who drove that car? He didn't think so.

Alex opened the door to see a woman a bit younger than him, dressed in black jeans and a black hooded sweatshirt.

'Hi,' he said.

'Hi. I'm really sorry to bother you. I've got a flat tyre.' The woman pointed to the black car. 'It's a bit embarrassing, but I've never changed a tyre before. Is there any chance you could give me a hand?' She looked suitably sheepish.

Alex looked around, up and down the road. No one else was in sight. He half wondered why she had parked outside his house in particular, but assumed that she just pulled up in the first suitable space once she realized there was a problem.

'Yes. OK. Just give me a minute.'

'Thanks so much. You're a lifesaver. I really appreciate it.'

Alex smiled and went back to the kitchen. He paused the music, and returned to the doorway to get his house keys just in case the wind blew the door shut. He and Bec kept their keys in a shallow wooden bowl on a high table just inside the hallway. Chloe had made it in her design and technology class at school when she was in Year 7 and it had served an admirable purpose ever since.

As he was picking up the keys he was aware of movement behind him. Then a sharp scratch on the right-hand side of his neck. He flinched and put his hand against where he felt the pain. He turned and saw the woman standing in the doorway looking quizzically at him.

'Everything OK?' she asked, a concerned look on her face.

'Yeah, I just . . . I don't know, it must have been an insect. A wasp or something.' But then it wasn't OK. As Alex took a step towards the open door his legs suddenly started to feel like jelly and his head started to spin. Then he knew he was falling to his knees and everything went black as he crashed to the floor.

The woman dressed in black walked back into the house and slowly closed the door. She looked at the man lying on the floor. It was time to make a phone call.

* * *

Bec Pope was unaware of the events unfolding at her home. She was wrapping up the day's work and considering their strategy for tomorrow. She genuinely wasn't sure whether Amy Weaver had escaped the city, or whether she was close by, waiting for an opportunity to wreak havoc on Pope and her team. Either way, Pope was ready for whatever Amy Weaver planned to throw at her.

At that moment Zahra Khan returned to the office and sat down in her chair.

'How's it going? Any luck?' asked Pope.

'It's ridiculous. It's like sorting through a colony of ants, looking at the CCTV around Covent Garden. Gazillions of people.'

'I take it you didn't find any sign of her?' asked Brody from behind his computer.

'No. Not yet. But Thompson's still looking. I need a break from staring at the screen. Good way to ruin your eyesight. I don't know how those guys do it,' said Khan.

'A misspent youth,' offered Brody. 'They spent their formative years glued to a screen, so this is natural for them.'

Pope smiled. 'I always suspected as much.'

Just then Pope heard her ringtone emanating from her pocket. She saw an unknown number and answered.

'DCI Pope.'

'Hi Bec, how're you doing?'

Pope froze, stared at Khan. She tapped the desk and Brody stuck his head above his monitor. He instantly clocked her expression. She put the phone on speaker.

'Hi Amy. Where are you?'

Brody and Khan stared at her intently.

'OK, so you've put me on speaker. Hi, team. How are we all doing?'

'What is it you want, Amy? Where are you?'

'You've already asked me that. The fact that I chose not to answer might suggest that I don't want to tell you. But, actually, I can't wait to tell you where I am.'

'OK, I'll play along. But I can't keep asking you the same question.'

'So why don't you ask me a different question, then?'

Pope thought Weaver was enjoying this too much.

'What do you suggest I ask you, Amy?'

'I had hoped that you would be able to come up with something on your own, but maybe that's too difficult. OK, I'll give you a clue. Why don't you ask me where I am *and who I'm with*?'

Pope's heart skipped a beat. She realized that if Weaver was talking like this, it was coming from a place of confidence. That meant she was either somewhere they would never find her or she was doing something they wouldn't like.

'OK, Amy. Where are you and who are you with?'

'I think it would be much more interesting if you tried to *guess* where I was. Don't you?'

'I have no idea.'

'I think you need a clue. Let me think. OK, got it. It's your house, Bec.'

Pope started. 'What did you say?'

'Oh, damn. I've given it away. Sorry,' said Weaver, the smile evident in her voice.

'What are you talking about, Amy? What do you mean? You're not at my house.' Pope was trying to convince herself.

'I'm afraid I am, Bec. Nice place. I've always liked open-plan kitchen and living rooms. Really opens the space up, don't you think?'

'You're fucking kidding me.' Of all the scenarios Pope had mapped out to keep her team safe, she hadn't even considered that Weaver might know where she lived. Pope suddenly remembered Alex's voicemail message telling her that Chloe and Hannah were out at the movies and he was there on his own. Should she mention him? What if Weaver didn't know he was there? But she had to know if he was OK.

'You're probably wondering at this stage about Alex, right? That is his name, isn't it? There is some junk mail here addressed to an Alexander. But I'm sure he goes by Alex, right?'

'If you've hurt him, I swear I'll . . .'

'OK, OK. Calm down. He's fine. A little woozy when he wakes up, I would guess. If he wakes up.'

Pope stood up. 'What have you done to him? Is he OK?'

'I've just told you he's OK. Listen, Bec. He's fine. A fast-acting sedative. I'll tell you what you'll need to do if you want to see Alex alive again.'

Pope flinched. 'If you fucking hurt him I will hunt you down and kill you myself.'

Weaver laughed. 'That's a little unseemly for a detective chief inspector. This is what you're going to do, Bec. You're going to pack up your work things and you're going to pop on that blue light and get here as fast as you can. If you're quick enough, you might just get here in time to save Alex. But you'll need to come alone. I've got enough cyanide in the needle I'm holding by Alex's neck to kill a horse. If I see anyone else with you, he's dead and I'll be away before you even see me. Is that clear?'

'Yes, it's clear. But you don't touch him. Not a single hair on his head.'

But Weaver had ended the call and Pope was talking to an empty line.

CHAPTER THIRTY-ONE

'Alex. Fuck.'

Brody walked towards Pope. 'How do you want to play it?'

Pope stared at Brody. 'How do I want to play it? I want to drive there now and teach Amy Weaver a lesson she won't forget.'

Brody didn't ask for details.

'Coming?'

'Of course,' he replied. 'Let's go.'

Khan got up to follow. Pope's initial reaction was to tell her to stay. She wanted Brody. But she knew this could escalate and they were a team after all. She nodded at Khan.

* * *

Pope had undertaken the Met Police Advanced Driver course years ago. She was used to driving at speed and in pursuit situations. But Brody had never seen her drive as fast as she was driving now. Her skill behind the wheel was not in question and she proved it multiple times on the way to her house.

They didn't talk much on the journey. Brody and Khan wanted Pope to be concentrating on the road. But as they drew close, Brody knew they needed to talk strategy.

'What's the plan?'

Pope looked as if she was considering the question for the first time. 'I'm going to drop you off at the end of the road. I'll call you and leave my phone on in my pocket and you can assess the situation.'

Brody looked concerned. 'I don't think you should go in alone. We know what Amy Weaver is capable of.'

Pope shook her head as she dodged past a white delivery van and swerved in at the last moment to avoid an oncoming black cab, who blasted his horn at her.

'No. She said to come alone. You're right that we know what she's capable of, but I'm more worried about Alex. I need him to be safe.'

She seemed to be saying the last part to herself rather than to Brody or Khan.

Brody tried to work out if Pope was right, or whether she needed to be convinced that this was a reckless plan. But he could see her expression set. She wasn't changing her mind.

He had to try. 'But you're aware that this is almost certainly a trap? You know it's you she really wants? The detective responsible for trying to track her down.'

'Maybe. But she threatened you and Fletcher. She knows the way to get at me is through the people I know. I thought it would be my colleagues. That's what she said. But it was to put us off the scent. She was going after Alex all along.'

Brody knew he wasn't going to win this argument. 'OK, maybe I'll go around the back, and Khan, you stay at the end of the road.'

Khan nodded her agreement. 'Do we need to call armed response?'

'No time,' said Pope. 'But call an ambulance. Tell them to come in quietly. I don't want Weaver hearing sirens.'

Khan made the call as Pope pulled up just before turning into her road.

'OK. Out.'

They both exited the car without argument.

'Be careful, Bec,' said Brody. 'What are you going to say if you need us?'

Pope thought about this. 'I'll say . . . "I'm going to have to call in my team."'

'OK. Khan?' said Brody.

'Got it.'

Brody closed the door. Pope took a deep breath and gently drove off, turning left into her road. She drove slowly, scoping out the scene. Everything looked ordinary. As she pulled up, she noticed a black VW sitting outside her house. Weaver. She stopped the car and took another look around.

The road was absolutely silent. Nobody walking their dog, no children playing outside. It looked just like any other day. But behind her front door, it was, of course, anything but ordinary. She shuddered to think of what was going on there. Time to find out.

There wasn't much planning she could do for this scenario. No time for reinforcements, which she couldn't risk anyway as Weaver had promised to kill Alex if she saw anyone else but Pope. All she could do was head in and see what happened. Try to save Alex. She felt a rising terror in the pit of her stomach. No matter how well you trained and prepared for confronting killers, the fear never went away. The fear of confronting a monster who had taken a human life. Or lives. But this was different. Not only was Weaver a manipulator, but it was Alex. Her Alex, who had proposed to her only yesterday. Weaver had murdered her own fiancé. She would have no qualms about doing the same to Alex.

Pope took another deep breath and got out of the car. Keeping her eyes laser-focused on the house, she walked slowly up the drive to the front door. She wasn't sure whether to open the door with her key, or knock. The latter seemed ridiculous. It was her own home. She put the key in the lock and turned. It felt ominous. She'd never felt it like that. Not even for a moment.

She stepped in. Inside, the house was still. The faint hum of the refrigerator was the only sound that dared to disturb the silence. The place was too quiet. Too empty.

She stepped into the hall, her footsteps barely making a sound against the hardwood floor. She didn't call out; she didn't need to. She knew where they were.

Then she heard a voice.

'You took your time, Bec. Mind you, it gave me and Alex time to get acquainted.'

Weaver was sitting in one of the armchairs. At her feet was Alex, lying on the floor. Weaver held a long kitchen knife which rested casually on Alex's neck. The one missing from the knife block in her flat. The one she had used to carve an inverted pentagram on the chests of Paul Ward and Tom Murray. Pope's heart pounded.

'He's quite a catch. You did well for yourself.'

'If you've hurt him . . .' Pope didn't finish the sentence.

'Oh, don't worry about Alex. He's fine. Just a bit groggy.'

Pope started to move slowly forward.

'But if you come any closer, I'll slice his carotid artery. Then he won't be fine.'

Pope froze. Stared into Weaver's eyes.

'Let him go, Amy.' Pope's voice came out hoarse, more a plea than a demand.

Weaver chuckled, the sound dark and sickening. 'You know I can't do that, Bec. Not until we have a little chat.'

Amy Weaver was a monster. Pope's mind raced for options, weighing the risks. She couldn't think straight. The only thing that mattered was Alex's safety.

'What do you want?' Pope managed, trying to steady her breath. She kept her distance from the chair, keeping an eye on both of them.

Weaver shifted in the chair, stretching her legs out in front of her, as if this were just another casual meeting.

'What do I want? Well, Bec, that's the million-dollar question, isn't it? I want you to understand something. You think you know me. You think you can stop me. But you've been playing this game all wrong from the start.'

Pope's jaw clenched. 'This isn't a game, Amy. Just let him go, and I'll do whatever you want. You can just walk out of here. There's nobody here but us. No one to stop you.'

'We both know that's a lie.' Weaver's smile was sharp, cruel. 'You think I'd believe you? You think he means anything to me? He's a pawn. Nothing more.'

Pope's eyes flicked to Alex again. He was out cold. She couldn't rely on him to do anything to help her. If she could work out what to do. The urge to run at Weaver, to tackle her, was overwhelming. But Pope knew that the moment she reached her, Alex would be the one to pay. And that was something Pope could never live with.

'You wanted to be a hero, didn't you?' Weaver's voice broke through her thoughts. 'A detective. All that power. Where's the power now?'

Pope took a step forward, her voice shaking, but she forced herself to stand tall. 'This needs to end now, Amy. It's over.'

Weaver's face darkened, the playful smirk fading into something more dangerous. 'You think you're in control? You're nothing. I'm the one who's been in control this whole time. You just didn't realize it.'

'I'm not letting you win, Amy.' Pope's voice grew colder, more certain. 'You hurt him, and I'll make sure you regret it.'

Weaver's eyes flickered to Alex, a malicious glint crossing her face. 'Oh, don't worry, Bec. I don't think he'll feel a thing.'

Pope's breath hitched. 'What do you want me to do? What's your plan?'

Weaver leaned forward in the chair, her eyes narrowing. 'I need to disappear. And you need to help me.'

Pope didn't say anything, their eyes still locked.

Weaver looked at her like she was a puzzle she was slowly piecing together.

'Because if you don't, I will make sure *he* pays for your stubbornness.'

Pope's body felt like it was suffocating under the weight of the decision. If she didn't give in, Alex might not make it out alive.

'Everyone's looking for you. Every officer in the country knows who you are. And every officer in London has a photo of you,' Pope said, her voice steadying as resolve flooded her. 'And you won't hurt Alex. Not while I'm here.'

Weaver's smile faded, replaced by an icy sneer. 'We'll see about that.'

'Look, you need to move away from Alex. Once I've checked he's OK, we can work it all out. How you can disappear.'

'So, your plan is that I give up the leverage I have and rely on your goodwill to help me get away? Good try. I'll need something better than that.'

'Such as what? You say you want to get away, but I can't see how that can happen. Just give yourself up and I'll explain that you cooperated.'

'I can tell you now, I have absolutely no intention of giving myself up. Alex here is my insurance against that. You're going to have to help me. Unless you want the same thing to happen to him that happened to Adam Miller.'

Pope started. Locked eyes with Weaver. She really was a planner. Had done her homework. Despite herself, despite her attempts to keep calm under almost unbearable circumstances, she was wrong-footed.

'This has nothing to do with Adam Miller.'

'I think it does, Bec.'

'I can't see how.'

'It's another example of you getting your friends and family into trouble. Do you really think it's possible to do the job you do and have a happy, easy home life? Of course it isn't. Everyone like me, cleverer than you and always a step ahead, knows that your weak point is your family, your colleagues. All you need is the ability to follow-through, to carry out your threats, and you lot haven't got a chance.'

'You say that, but the man who murdered Sergeant Miller didn't do so well.' She used his rank and surname in an attempt to distance him from Weaver. Pope wanted no connection between Adam Miller and Amy Weaver.

'Yeah, well, not everyone's as careful as me.'

Pope suddenly regained her composure. She remembered who she was and what she was capable of. She was easily a match for Weaver.

'It doesn't look like you've been very careful, Amy. You're in my house with nowhere to go and everyone knows you murdered two men. I'm assuming us finding out it was you so early wasn't part of your plan?'

'That's true. But it's important to have a plan B. You did find out it was me and that was quite impressive, actually. But the only reason you found me was because I called you and told you exactly where I was. And I managed to get into your house and subdue your boyfriend. And the only thing between him living and dying is you doing exactly what I want. So, I wouldn't be slapping yourself on the back just yet, Bec.'

It infuriated her that Weaver insisted on using her first name. She knew she was trying to get under her skin. It was working.

'OK. You say you want help to get away. What did you have in mind?'

'Now we're getting to it. You've finally realized you're in a classic no-win situation. First, you'll need to get rid of the other officers you've undoubtedly got outside. I'm guessing Brody and Khan? Maybe a few uniforms? I imagine Superintendent Fletcher doesn't get his hands dirty by turning up to active crime scenes.'

Weaver had got it more or less right. It was useless to deny that her team were close by. She stared at the woman opposite her.

'Then what?' she asked.

'Then I want an unmarked car outside the house within thirty minutes. And absolutely no police anywhere near here.'

'If you want a car, why didn't you just leave in your own car? Why come here?'

'My car is marked, as you told me, by every police officer in the country. I wouldn't get very far. And I can't very well use public transport. I need a clean car and the space to go.'

Alarm bells were starting to ring for Pope. More than those already clanging in her head. Weaver would have to know that if she got what she wanted, that car would also be tracked and it would be absolutely no different to escaping in her own car. And she would also realize that she would be followed as soon as she left Pope's house. She wouldn't make it a mile before she was stopped. What, then, was Weaver's plan? Clearly escape wasn't the only thing the woman had in mind. She wanted revenge. She knew then that Weaver's plan was to kill Alex.

Weaver was watching her closely. Did she know that Pope had realized what she had planned?

'I'll give you one more chance to walk away, Amy. To just walk out of here and take your chances. We both know that if I call in a car you won't get very far in it.'

Weaver smiled at Pope. 'Ah, the penny's dropped. Well done, Bec. You've finally got it. I am going to escape. But you've caused me so much trouble, there's one more thing I need before I finally say goodbye.'

'Don't do anything you're going to regret, Amy. Please.'

Then it all happened so quickly. Weaver lifted the knife from Alex's throat and in one fluid movement plunged it into his chest. Pope watched in horror as the knife drove deep and blood started to pour out and pool on his shirt. Before she could react, Weaver withdrew the knife and pushed Alex's body away. She rushed towards the door to the garden.

Pope leaped forward and fell down by Alex, lifting his head gently and cradling it in her arms. 'Alex! Alex! No! Alex!' She kept repeating his name as she stared at the incongruous sight of the man she loved lying in her arms with a large knife wound in his chest. She didn't even see Weaver run through the door and out into the back garden.

Pope just about managed to take her phone, still connected to Brody's, out of her pocket. 'Brody, get an ambulance now! It's Alex . . . Weaver's gone out the back.' She dropped the phone on the floor and quickly wrenched her jacket off, balling it up and pushing it against the chest wound. Alex groaned. At least he was still alive. Just. She held him closely. His eyes were closed and there was no response as she called his name.

'Alex. Alex. Stay with me. Come on. The ambulance is on its way. We had it standing by so it will be here any minute. They'll look after you. It'll be fine.' Pope was rambling, terrified.

Pope looked around the room, looking for something that would help. It looked strange, in this completely different situation. The things which usually seemed comforting were suddenly alien, disconnected.

She looked down at Alex, who had now stopped groaning, stopped making any noise at all.

CHAPTER THIRTY-TWO

'Alex. Come on, Alex. Open your eyes, Alex.' Pope felt a rising panic.

Suddenly a paramedic came rushing in through the front door and into the living room, followed by another.

'OK. Move back. Let us get in there,' said the first. Before she could protest, he gently moved Pope away from Alex and the two men started working on him. Pope stood up and backed away, her hand held to her mouth.

Pope was vaguely aware that Amy Weaver had escaped, but she couldn't focus on that. Brody had been at the back of the house and she had to hope that he and Khan had found her. Her only priority was Alex. And in that regard, she was utterly helpless. Pope was used to being in control. This was hell. She could only watch as the two medics removed her jacket from on top of Alex's chest, exposing the blood seeping from the wound. Pope looked away. She had faced some tough times in this job. But nothing like this. She was paralysed with fear of what might happen to Alex.

They worked quickly and professionally, calm under extreme pressure. Pope looked back and saw that they were applying a dressing to the wound. That had to be a good sign.

Suddenly the temperature in the room rocketed and the medics' voices rose.

'He's stopped breathing. Start compressions.'

Pope thought she was going to be sick. The cliché was that everything happens in slow motion, but this most certainly wasn't the case. They were working quickly, one trying to manually work Alex's heart, the other retrieving a small electric machine from a nylon case, then fixing pads linked to the machine by wires to Alex's chest. One of the paramedics was carefully checking the settings on the machine.

'Clear!' he shouted. The other man took his hands off Alex.

'Clear,' he responded.

Then the first shock was administered. Then another, then another.

Both men stared at Alex.

Pope didn't breathe.

'We have a rhythm,' said the medic who had administered the shock. 'OK, let's get him in the ambulance.'

One of the men went out to the ambulance to get a stretcher for Alex. The other was carefully removing the electrodes from his chest.

'Is he . . . ?' Pope wasn't sure she could say the words.

'We lost him for a minute, but he's back. We need to get him to a surgeon immediately. He's losing a lot of blood.'

'Is he going to be OK?'

'We've stabilized him. We need to get him to a surgeon.' The medic repeated, used to having to repeat information to people in shock.

Pope simply nodded. She was indeed one of those people.

When the other man returned, they lifted Alex onto the stretcher and carried him towards the ambulance.

'Can I come with you? In the ambulance?' asked Pope.

'Yes, sure,' said the older of the two medics.

Suddenly Pope was aware of a commotion coming from the garden. Then Amy Weaver was thrust through the open door and into the house. Her hands were cuffed behind her back, held by Brody, with Khan close behind. She was struggling to get free.

'Get your hands off me!' she screamed. Brody had to work hard to contain her, and once through the door Khan assisted in the restraint.

Then she saw Pope. Her whole temperament immediately changed and she seemed calm again.

'Bec. How's Alex?'

Pope saw red. She'd been numb, in shock, but the floodgates opened.

'Weaver. You . . .' She lunged forward towards Weaver, arms outstretched. She wanted to kill Amy Weaver.

Brody saw it just in time and leaped in between the two women. Pope tried to get around him, but he was immovable, too strong for her, and he managed to hold her back even as she tried to get at Weaver over his shoulders.

'Bec!' he shouted. 'Bec, that's enough. That's enough!' He pushed her backwards as Khan kept a hold of Weaver.

The woman was laughing. 'It's annoying when things don't go your way, isn't it Bec?'

Pope made a renewed and, Brody had to admit, an extremely powerful attempt to get at Weaver.

'Get her out of here,' he said to Khan, who walked the woman, still laughing, out to a waiting police car.

Brody forced Pope to make eye contact as he held her shoulders.

'Enough. She's gone. She's gone, alright? It's over.' Pope turned away. 'We've got her, Bec. She's done.'

Pope looked at Brody, took a deep breath and burst into tears. She'd held too much in for too long. She hugged Brody, who stood firm as she sobbed.

'How's Alex?' he asked.

She shook her head. 'I don't know. His heart stopped and they had to use a defib to bring him back. They're taking him to hospital.

'Are you going with him in the ambulance?'

'Yes, I need to.' Pope extricated herself from Brody and walked towards the door, but then stopped. 'Hannah and Chloe? Oh no. They're out at the movies. I need to—'

'Go to the hospital. I'll wait here until they get back and bring them over. Text me which hospital when you get there.'

Pope looked at Brody. He would do that for her. 'Thanks, James. I will.'

She left and climbed into the ambulance with Alex.

Brody watched them drive away. He now had to work out how to explain all that had happened to Alex's daughters.

CHAPTER THIRTY-THREE

Saturday evening

Brody had to wait two hours for the girls to return so he could break the news. It had been two of the longest hours of his life. Khan and two uniformed officers had taken Amy Weaver back to the station and safely secured her in the cells.

When Chloe and Hannah had arrived back from the cinema, they had been greeted by a number of police cars and Forensic unit vans outside their home, as well as DI James Brody. He had wanted to meet them outside the cinema, but Pope had absolutely no idea which cinema they might have attended. He had only met the girls a handful of times and didn't feel he was the right person to deliver such awful news, but he knew it had to be done and it was at least better than a complete stranger.

Both girls had been shocked, then they had both sobbed, and Brody had been in the position of trying to comfort two teenage girls he hardly knew. On the way to the hospital, there had been a stunned silence. He had parked in the bay allocated for police vehicles and taken the girls to the ward on the eighth floor, as Pope had texted him to.

When they found Pope, both girls had again immediately started crying. Brody decided to hang back while she explained the situation with their father. Then she took them into his room. Soon after, she came back out and walked over to Brody and gave him a big hug.

'Thanks so much for bringing them. I'm really sorry you had to deliver the news. It can't have been easy.'

'No problem. How is he?'

Pope leaned back against the wall. She was utterly exhausted.

'The knife wound was pretty deep and the injuries are serious. They operated; it was pretty quick. They've patched him up, but the surgeon says they'll need to do further procedures once he's properly stabilized. They've put him in an induced coma to protect him and let his body stabilize properly.'

Brody looked towards Alex's room. 'What's the outlook?'

Pope took a beat. 'They're not sure. They'll know more when they bring him round, see how he's doing.'

'And how long will that be?'

'They can't tell me that at the moment. A day? Two days? Longer? He can't breathe unaided . . .' Pope's voice tailed off.

'Oh, Bec. I'm really sorry. Is there anything I can do?'

'Just hold things down at work. Nail Amy Weaver in every way possible.'

Brody nodded. 'I'm headed into work after this to see her. We'll probably do the interrogation in the morning. Give her time to stew.'

'It'll be two counts of murder and one of attempted murder.' Pope's voice caught. She wasn't ready to talk about Alex as a victim yet.

'Don't worry. We've got her cold. We just need to get a clear confession to make things quicker.'

Pope nodded. She knew she could trust Brody.

'Are you going to be alright here? Is there anything you need?'

'I don't think so. I've called Alex's parents and they're on the way.' Pope turned around and looked at Chloe and Hannah sitting by their father's bedside, the room dark and sombre, the panel of flashing lights above their bowed heads.

'Go and be with them. I'll let you know how we get on with Weaver.'

'Thanks again, James. If anyone had to tell the girls, I'm glad it was you.'

Brody wasn't sure he shared her conviction that he was the best person for the job, but he didn't offer that opinion.

'Text if you need anything. Anything at all.'

'Will do. Talk soon.'

Pope turned and walked away. Brody watched her go. Pope had dealt with so much over the last couple of years, he wondered how much more she could take. Not a problem for today.

He checked his phone for messages, then dialled Zahra Khan and updated her on Alex's situation. He was planning to return to the station and check on Amy Weaver. He would book an interview room for tomorrow morning, and start the process of making Weaver pay for the crimes she had committed.

* * *

When he arrived back at Charing Cross Police Station, it was late on Saturday evening. Drunken revellers were swaying their way around Covent Garden and past the entrance to the station. None were working on a Saturday evening. Brody knew he'd be working all weekend. Luckily, Lizzie was also on shift. It made things much easier when their schedules matched up.

He walked up the stairway, stopping several times to fill in concerned officers on how Pope was doing. It took him a while to arrive at the office.

'How's Pope?' asked Khan as he walked in, adding to the chorus.

'As you'd expect. They've done a preliminary operation on Alex to get him stabilized, but he's in an induced coma. She says there was quite a lot of damage from the knife wound.'

'That's terrible. Is there anything we can do?'

'I think the only thing we can do is get Amy Weaver's confession sorted. That'd be a weight off her mind. How was she when you brought her in?'

'Fairly quiet. She seemed to have accepted it. I mean, she was caught red-handed and we've heard her confess to Pope. What else can she say?'

'Yeah. We need her to admit everything on tape and under caution. I'm going to pop down and talk to her. Tell her we're going to interview her tomorrow morning and see if she wants a solicitor.'

'Do you want me to come with you?'

'Yes, why not? Strength in numbers.'

Down in the bowels of the station, the duty sergeant opened Weaver's cell for them. She was sitting cross-legged on the narrow bench along the back wall. She looked up when Brody and Khan entered, but her face was expressionless and she said nothing. Brody wondered if the gravity of her situation had finally hit her.

'Ms Weaver, you're aware that you've been arrested on two counts of murder and one of attempted murder,' Brody said. 'We'll be interviewing you tomorrow morning. Do you want to arrange for a solicitor to be present? Or we can arrange legal representation via the duty solicitor on call if you'd prefer that?'

She didn't say anything for a moment. Then she spoke with a hint of a smile. 'How is Alex? And how is DCI Pope coping? Not well, I suppose.'

Brody ignored the comment. 'Do I take it that you don't require legal representation?'

She smiled again. 'No, I don't need a solicitor. But I'll only speak to DCI Pope. Alone.'

'I'm afraid that won't be possible,' said Brody.

'Who do you think is going to interview me?'

'Myself and DS Khan here will be doing the interview in the morning.' He indicated his colleague.

'I'm afraid that won't work for me, DI Brody.'

'It's not about what works for you, it's—'

'Yes, it is,' interrupted Weaver. 'If you want me to say anything, anything at all, it will have to be with DCI Pope. I'll give her a full confession. But if it's not her, I won't say a word. Your choice.'

'DCI Pope won't be available.'

'You've already said that. I get it, she's playing the grieving partner at Alex's bedside. But that's the deal. Pope or nothing.'

Brody looked at Khan. 'Let's go.'

'I'll look forward to hearing from you, DI Brody,' Weaver called after them, as the cell door was locked.

Brody and Khan were silent as they climbed the stairs.

'What do we do?' asked Khan when they had returned to the office.

'What can we do? Pope's in the hospital. She's not going to want to leave Alex and the girls to interview Weaver.'

'She might, if you explain the situation.'

'Do you think she's going to be in any shape to be able to handle an interview with the woman who stabbed Alex? It's too much to ask.'

'I get that. But do you think she would want to make the choice herself? Should we at least talk to her about it?'

Brody didn't know what to think. He didn't want to disturb Pope when she had more important things to take care of. And he seriously doubted if she was the right person to interview Weaver at this point in time. But he also knew that a full confession would make everything much easier as the case went through the criminal justice system. And Pope would want that, at any price. He made a decision.

'OK, I'll run it by her.'

'Are you going to call her now?'

'Yes, will do.'

244

Brody dialled Pope's number. She didn't answer and it went to voicemail. Brody didn't leave a message.

* * *

Pope felt her phone vibrate in her pocket.

'I'll be back in a moment,' she told Chloe and Hannah.

She didn't get outside the ward in time to pick up, so she called back and Brody answered on the second ring.

'Hey, what's up?'

'Bec, how are things? Any change?'

'No, nothing yet. He's comfortable, according to the doctors. They're taking good care of him.'

'I need to talk to you about something.' His voice sounded hesitant and Pope was immediately on her guard.

'Is it Weaver? Is there a problem?'

'Not a problem, but let's say a situation.'

'What's happened?'

'Don't worry, it's nothing serious. But we're planning to interview her in the morning. She says she's only willing to speak to you.'

'Well, she doesn't have any choice. She can't choose who interviews her.'

'Of course. That's right. But she says she'll say absolutely nothing to us. Not a word. She says she'll give a full confession, but only to you. She also doesn't want a solicitor.'

Pope was silent.

'She's probably bluffing,' said Brody, suddenly feeling guilty for disturbing her in the hospital.

'Knowing Weaver, I doubt it.'

Pope considered the situation. Alex was likely to remain in a coma for some time. His parents would be here any moment and could stay with the girls in the morning. She wouldn't be gone long. And a full confession would be an excellent outcome. She knew what Alex would say. But she also wanted to nail Amy Weaver for her crimes and send her to prison for the rest of her life. She weighed it up.

'I'll be there. What time?'

'Are you sure, Bec? Everyone would understand if you didn't feel up to it.'

'I'm fine. I want her confession. If there's a chance she's going to give it to me, I have to do it.'

'OK. Shall we say nine?'

'I'll be there. And thanks, James. I know that can't have been easy.'

Pope ended the call. Tomorrow morning she would face the woman who had murdered Paul Ward and Tom Murray. And had stabbed Alex. This time, she would be ready.

CHAPTER THIRTY-FOUR

Sunday morning

Pope was exhausted. She'd managed around an hour's sleep in an uncomfortable chair beside Alex's bed. But as she woke, the adrenaline kicked in as soon as she remembered what she was going to be doing in three hours' time.

Alex's parents had arrived last night and they talked for a long time about what had happened and what would happen next. His mother had cried. His father had tried not to. They had understood completely when Pope explained what she was planning to do this morning. When she broached the subject with Chloe and Hannah, they were initially shocked that Pope was going into work. But when she explained that Amy Weaver would only talk to her, and that a confession would ensure that she was in prison for life, they saw the sense and gave their blessing.

Pope had managed to convince the girls to go home with their grandparents, with the promise that she would call them immediately if there was any change. There hadn't been. Their arrangement was that they would be back by 8 a.m., so that that Pope could get to the station and prepare for the interview. Sure enough, they arrived at 7.55 a.m.

Before she left the hospital, Pope changed into the clothes Chloe had brought from home for her. She also checked with the nursing staff that they weren't planning to do anything with Alex over the next few hours. Pope promised Alex's family that she would be back as soon as she was finished.

'Bring us good news,' said Alex's father.

'I'll do my best.'

When Pope got outside the hospital, the fresh air hit her like a slap to the face. Fourteen hours in the sterile atmosphere of the hospital had left her deprived of the outside world. Only fourteen hours? It felt an awful lot longer. She breathed deeply and relished the experience.

* * *

By the time she arrived at the police station Pope had regained her equilibrium. Or at least she was running on adrenaline and caffeine, which gave the same impression. She wondered if the four cups of mediocre coffee she had drunk at the hospital was too much. Probably not.

Brody and Khan were already there when she arrived. On a Sunday. The loyalty almost made her tearful, but she held herself together.

'Thanks for coming in on a weekend,' she said. 'We'll get this done quickly so we can all get back to what we were doing.'

'How's Alex?' asked Brody.

'No change. He needs assistance breathing at the moment. The doctors are hopeful, but there's no timeframe.'

'How are the girls?'

'They're holding it together today. Yesterday was really difficult for them, but a good night's sleep seems to have made a difference. Alex's parents are with them at the hospital.'

'Sorry we had to drag you away. I know it's a terrible time.'

'It's Amy Weaver who's dragged me away. Another of her petty games. But to be honest, if it means we finish this now, it's worth it. I'll play along.'

248

'Do you want us in there with you?' asked Brody.

'She might be more forthcoming if it's just me. Are you going to observe?' She looked from Brody to Khan. They both nodded.

'Yes. We'll be next door if you need us.'

'OK. I'm going to see how she plays it. I have some questions, but I really just want her to say she committed the murders. How we get to that point might have to be led by her. Can you get her into the interview room? I want her in there first so she feels like she has the upper hand. Hopefully the arrogance we've seen in her will take over and she won't be able to stop herself boasting about what she did and how clever she was.'

Brody and Khan left to get Weaver while Pope went into the bathroom. She checked her appearance in the mirror. She looked like she had been up all night, which was a fair reflection of events. She wondered how many times she had stared in this mirror and prepared herself for an interview. Or tried to control her irritation after a frustrating encounter with Fletcher. One thing she did know, she had never prepared to face a multiple murderer who had also put her fiancé in the hospital. She splashed water on her face, dried it with paper towels and steeled herself.

When she opened the door to Interview Room One, Amy Weaver was sitting in one of the chairs, just as Pope had planned. Pope nodded in acknowledgement to the officer standing at the back of the room, which he returned. By now, everyone in the station would know who this was and what had happened to Alex.

'Bec, nice to see you. Why don't you have a seat?'

Pope had been right. Weaver was acting like she owned the place. Pope suddenly felt a rage inside her — not building up, but fully formed in her chest. She had been ready for this and knew it would happen. So she ignored it. She'd play Weaver's game for a while. She sat down opposite Weaver and took a sip of her coffee. She pressed record on the tape and read Weaver her rights.

'Didn't you bring me a coffee?' she asked, her tone light, relaxed.

Pope ignored the question.

'Everything alright in the cells? Are you being treated OK?'

'Oh, very businesslike. No complaints. Terrible breakfast, though.'

'Sorry to hear that.'

'I expect it's similar to hospital food. How's Alex?'

Pope had known this was coming too. On the drive here, she had tried to anticipate how Weaver would behave in the interview. So far, Pope had guessed right. Blasé, trying to get under Pope's skin.

'I'm afraid we won't be talking about that today. But I'd like to know about how you killed Paul Ward and your fiancé. And why.' Pope looked straight at Weaver.

'So, Alex is not doing so well. To quote you, sorry to hear that. I'll keep my fingers crossed for a swift recovery.'

'I'm sure,' said Pope. 'Why don't you tell me why you murdered your fiancé? We found a wedding planning folder in your flat. It all seemed to be going to plan. What happened?'

Pope saw a brief look of regret play across Weaver's face. She knew it: Weaver would not be able to resist talking about what she had done. She wanted to tell the story from her perspective. To be understood.

'You're right, Bec. We had everything planned. It was Tom who proposed. He had bought a ring already. It was great. We had all these amazing plans.'

'What happened? It must have been something pretty drastic.'

'Simple really. He changed his mind. He got cold feet and started talking about postponing it for a couple of years. We talked for hours, but I could see that all of a sudden he wasn't into it.'

'So you decided that the only thing to do was to murder him?'

'You don't understand. I couldn't tell everyone that we'd made all these plans and suddenly Tom had decided he didn't want me anymore. It was so humiliating.'

'It happens.'

'Not to me. Not to me, it doesn't.'

Pope let that hang in the air for a moment. Weaver was clearly unhinged. Why else go to such dramatic lengths for retribution?

'What about Paul Ward?'

Weaver shook her head dismissively. 'He was just in the wrong place at the wrong time.'

'And by "wrong time", I take it you mean midnight?'

'I needed someone first so that Tom would look like just another in a line of killings. He was nobody. Just a convenience.'

'"A line of killings". Had you planned more victims?'

'I guess we'll never know now, will we?'

'I suppose we won't. Murderers never plan to get caught.'

Weaver smiled. 'Remember I told you where to find me, Bec. You can't claim the credit for that.'

'Whatever you say. We found the books you ordered online from the States. The satanism material, the pentagrams carved on their chests. Are you a true believer?'

Weaver laughed out loud. 'Of course not. All that devil-worship nonsense? That was just a smokescreen. And it worked pretty well.'

'Did it?'

'Well, it had you looking in all the wrong places, so I guess it must have done.'

'But carving an inverted pentagram on the victim's chests? On your own fiancé? It's pretty extreme stuff. How could you do that?'

For the second time today, Pope saw a look of regret in Weaver's expression.

Weaver's voice was a little quieter. 'It had to be convincing. And it certainly convinced you.'

'But that's an odd thing to come up with. It must have taken you a long time to plan. Did you actually read the books?'

'Of course I did. I needed to know as much as possible to make it look believable. I had a boyfriend when I was younger who was into all that stuff. I remembered the moral panic at the time. It was the perfect cover.'

Pope shook her head. She had a feeling Amy Weaver was someone she would never understand.

'But I'd rather talk about you, Bec. How are you dealing with Alex in hospital? Is it weighing heavily on you?'

Pope knew Weaver would want to taunt her. But she felt strangely calm. She was completely in control, even if she had allowed Weaver to think that was not the case.

'I can't deny it's difficult. You've caused a great deal of pain and anguish. What I don't quite understand is why you decided to attack Alex. You must have known there was a good chance you wouldn't escape. Why take the risk?'

'You came after me. I wanted you to feel what I had felt. The pain of losing a loved one. A partner.'

'That simple? Revenge?'

'You could call it that. Or justice.'

'There is absolutely nothing about this that is just by any sane definition. Except the part where you're behind bars and will stay that way for the rest of your life.'

Weaver laughed. 'We'll see about that. Never seen a good lawyer get the accused an innocent verdict?'

'You've been watching too many crime dramas on TV. You won't have a chance.'

'It ain't over 'til it's over.'

'OK, whatever you say.'

'I suppose after losing your sergeant recently, Alex must be a double blow for you. What was his name again?'

Pope was determined not to lose her cool, no matter how many buttons the woman pushed.

'I can't deny you've caused me some trouble, Amy. And if it were up to me, I wouldn't mind you and me in a dark alley and save the taxpayer a lot of money. But it isn't up to me and that's probably a good thing for you. But I can tell you one thing.'

'Oh, yeah. What's that?'

'In a minute's time, I'll be walking out of here and you'll be led, in handcuffs, back down to the cells. Then you'll be held on remand until the trial date, then you'll be sentenced to life without parole. And I'll never have to look at your face or think about you ever again.'

Pope got up and pushed her chair under the table. She nodded at the officer in the corner of the room.

Weaver suddenly looked enraged. 'Bec, sit down. I haven't finished.'

'You don't get to decide that, Weaver. In fact, you don't get to decide much of anything from now on.'

'Sit down!' Weaver shouted.

Pope ignored her shouts and opened the door to the interview room. Weaver was still screaming her name when Pope closed the door behind her.

CHAPTER THIRTY-FIVE

Brody offered to drive Pope back to the hospital. Given how little sleep she'd had the night before, she gratefully accepted. Khan stayed at the station to liaise with the duty sergeant and compete the paperwork on Amy Weaver. Pope had been impressed with how Khan had handled herself on her first case out of Charing Cross. She'd had a moment, but had composed herself. Pope hadn't had the time to call her contact at Hackney to get the info on Khan. Now she thought she wouldn't need to.

Pope was convinced Khan was going to be a good addition to the team.

Brody seemed to read her mind as he drove along the Strand towards Waterloo Bridge.

'Khan did pretty well, I thought. It was a tough case but she did alright.'

'Yeah, I think she's going to be good.'

'Is she here on any sort of probation period, or is it permanent?'

'Permanent, as far as I know. Fletcher didn't give me much background and we were already on the case at that point. Not much time to talk about her. I'm still not sure why he chose her for the team, but he didn't do a bad job.'

'Miller would have liked her,' said Brody.

'I think you're right.' Pope was feeling fragile after the last twenty-four hours and wasn't ready to discuss anything even remotely emotional, let alone this. She changed the subject.

'How are things with Lizzie?'

Brody caught the change. 'All good.' He hesitated. 'I think I might ask her to move in with me.'

She turned to look at him. 'That's great news. Congratulations.' Pope was genuinely happy for Brody. 'But your flat? I mean, has she seen it?'

'Funny. I was actually hoping she might suggest hers. It's bigger. And a lot nicer.'

'Good idea. That's exciting.'

'Yeah. Well, we'll see. Still thinking it over.'

Pope almost said something about not waiting too long as you never know what's around the next corner. But she stopped herself. Their relationship wasn't based on empty platitudes.

'I'm going to have to take a bit of time off. To be there for Alex and the girls. I don't know how long. I'll talk to Fletcher later.'

'Of course. The most important thing is to look after Chloe and Hannah, I get that.'

Pope was quiet for a while as Brody drove.

'After losing their mum, this is going to be really hard for them.'

'Will Alex's parents be able to help out?'

'I'm sure they will. But they're grandparents. At seventeen and thirteen . . . well, they can be a handful.'

'So there's no indication how long Alex will be in the hospital?'

'Not as of this morning.'

'Anything I can do, just let me know.'

'I will. Thanks, James.'

Pope was quiet for the remainder of the short journey, until Brody pulled the car up outside the front entrance.

'Do you want me to come in?' he asked. 'A bit of moral support?'

'No, thanks. I think there's enough of us round the bed-side if Alex wakes up.'

'Let me know how it's going.'

'Will do.'

Brody watched Pope walk in through the revolving doors at the entrance to the hospital. She had a long, difficult road ahead of her. He didn't envy it.

He decided to head home. He had a big decision to make.

EPILOGUE

One week later

After negotiating her leave with Fletcher, Pope had spent the next four days by Alex's bedside at the hospital. Hannah and Chloe had divided their time between staying with Pope and being at home with their grandparents. Pope had dashed home for a shower and a change of clothes each day and was never away from Alex for more than a couple of hours.

But Alex had not come out of the induced coma and now was on life support. The doctors had explained that the knife wound had done serious damage and his body had shut down to try to repair itself. The prognosis was unclear. When Pope pushed the doctors, they had told her that it was fifty–fifty whether Alex regained consciousness. Pope didn't share this figure with Chloe and Hannah.

On the fifth day, Pope had decided to spend more time at home. The hospital had promised to call her if anything changed. She still visited every day, but slept at home and tried to be there to cook meals.

Pope had sat down with Alex's parents and laid out the situation. It could be weeks, or even months, before they knew what was happening. They had to make a decision about the girls. Pope felt a connection to the couple that she hadn't fully realized until this moment. This situation had changed the way she saw them and she knew they were family now. She felt overwhelmed. Pope had very few genuine personal connections in her life.

They talked for a long time. But the best option was clear to all three of them. Alex's parents were prepared to have Chloe and Hannah if that's what Pope wanted, but they expressed reservations about their ability to deal with two teenage girls. In addition, the girls needed to be able to visit Alex in hospital, to be there if, *when*, he woke up. They also had school. Chloe would be taking her A levels. They had friends. Chloe had Dylan. It was obvious. The girls had to stay with Pope in London. The only thing now was to see what they thought.

* * *

The five of them talked it through. It was a lot easier than Pope thought it might be. Hannah was adamant that she needed to be near to Alex so she could visit him every day. She also had friends at school. That was important. Chloe informed them that she had decided to apply to university in London. She wanted to stay at home initially. Pope realized that her boyfriend was a key driver in this decision. But, of course, she too wanted to be near her dad. There was a determination in Alex's daughters that impressed Pope. Alex would be proud of them.

It was decided. Alex's grandparents would return home in a couple of days. The girls would stay.

* * *

After the discussion they all gravitated to different parts of the house to be alone with their thoughts about this arrangement. Hannah and Chloe went upstairs. Alex's parents sat in the living room. Pope took a coffee out into the back garden.

She stared out at nothing in particular. She was numb. Amy Weaver's callous and brutal crimes had shocked her. But the senseless and vindictive attack on Alex had flattened her. She knew she'd return. She didn't have any choice. She was now acting as mum, as sole parent to the girls. She didn't have the luxury of worrying too much about herself. Pope had been a stepmother for three years. But this was different. An extra level of responsibility. Was she ready? She guessed she'd find out.

Pope knew she would need to think about getting back to work. She couldn't leave Brody and Khan holding the fort for too long, capable as they were. For today, though, she would focus on steeling herself for what was coming. On being strong for Chloe, for Hannah and for Alex.

Alex. His proposal seemed a very long time ago. Pope smiled to herself. She knew that the first word she would say when Alex woke up would be to repeat the word 'yes'.

THE END

ACKNOWLEDGEMENTS

I'd like to thank the team at Joffe Books, who always work on the Bec Pope novels with dedication and creativity. Thanks to my early readers for the feedback, ideas and mistake-spotting. Your dedication is much appreciated. Thanks to Moira, who is usually my first 'real' reader, although this could possibly be aided by the Antipodean time difference on release day! Thanks to JJP and BSF for the encouragement. Matt — stay lucky. As always, love and eternal thanks for everything to Nik, Livi and Martha.

THE JOFFE BOOKS STORY

We began in 2014 when Jasper agreed to publish his mum's much-rejected romance novel and it became a bestseller.

Since then we've grown into the largest independent publisher in the UK. We're extremely proud to publish some of the very best writers in the world, including Joy Ellis, Faith Martin, Caro Ramsay, Helen Forrester, Simon Brett and Robert Goddard. Everyone at Joffe Books loves reading and we never forget that it all begins with the magic of an author telling a story.

We are proud to publish talented first-time authors, as well as established writers whose books we love introducing to a new generation of readers.

We won Trade Publisher of the Year at the Independent Publishing Awards in 2023 and Best Publisher Award in 2024 at the People's Book Prize. We have been shortlisted for Independent Publisher of the Year at the British Book Awards for the last five years, and were shortlisted for the Diversity and Inclusivity Award at the 2022 Independent Publishing Awards. In 2023 we were shortlisted for Publisher of the Year at the RNA Industry Awards, and in 2024 we were shortlisted at the CWA Daggers for the Best Crime and Mystery Publisher.

We built this company with your help, and we love to hear from you, so please email us about absolutely anything bookish at feedback@joffebooks.com.

If you want to receive free books every Friday and hear about all our new releases, join our mailing list here: www.joffebooks.com/freebooks.

And when you tell your friends about us, just remember: it's pronounced Joffe as in coffee or toffee!